"JOSH, YOUR FATHER WAS SHOT. HE'S DEAD."

Now the Catlin plot out at Sunnyvale Cemetery was marked by another headstone. *It shouldn't be this way!* Josh thought through his grief. At any moment he expected to hear his father's voice come singing out through the screening trees. Josh's train had pulled in this morning, where he'd been met by Dr. Paul Catlin, his uncle.

"About how your father died," said Dr. Catlin. He was gruff of manner, blocky of build, had no interests other than his medical career—which included being Denver County Coroner. "I grieve as much as you do, Josh. Your father, my brother, committed suicide."

Josh Catlin pulled up short, his mind reeling. *No! Not my father!* If he'd been told that Jarvis Catlin had robbed a bank, had squared off in a gunfight, those were believable, but to take his own life . . . ?

Never!

Josh settled into the seat of the carriage. He knew that his father hadn't taken his own life . . .

That meant that someone had taken it from him . . . and Josh meant to find out who that was.

SMOKE JENSEN
IS
THE MOUNTAIN MAN!

THE MOUNTAIN MAN SERIES
BY WILLIAM W. JOHNSTONE

ROBERT KAMMEN
THE BULLET

ZEBRA BOOKS
KENSINGTON PUBLISHING CORP.

to the National Rifle Association
Keep up the good work . . .

ZEBRA BOOKS are published by

Kensington Publishing Corp.
475 Park Avenue South
New York, NY 10016

Copyright © 1994 by Robert Kammen

Zebra and the Z logo Reg. U.S. Pat & TM Off

First Printing: November, 1994

Printed in the United States of America

Prologue

Tucking in closer than the autumn wind were Jarvis Catlin's fears that he had gotten in too deeply. With him in the carriage pulling away from Rocky Mountain Arsenal were Mexican Legate Arsenio Valdez and three Colorado ranchers. Dire thoughts tumbled through gunsmith Catlin's mind, in that someone back at the arsenal had tipped federal agents off to this clandestine plot to sell arms to Mexico. But just before leaving the arsenal Luther Radford, the bulky, square-jawed man settled in between the other ranchers, and whom Catlin studied covertly, had reassured him that except for the occupants of this carriage, only Kevin Mulcahan was involved in this.

Jarvis Catlin waved away the flask held out to him by the Mexican, this through a calm and toothy smile, as Catlin switched his mindset to just why Mulcahan, the civilian manager of Rocky Mountain Arsenal, would jeopardize his government career. Over the last three years he had come to know Kevin Mulcahan as more or less of a glad-handing politician and ladies man. As a master gunsmith employed by the famous Samuel Colt Firearms Company, Jarvis Catlin had been sent out here to certain the Colt Peacemakers purchased by the armory were in perfect working order. Though he would leave from time to time to do other gunsmithing jobs throughout Colorado, back Catlin would come to Denver.

Seated to cattleman Radford's left was Benton Wade, a wiry, erect man, with smoky gray eyes and weathered skin stretched tight across the bony contours of his face. Smoke from his cheroot flicked out an open side window and fled into the gathering haze of night, with the outlying streets of Denver reaching to embrace their rolling carriage. Opposite sat Reese Tillman, an old-time cattleman spouting off about notions to turn over his ranching operation to a pair of sons. Like the others, Tillman had money spread about in several Colorado banks, and their attire was leather coats, fancy shirts and string ties, and low-crowned hats and hand-tooled boots.

There was more, Catlin knew, as over the years he'd done gunsmithing work out at their ranches and been party to some big-game hunting. These three were part of an inner group controlling Colorado politics. About them was an aura of quiet surety, and if one was sharp enough to catch it, sometimes there'd be a cocky glint of the eye or a chance remark, then the masks would come back on in the form of friendly smiles and remarks. He'd sat in on some high-stakes poker games, which would take place again once they arrived at the Colorado Club.

Gunsmith Jarvis Catlin was tall but gaunted out some. Between chin whiskers and black bushy brows a long nose tapered toward a wide mouth generally cloaked in a smile. He wore a plain gray vested suit, and in an inner coat pocket reposed a pair of bifocals, which he'd put on when doing close work with a firearm. He ate sparingly, a habit he'd gotten into ever since his wife had passed away a couple of years ago. Sometimes a letter would arrive from London, sent by his only son, Josh, while here in Denver lived a doctor brother.

His involvement in this, mused Jarvis Catlin by way of silent justification, was superficial, simply that of a go-between. He had introduced Mulcahan to the cattlemen, had in fact brought them out to the arsenal at least five times within the last month. As for the man he shared a seat with, Legate Valdez, Valdez had been invited along by rancher Luther Radford. Most worrisome to Catlin was that he simply couldn't disassociate himself, that he was a part of whatever happened next. To distance himself from the presence of these ranchers and Denver, would without question prove hazardous to his health, as men like Radford and Wade and Tillman lived by the law of the gun. They'd bragged on this enough, mostly when they were out at their ranches pouring down some prime whiskey.

In Jarvis Catlin's room at the Colorado Club was an unopened envelope bulged out with greenbacks. The envelope had been presented to him quite openly in one of the club's smoking rooms by Luther Radford along with these words of explanation.

"For your help in this." Carelessly, ashes from Radford's cigar strewed over the arm of the chair.

Jarvis Catlin cast a worried glance at other men taking their ease in the room, and gazing at Radford he said quietly, "You did mention the sale of firearms?"

"To Mexico."

"I . . . see? This, I gather, is sanctioned by our government—"

"Don't fret now, Jarvis, we've got all of our options covered. All of us should make a killing out of this. Tomorrow afternoon Tillman an' me and Wade are headin' out to the armory for a final get-together with Mulcahan."

A meeting barely an hour over and which, to Jarvis Catlin's surprise, had included Arsenio Valdez. And now as Catlin gazed westerly toward the upthrusting Rockies, it was with the grim knowledge that he was neatly trapped in this gun-smuggling plot. But why, why should men like Luther Radford, with all of his riches and power, get involved in such a dangerous game? Perhaps part of the answer lay in the fact the Indian and the outlaw had been subdued and there were no more dangerous games to play. The West was changing in this year of 1888, was getting

halter-broke to neck-choking civilization, the rancher as
much as the gunfighter a forgotten breed.

Reese Tillman's raspy drawl cut through cigar smoke at
Catlin. "How's that son of yours doin' amongst them
Brits?"

"Ah, splendid, Mr. Tillman."

"Should make a helluva gunsmith," said Benton Wade.
"You know, Jarvis, that over-an'-under you fixed—damn, I
love that gun."

"As I gather," jibed Radford, "you was gonna shitcan
that thing." His guffaw was matched by Benton Wade's,
and with the Mexican tending to the business of emptying
a flask that Radford had brought along.

Jarvis Catlin's toothy smile pushed away a few worries.
He got to thinking that here he was, accepted as an equal
by these cattle barons. They knew him as a close-mouthed
man, and more importantly, a sharer of their love for firearms. Matching that with what he knew about them, he let
more worries ebb away. If they were involved in this, certainly it was with a great deal of protection from government interference. With the unexpected passing of his wife,
there'd been moments of deep loneliness, and Catlin found
he needed both the acceptance and company of these
men. As for gunsmithing, it was merely a means to an end,
and no pot of gold when he retired. That money given
him by Radford, there probably would be more, and if
that happened, Jarvis Catlin realized there'd be no backing
out.

A street sign fell behind, and Reese Tillman said, "Another block and we're there. The first round of panther
piss is on me."

Around a smile Radford said, "Sorry you can't join us,
Senor Valdez. My driver'll get you back to your hotel."

"*Si*, and I am grateful all is arranged."

"Just make sure," said Radford as the smile went away,
"your people handle this thing right."

"There will be no *faltas*—by my people, senor." Suddenly Legate Arsenio Valdez seemed a more threatening person as his dark brown eyes took in the trio of ranchers.

"Yup, sure, Valdez," Benton Wade said easily, "we've always kept our word. No need to change hosses in the middle of the stream now."

In the midst of dealing out cards, Jarvis Catlin paused to spear a hand out to finger it around his shot glass. Hefting the glass tumbler, a little whiskey slopped out as he glanced about through the thick pall of cigar smoke. The cards had been coming right to him, as attested to by the tidy piles of poker chips stacked before him on the table. The whiskey had been going down smooth as silk, and maybe just a shade too much, he reckoned. But he didn't seem to mind, as the whiskey had helped to ease his worries.

He said with mock solemnity, "Obliged, gentlemen, for letting me win."

"Like you've got them cards spellbound, Catlin. This hand is shapin' into somethin' though."

"Scares me when you say that, Benton," said Radford.

Finishing his deal, Jarvis Catlin picked up his cards and gave them a quick peek, and shrugging, discarded them. The other five players were ranchers, their drinks being served to them by uniformed valets who'd placed trays of food on side tables. Pushing up from the table, Catlin's glance at a wall clock told him it was five minutes shy of ten o'clock. The valet who'd entered as Catlin moved to a side table and reached for a cup slipped up to say, "Mr. Catlin, suh, you have a visitor?"

"I'm not expecting anyone."

"A Mr. Rodriques."

Through a remembering frown Catlin said, "Yes, tell Mr. Rodriques I'll see him privately." He left the cup there as he followed the valet out into a hallway. Silently Catlin chided himself for going over to the Mexican Consulate. But he had, only to find that everyone was out but for a woman secretary. Somewhat hesitantly he'd left a message behind that he wanted to see Pedro Rodriques, whom he had met years ago down in Mexico City. Here in Denver there'd been some chance meetings. To have Rodriques show up tonight . . . some of his worries of that afternoon came eeling back.

By a door leading into the club's gun room he dismissed the valet, and when Catlin entered the room, it was to return Pedro Rodriques' questioning smile. The Mexican said, "I expect, my friend, that some of these guns are yours . . ."

Catlin's eyes flicked to gun racks hooked to the oak-paneled walls. "You know ranchers, Pedro, they like to show off their guns and prize cattle. But yes, I brought over some of my guns to display. I . . . wasn't expecting you . . . at this late hour . . ."

"And I apologize for this intrusion. I was just passing by your club when I recalled that you wanted to see me. Another reason, Jarvis, is that I'm leaving on diplomatic business, in the *mañana* as a matter of fact."

"I see," Catlin murmured, as the sound of someone entering the club penetrated into the room. He stepped over and closed the door leading into the gun room, and came back to add, "Perhaps, Pedro, my fears are unfounded."

"Your message, Jarvis, mentioned Legate Valdez? Also that I must not mention this to anyone. *Asi*, is there some matter for concern—"

"No," he said quickly, "it was all a mistake."

Rodriques shrugged as he dipped a hand into a coat pocket and lifted out a small manila envelope, from which he retrieved a tintype picture. "This is, of course, Legate Arsenio Valdez, the man you were inquiring about."

A wondering shock ran through Jarvis Catlin. The man in the picture was not the same man that Luther Radford had brought out to Rocky Mountain Arsenal. Where the real Valdez had a thin but prominent face, the man claiming to be the legate was the Latin lover type, possessed of slicked-back wavy black hair and smoldering dark brown eyes, along with a certain calm indifference. What was he to say to Rodriques now, that he, Jarvis Catlin, was involved in an international *conspiracion?* He was fluent in Spanish, and in that language Catlin said, "Yes, that is Legate Valdez. Ah, perhaps you would care for a drink, my old friend . . ."

"The hour draws late, Jarvis. And a woman awaits me in my carriage." They moved up, where Catlin opened the door, and they sauntered past the cloakroom to the front door, to have a servant hand Rodriques his coat. "We must go hunting again, and soon. Until then, *adios,* Jarvis."

Somehow, after Rodriques had left, Jarvis Catlin found himself reentering the gun room accompanied by a batch of new fears. To the corner bar he went to pour brandy into a glass. If not the Mexicans, his mind spun, then who? There were any number of Central American countries that could be involved in this.

"How stupid I've been," he chided himself angrily. "The price one must pay to rub elbows with these money men . . . it just isn't worth all this worry."

With drink in hand he moved to a curtained window, and gazed westerly along Cambridge Street rising toward the deeper blackness enshrouding the mountains. For some reason London's Cockspur Street came to mind, that last time when he and Josh had groped their way through fog in search of a pub. They'd gotten hopelessly lost in the maze of twisting, narrow streets, the touch of cold brick walls to either side, until suddenly they had found themselves in an alleyway running up to a blocking wall. Impishly then the fog had lifted to reveal a flickering lantern throwing down reddish light onto a doorway, the sign above it proclaiming that within was the Red Dragon Inn. Curiosity drew them inside to an evening of ale and good talk, and the exotic dances of a beautiful Eurasian woman.

It was his son, Josh, who'd caught the woman's eye. But that evening had served to bring him closer to his son, as in the past his travels as a gunsmith had kept him away from home much, much too often and long. He simply had not wanted Josh to take on the vagabond life of a gunsmith. But Josh had taken to gunsmithing, spurning the more honorable professions of medicine and law. Jarvis Catlin knew that once guns became part of a man's life, the fever lasted a lifetime. That was the reason Josh was now in London, to learn more about his chosen profession from the master gunsmiths employed by Samuel Colt's London factory. His son, he knew in the final days before he set sail for America, had been seeing the Eurasian woman.

"Lanai Meling," he said enviously. "An exotic name for an exotic woman. Cheers, my son."

Regretfully Jarvis Catlin realized he had to get back to the game. Generally these affairs lasted through the night. As for what he'd just learned from Pedro Rodriques, it would be his secret. It could prove dangerous, and would serve no purpose, to voice his concern about this to Radford or the others. To disclose what he knew would cause a ripple effect, like casting a pebble out into calm waters. First there'd be a small ring of disturbance, which would enlarge and spread to riverbanks, or be carried by the current until someone noticed the concentric rings of disturbance and came to investigate.

Turning away from the window, he deposited his empty glass on a table, and as he did, Catlin picked up on the low murmuring of voices, his attention going to a previously unnoticed door that stood slightly ajar. He would have gone on had he not recognized Luther Radford's deep baritone voice. Hesitating, he started to leave, then Catlin heard someone else mention his name, and quietly he eased over.

"Are you sure he's from the Mexican Consulate—"

"It was most assuredly Pedro Rodriques."

"Okay, Major Devlin, no need to get your dander up,"

said Radford. "Catlin's an honest man—maybe too much so. The question is, what does he know?"

"We do know that Catlin had spent time down in Mexico City. Perhaps they're old friends . . ."

"It worries me, Catlin's knowing this Rodriques. Though he did accept as cold fact the man who went out to the arsenal with us was Legate Valdez."

"True, Mr. Radford. But if Catlin were to learn that we're really planning to sell these guns to the Cuban Junta, a bunch of renegades at best . . . Especially now when our State Department is trying to keep things on an even keel with Spain."

"Well, hoss-shit, Major, we're gonna hafta fight the Spanish sooner or later. What we're doin' is merely arming the winnin' side an' makin' a tidy profit to boot. What was that noise?"

Anxious eyes went to the door leading into the gun room. And just as quickly it was yanked open, to have a man lean in and say urgently, "Major! Caught this gent I just cold-cocked out here eavesdropping." Like Major Devlin, Sergeant Guy Hogue was wearing a civilian suit, with both officer and enlisted man assigned to the Army Ordinance Corp. Hogue held there as Devlin and the rancher hurried over.

"Dammit, it's Catlin!" muttered Radford. "We sure as hell spilled the beans to him. But, I reckon there's only one way to handle this."

"We simply can't do it here, Radford."

"Nope, Major, best we get Catlin up to his room. We'll use the back stairs. Which'll be a job, Devlin, for you and your sergeant."

Major George Devlin stared back at the rancher. In Devlin's eyes was this naked reluctance to just simply up and commit murder. But for gambling debts and assorted other bills amounting to nearly ten thousand dollars he wouldn't be here. But he was here, and what he saw stamped on Luther Radford's cold-chiseled face told Major Devlin murder and more would be expected of him.

"I'll fix this to make it look like he committed suicide."

Both men swung their attention to Sergeant Guy Hogue, who said, "Sergeants are like shadows—nobody ever notices they've been around. Or when they leave. If the major will help me get Catlin up to his room, before he comes out of it and starts yelling bloody murder . . ."

"Yes," agreed Radford, "do as the sergeant says, Devlin."

From a shoulder holster Sergeant Hogue had removed the gunsmith's presentation Colt .31 caliber revolver. The engraving on the cylinder showed a stagecoach holdup, and the weapon had solid ivory grips. He spun the cylinder while grinning his appreciation. "Too bad I can't take this with me." He shoved the gun into his waistband. "Once we get up there, I'll hold off doing the job until Major Devlin has had time to take his departure."

Nodding, Radford said, "There is something you can take with you, sergeant. In Catlin's room you'll find an envelope containing a considerable sum of money. You'll handle this right, I'll expect." He returned Hogue's gap-toothed grin.

Major George Devlin voiced no objections as he crossed the threshold and bent to wrap his hands around Catlin's ankles. With Hogue grasping the upper body, they found a back door and the staircase pushing up to the third floor. The perspiration beginning to stain Devlin's face was more from his fear of being caught than anything, which proved to be unfounded when at last they were pushing into Jarvis Catlin's third-floor room, set on the extreme southeast corner of the large brick building. They'd barely dropped the unconscious gunsmith on the living room sofa when Devlin made a hasty departure.

Patiently Guy Hogue, a scorning smirk on his face for the way Devlin had acted, moved over and locked the door leading into the hallway. Now his first order of business was finding that envelope. When he did come upon it nearly ten minutes later, it was under some clothing in a bottom dresser drawer. Depositing the envelope down the front of his shirt, he crossed to a bedroom window where, as he'd taken notice of earlier, a balcony ran along both the second and third floors. His eyes caught movement on a side street, and Hogue grinned at the sight of Major Devlin hurrying furtively through the glow cast by a street lamp. Turning, he brought a pillow from the bed with him into the living room of the two-room suite occupied by Catlin, who was beginning to stir on the sofa.

"Reckon," muttered Hogue, "a slug from my Colt .45 will cure that headache, Mr. Gunsmith."

Unleathering his six-gun, Hogue lowered the large fluffy pillow down onto Catlin's head, and quickly he shoved the barrel of his Colt in hard. When he jerked back the trigger, the gun bucked in his hand and emitted a muffled crackling sound, as of a man tromping over ground strewn with acorns. Shoving his gun back into its holster, he pulled Catlin's gun out of his waistband as he hurried over and triggered a bullet from the gun out through an open window. He moved back and wrapped Catlin's right hand around the butt of the gun. He lifted the pillow away from Jarvis Catlin's head to reveal the purpling, blood-stained hole in the forehead. When Guy Hogue crawled through the open bedroom window, it was while holding the pillow and wondering just how much money there was in the envelope tucked under his shirt.

Downstairs, Luther Radford had gotten back into the poker game. He'd shucked out of his coat and rolled his shirtsleeves up to his brawny elbows, and was puffing calmly at the moment on an imported Cuban cigar. There'd been some comment about Jarvis Catlin's prolonged absence, which Radford had ignored. Spearing his eyes across the table, Radford said, "Dammit, Benton, I think you're bluffin'—I'll raise that another fifty."

When the hand was played out, a smiling Luther

Radford started raking in poker chips as one of the valets came rushing in to announce that something had happened to gunsmith Jarvis Catlin.

"There was a shot! It appears . . . that . . . that Mr. Catlin has killed himself—"

One

There was a brief and unsettling moment when the barrel of the .45 Colt revolver seemed to be pointed at Josh Catlin. Then the man grasping the revolver, an Englishman named Tucker, pivoted slightly as he centered the gun in on the round bull's-eye target.

As a bullet from Hiram Tucker's revolver struck into the target near an outer ring, Josh Catlin let out a delighted war whoop and said, "How very kind of you, my good Mr. Tucker." Quickly Josh brought up his own weapon, a matching Colt, and when he fired a bullet punched into the small bull's-eye circle of the adjoining target. He turned and laid the empty gun on a table cluttered with other weapons and gunsmithing tools.

Hemming in this firing range out back of the large brick building housing the Colt Firearms factory was a high brick wall encrusted with ivy. The firing range was composed of wooden frames holding up ten-round targets, with sandbags piled up behind the targets and to the height of the high wall. Leftward, away a little where the rear fence wall pushed along in the direction of Vauxhall-Bridge, there stood a large, gnarled oak tree through whose thick branches pierced afternoon sunlight.

Now the pair of them began trudging back toward the targets. Tucker, reaching up with his left hand to thrust away from his forehead a wayward lock of brown hair, said in self-reproach, "But for that last errant shot . . ."

"What's a pound to a bloody rich Englishman," chided Josh Catlin.

"Rich my Limey arse," countered Tucker. "But I promise you, Catlin, tomorrow I shall exact revenge." Reaching the target he'd been firing at, he grimaced. "One errant bullet . . ." Then he bent to the task of detaching the target from its moorings.

Hefting their respective targets, which were covered with heavy white cloth and thickly padded, they retraced their route past the table to use a back door. As they passed into the building, the rangemaster came out to take charge of their revolvers. Tucker led the way into a small room where they worked. For the past couple of weeks they'd been testing out a new method of casting gun barrels called the Metford Rifling System. As they set about using knifes to pry leaden slugs from the targets, Josh Catlin was coming to realize this new system had indeed improved the accuracy of every Colt he'd fired.

He was a week away from celebrating his twenty-third birthday. Taller than his father at five-eleven, he had coal-black hair and chiseled handsome features. A gunsmith, as Tucker was, he was just starting to appreciate the other benefits, which had been pointed out to him by the more scholarly Englishman, of this new system. For the Metford form of rifling consisted of seven lands and grooves cast into the gun barrel, though shallow enough to be all but undetectable to the naked eye. These groovings, they'd found, did away with the need to cut into the bullet to give it spin. Where before a bullet had to be loaded from the muzzle, this rifling system would pave the way for more breech-loaded weapons. In the past, Josh had encountered as a gunsmith other forms of grooving the barrel of a gun, but none as advanced as Metford rifling.

Dropping a slug he'd pried out of the target onto his work bench, he paused to look over at Tucker. "It's really amazing, Hiram, the distinctive markings each barrel impresses on a bullet fired out of it."

"They say," said Tucker, "no two snowflakes are alike. Tell me, Catlin, just why is it a beautiful tidbit like Lanai Meling prefers your company . . ."

"Seems we colonists have a certain charm."

"Which consists chiefly of baying at the moon on a dark night." Tucker settled one of the slugs he'd pried out of the target under the lens of his microscope. "I have truly been considering accepting that invitation to have dinner with you and your lady. Then perhaps after a night on the town the pair of us will do some moon-baying."

Josh nodded as he used his microscope to check out the markings scoured into a leaden slug. During the course of this experiment he'd pitched at Tucker the possibility of the Metford system being adopted by the London police, only to be told by Tucker that it was still considered suspect as evidence, much like this new-fangled thing called fingerprinting. But Josh suspected that in time the Metford system would become as much a witness to a crime as the human eye.

He gazed out a window and saw to his dismay that clouds were beginning to stain the late afternoon sky. "What's another day here without a cold, drizzling rain?"

"One gets used to it, I suppose. What you told me about your American West does whet my interest."

There rose in Josh Catlin longings he'd suppressed, and the fact that he wanted to cut out of here for home, even though in another couple of months he'd return to take up the job of promoting Samuel Colt's wonderful firearms in Western cities and towns. What had made it bearable was of course not only the friendship of Tucker and others working there, but mainly the presence in London of sloe-eyed Lanai Meling. The beautiful Eurasian woman was still as much a mystery to him as the fog-encrusted streets. Though slowly, ever so subtly, Lanai was revealing parts of herself to him.

A smile danced in Josh's eyes, at the reaction his old Denver chums would have once they set eyes on Lanai. As for his feelings toward her, they were partly defensive, for shortly he'd be leaving, and the feelings were of a man on the verge of falling in love. At the moment he was glad that his father wasn't there, since that worthy would take one look at his son and remark caustically he'd been "moonstruck by a good-looking filly." He said to Tucker, "It would disappoint Lanai mightily if you declined our dinner invitation."

"This friend she's bringing along," grimaced Tucker. "So far for me all they've been are either heifers or fat cows or their dimples hide their warts." Sighing, he began untying the long blue apron that protected his clothing. "But, Catlin, once again it seems I must sacrifice my body to please you and your Lanai. Oh . . . it appears the sanctity of our laboratory is being invaded."

Entering first was factory manager Buckley, who stepped aside to turn the thrust of his smile upon Von Oppen, a Prussian, and the man in charge of the London sales office. A black cape hung over Von Oppen's ample shoulders, and he had on a black suit and a gray vest, and gloves, which he was busy removing as he nodded at the gunsmiths. His full name fitted his ample frame; Freiherr Frederick Augustus Kunov Waldemar von Oppen. Removing his felt hat, he thrust his gloves into the hat as he came toward the workbench. Abruptly, he said through a searching gaze, "What do you make of all of this, Catlin?"

"Sir, Mr. Von Oppen, we have sent you reports on our research—"

The Prussian flicked a finger against his mustache and said, "Papers cannot tell the whole story."

Josh nodded in agreement. "So far all we've tested are revolvers, but enough to make me want to carry a sidearm equipped with the Metford system. We've gained a lot more accuracy."

"I can attest to that," affirmed Hiram Tucker.

"Good," beamed Von Oppen as the plant manager, who'd slipped out of the room, returned bearing a gun case. The Prussian's gesture brought everyone over to a table on which Buckley had set the case.

"I've heard of William Cashmere," Josh said, in reference to the name embossed on the top of the gun case.

"One of England's best gunsmiths," affirmed Von Oppen as he lifted out of the case a fully engraved rifle. "Forty-four caliber, carrying forty grains of powder and two hundred grains of lead in the cartridge. As you can see, gentlemen, the barrel has Metford rifling machined into it." He handed the rifle to Josh, who ran a caressing hand along the rosewood stock.

Butting the rifle against his shoulder, Josh ran an appraising eye down the sights atop the long barrel. "It's wonderfully balanced."

"Yes," said Von Oppen. "Cashmere has been working with our people on this rifle. And now your chore, Tucker and Catlin, is to see how it performs out in the field. But you won't be doing the test firing."

Josh shot quizzical eyes at plant manager Buckley, who responded with a catlike grin.

The Prussian went on. "Are you a wagering man, Catlin?"

"To some extent," said Josh, as he handed the rifle to Tucker.

"Anyway, we are wagering that this rifle can be most deadly, and profitable to us, in the proper hands. Cashmere has produced three more rifles identical in every way to this one. Which you, gentlemen, will deliver into the hands of the man known as the 'Spirit Gun of the American West'."

Interest slitted Josh's eyes, and he said wonderingly, "That of course would be Doc Carver?"

"Possibly the greatest marksman in the world," said Von Oppen. From the folds of his coat he produced a copy of an English sporting publication called *Bell's Life of London*. He rapped a finger against the cover. "The illustrious marksman came like a thief in the night, which displeased formal Englishmen mightily. But here is Doc Carver's challenge, for all to see and ponder."

All of them took in the gist of the main article in the publication, in which Carver challenged all comers to every phase of rifle and shotgun shooting, on horseback or on foot. More, Carver dared any man in England to meet him on that gentleman's own terms. Josh, having seen Doc Carver perform his magical shooting feats on two occasions back in America, wagered silently that Carver was a formidable foe. Still, during his sojourn in London, Josh had engaged in several matches with the English, men just as capable with firearms as Carver. These matches could run up to several hours or days, with two marksmen squared off to fire at glass balls tossed overhead by assistants.

Said Josh Catlin, "I saw Doc Carver take on Pawnee Bill down in St. Louis. A fifty thousand glass ball match. Just hefting a rifle in a match like that would darn near cripple an ordinary man."

"Carver is extraordinarily strong," said Von Oppen. "He'll need his strength when he appears at the Trentbridge Shooting Grounds. We've managed to arrange a match, a hundred thousand ball affair, against the · European champion Krueger." He reached for his hat. "So, Catlin, we're gambling that this new rifle will give Carver the edge. At precisely nine o'clock tomorrow morning you and Tucker will present yourselves at 20 Onslow Terrace. Fetching along, of course, these new Cashmere rifles."

"We're honored," said Tucker, "by this gracious trust you've placed in us, sir."

Ominously Von Oppen responded, "Just don't let us down. As I've wagered my chicken coop, as you Yankees coin it, Mr. Catlin, that Doc Carver triumphs again." He left trailed by Buckley.

Josh turned to Hiram Tucker, placing the rifle back into the case, and Josh said, "There are more experienced gunsmiths working here?"

"But none of them have tested out this new Metford system. Carver, they say he's the nonpareil rifleman in the world. But of course all Carver has faced are American shooters."

"Then Krueger's your man—"

"No, I didn't say that. Not when Carver will be firing a Cashmere rifle."

"We can start wagering right now, Mr. Tucker. Say a pair of shillings that Lanai's friend will be enchanting and pretty."

He followed Josh over to the coat rack. "With my luck, a remote possibility. Say, two shillings and the price of dinner . . ."

"Taken."

With evening settling on London as if it weighed more than the afternoon, lamp light began poking along main boulevards and cobbled streets. In the district of Mayfair, as elsewhere in the city, many buildings were made of white limestone from Portland, a small island off the southern coast of England. Over the years clouds of smoke from thousands of chimneys had thickened the fogs which often embrace London, causing a thick soot to fall upon the buildings, griming the limestone into shades of dark gray or black.

Tonight above the spreading glow of the city the sky was clear, the glow pushing back starlight, and the eyes of Josh Catlin fixed upstreet as he strode briskly along, accompanied by Hiram Tucker. They wore toggery purchased on fashionable Bond Street, though Josh would have felt more comfortable in Levi's and a pair of Justin boots. It seemed to please Lanai Meling, his playing the role of English gentry. And tonight that was all that mattered.

Ahead of them lay Piccadilly, a fashionable shopping district, and somewhere in the immediate vicinity, Josh recalled, lay Onslow Terrace, where Doc Carver had taken up residence. The temptation was strong in Josh to drop by and pay their respects to the world-famous sharp-shooter, and he voiced this to Tucker.

"Lowly gunsmiths do not entertain such ideas," scolded Hiram. "Right this very minute I assume Carver has as his house guests some dukes and their ladies. I daresay, Josh, you saw Carver perform—is he all that good?"

"Tell you what, Hiram, perhaps I can arrange a match for you with Doc Carver, winner take all." Coming abreast of a display window filled with clocks, he added worriedly, "We're late. Perhaps we should catch a hack?"

"Or perhaps," came back Tucker, "your lady of the evening has found someone else to squire her around town. Patience, as we're but three blocks away from Hyde Park Corner. And about our bet, what say we make it four shillings and dinner . . ."

Josh merely nodded as his pace picked up. The sidewalks were clogged with others converging on Piccadilly. The clatter of shod hoofs striking cobblestones and the heavier thudding of iron wheels added to the murmur of the streets. Though London had a special appeal for Josh, in him was this longing to push away the buildings and replace them with mountain crags hazing in the distance. He'd discussed with Lanai Meling the off chance she might return with him to Denver. She hadn't said no, nor had Lanai ever told Josh why she preferred his company to the more sophisticated Londoners.

Coming to an intersection, they darted across, barely ahead of a pair of bays pulling a transom hack. Another block brought them to the north side of Green Park, the sidewalk they followed finally ending at Hyde Park Corner. Here a crowd had gathered to listen to a man perched on a box speaking out on some social issue. As for Josh, his eyes were stabbing anxiously about in search of Lanai.

"Awful crowded."

"There," said Hiram, "could be your lady love?"

Then Josh sighted a white gloved hand waving over the bowlered heads of some onlookers, and he began shouldering through the press, to have her come to reach out for his hand. He could only think that tonight Lanai looked stunningly beautiful in a dark blue velvety dress. The veil hooked to her black hat brushed just below her large purpled eyes. Over her dress she had on a light summer coat. She smelled of jasmine, her eyes still holding that delightful smile, and then, bodily, she leaned in to receive his kiss.

He murmured huskily, "Tonight I'm the luckiest man in town. Oh, you remember Hiram Tucker ..."

Now they had to smile at the way Tucker stood there staring at Lanai's woman companion. He'd managed to remove his hat, and held it awkwardly with both hands as he took in Sybil O'Mara's mass of reddish hair piled up under a brimmed hat pulled cockily down over her forehead. She was comely, with delicate features and sky blue eyes. In a lilting Irish brogue she said, "So you are Mr. Tucker." When she held out her hand, color splashed across Hiram Tucker's face.

Lanai Meling said, "And this is Sybil O'Mara. Perchance we live at the same rooming house." Now she threw in teasingly, "Do you approve, Mr. Tucker?"

"I ... yes, I find you so ... enchanting, Miss O'Mara."

"Hiram, did you say something about buying supper?"

"Why, I ..."

Josh stepped out ahead with Lanai Meling. He threw back, "At the Grosvenor, wasn't it ..."

Lanai protested, "That place is dreadfully expensive."

"Nonsense, our dear Mr. Tucker has lots of money. And the Grosvenor is where the sporting crowd hangs out." Now Josh told of how the famous marksman Doc Carver had come to be in London, and of the role he and Hiram Tucker would play in upcoming shooting matches involving Carver, especially the match involving the European champion. "As for us, Lanai, I'll miss you terribly when I go back home. Perhaps I ..."

"Will stay here?" she ventured.

"Something to ponder over. I doubt if the Colt people

will support that decision. But I suppose I can always hook on elsewhere. What about you, Lanai, surely you can't like London all that much?"

"The world has been my oyster, Josh. That is, until my parents perished in a shipwreck . . . on their way back to Hong Kong. There wasn't much of an estate. But why bother with all of that." Tilting her head up, she leaned in and brought her lips caressing across his cheek, to have Josh redden. "The night is young—and we have each other."

But for the trees standing there in stately rows along the roadway, the flat Norfolk countryside reminded Josh Catlin of the plains of eastern Colorado. False dawn had seen them pulling out of London, this after a span of six days in which Josh had seen the incomparable Doc Carver best Webster, a famous English shot, at the Trentbridge Shooting Grounds in no small measure, as attested to by Carver, by the modified Cashmere rifles. After this tune-up match, they were about to entrain for the Crystal Palace in Sydenham to take on the European champion, when word came that the match would be held at Sandringham instead, the summer home of British royalty, at the behest of the Prince of Wales.

To actually be in the presence of nobility added to Josh Catlin's anticipation. Not so Hiram Tucker, seated facing him in their enclosed carriage, for Tucker had revealed that he was a distant relative of some duke or other. Seated alongside Tucker was Doc Carver's colored assistant, a pleasant, bony-faced man in his late thirties named Jim Williams. He was dressed especially for today's match in a Union army blue uniform and cap. Possessed of a deep melancholy voice, Williams liked his Cuban cheroots, the smoke from one curling out through a side window. Behind them a heavier wagon carried some of their equipment and Carver's famous shooting-horse, Winnemucca. Out front rolled another carriage holding as occupants

Doc Carver and match promoter Alf Jowett of London, along with the Earl of Oxford acting as personal representative for the Prince of Wales.

As for Josh Catlin, he'd developed a quick friendship with Williams. Not only did Jim Williams have to take on the strenuous task of casting glass balls up into the air during a match, but he tended lovingly to Doc Carver's many guns. It was the shared love of firearms that made him realize that perhaps Williams knew more about gunsmithing in general.

"This is a far piece from Cajun country—"

"Or Denver for that matter," said Williams. "I nevah reckoned I'd evah get to see New Orleans or even London. That Doc Carver's a fine gennulman . . ."

"Has amazing strength," said Hiram Tucker. "Which he'll need against the German."

"Does this mean you're placing your money on Krueger?"

"You'll not trap me that easily, Josh. I'm for Carver, as he'll be firing a superior weapon."

"Seems," said Williams, "we're about here."

Through a break in the treeline Josh fixed in on a large, hideous, rambling pile of a building composed of dark orange brick like a station hotel. There was a profusion of lawns, gardens and sculpted shrubbery. They passed through open gates embossed with coats of arms, went up a long driveway, and as they did, people began to assemble out in front of Sandringham Hall.

"The proper etiquette, do we curtsey or bow," teased Josh to the Englishman.

Williams muttered, "I don't know as but I's staying right in here until we get around to the stables."

"We remain respectfully silent," grimaced Hiram Tucker. "Until we're called upon to speak, if that shall ever happen, for they are out to greet the Spirit Gun of the West."

"Anyway," said Josh, "before he goes against the European champion, Carver is slated to put on a shooting exhibition. Said he'd use one of his Winchesters."

"Save the Cashmeres as a sort of surprise for Krueger," said Tucker.

"Don't matter none what Carver shoots with or against." Jim Williams had a knowing smile etched on his face. "So ev'ry match I bet my life savings, as I aim to retire young an' wealthy back in Cajun country."

As soon as their carriages were reined to a stop, liveried servants scurried forward to open carriage doors, and somewhat timorously Josh Catlin dismounted. He stood alongside Hiram Tucker under the scrutinizing eyes of at least thirty people clad in hunting garb. Then Josh was aware of Doc Carver's beckoning arm.

"Mr. Catlin, please come over so I may present you to the Prince and Princess of Wales—"

Onto a back lawn the length and breadth of an American football field came Doc Carver astride his frisky palomino. Acknowledging the onlookers with a graceful wave of his black Stetson, he reined up to gaze down at Josh Catlin. Carver was a big, broad-shouldered man with long red hair and a sweeping mustache. Some of the medals he had been presented with by European royalty were pinned to his black velvet shirt.

He leaned closer and said softly to Josh, "If I'm to be accepted as the genuine article by these folks, today I've got to surpass my previous exhibitions—or for sure they'll have my scalplock."

"You'll be using one of the Winchesters?"

"Yup," Carver said laconically. "Save those Cashmeres for the German. What do you make of Krueger?"

Josh turned his head slightly, where among the assemblage stood Otto Kurt Krueger. The German had a blocky head and seemed even bigger than Carver. "He does have a steely grip and eye, and he is the best Europe has to offer." Reaching to a nearby table, Josh picked up a Winchester rifle, which he handed to Carver. "Before we pulled out of London I cleaned out my bank account. All of which I have wagered on you, Doc."

"You've been talking to my man, Williams." Carver grinned as he added, "The Santee Sioux, whom I grew up amongst, coin it a shade different—to them I'm known as the Evil Spirit of the Plains. Could be you'll be cussing me out after this set-to with Krueger. Jim, you about ready to work up a sweat?"

The Negro Jim Williams nodded from where he stood close to wooden boxes containing glass ball targets. Behind this reposed a table holding more guns and presided over by Hiram Tucker. It was a day favored by hunters, windless, in the high seventies, and with cloud cover to cut the glare of the late morning sun. Reining on, Carver rode around the tables set end to end and toward the Prince of Wales grasping a timing watch.

He returned Carver's smile and said, "Now, sir, will you please give the ladies present an evidence of what you can do."

Eagerly the palomino responded to Carver's reined command, and at a nod from Carver, the first glass ball was thrown up by his assistant, to be immediately shattered, and the next, and the next. When he'd emptied one rifle of its shells, Josh would dart forward to hand Carver another and take the empty one back to reload it with fresh shells. The next time Tucker would have the honors, as all the while the glass balls being thrown up by Jim Williams were shattered to rain down upon him bits of glass and feathers.

Suddenly the Prince of Wales shouted out, "Carver has broken one hundred glass balls consecutively!"

Wheeling back toward the tables, Carver thrust his empty rifle at Josh, to comment that this was the first time he'd ever fired at one hundred glass balls, without missing, before an audience. "I expect," Carver went on, "that all of this will wear me out for tomorrow's match." Hefting the shotgun passed up to him by Josh, he broke away.

Then, using that shotgun and others passed to him by

Josh and Hiram Tucker, Carver quickly equalled his just-set record with a rifle by not missing with a shotgun the one hundred glass balls pitched into the air by Jim Williams. A moment after Carver finished firing, the Prince of Wales turned to the Earl of Romney and exclaimed, "Bravo! I will bet one thousand pounds that Doctor Carver will break one hundred and fifty balls without error or intermission, with his rifle!"

Coming in to swing out of the saddle, Carver said, "That bet about cuts the mustard."

Josh took in the marksman's sweat-stained face, the anxious glitter in Carver's eyes. "Nobody took the Prince up on his bet , . ."

"Maybe so, Josh, but it's a challenge I have to pick up on or go slinking home in disgrace. Best I've ever done is about a hundred-thirty of them glass walnuts down in Missouri. Hiram, I think I'll avail myself of one of those Cashmeres. You boys"—his glance took in the pair of them—"have bragged them up enough."

"They're a trifle lighter than a Winchester."

"Which should help my ailing shoulder," said Carver.

As Carver hefted a Cashmere rifle and walked his horse over to confer with Jim Williams, Josh Catlin glanced incuriously at a carriage just pulling into the circular driveway. Then the carriage was pulling up, and London Colt's agent Von Oppen emerged. Probably here, Josh mused, to take in the shooting festivities. Josh's eyes flicked back to Carver reclaiming his saddle. It began again, Williams casting glass balls skyward, the American Carver blasting them into shattering pieces.

A heavy hand pressed upon Josh's shoulder.

Turning, he saw it was Von Oppen.

The Prussian said gravely, "I have just received a letter from Denver. It concerns your father, Josh."

He studied Von Oppen's face briefly, and then he knew, and the words tumbled out, "My father is dead."

Von Oppen lowered his head in agreement.

TWO

The Cuban took pride in the fact that he was one of the very few who'd managed to escape from Havana's infamous fortress prison, Morro Castle. But at a price, for afterwards the Spanish rulers of Cuba had killed Felix Casandro's wife, three children and nephew. Word of that had been brought to Casandro, hiding out in Key West. He'd been smuggled there by members of the Cuban Junta, an organization whose authority came from Maximo Gomez, the commander of the Cuban insurgent army. While in Key West, Casandro had learned that over three hundred Cuban revolutionary clubs could be found in America and Europe.

Before Felix Casandro had learned that his family had been murdered, he had succumbed to the lures of southern Florida. Oftentimes he would slip in to watch the action at gaming casinos or stroll along the wide boulevards with their fancy shops, in an effort to forget all that was happening in Cuba. He'd been on the verge of heading up the Atlantic shoreline in hopes of finding work in New York. Only one of Senor Palma's agents had found him to tell of the murders. Even in the midst of his grief Felix Casandro agreed to work for the Cuban Junta.

A week later he was part of a crew aboard a fast steamer slipping out of Port Brunswick, the low hulk of St. Simons Island to larboard, the prow of the *Black Swan* pushing further into the beckoning waters of the Atlantic. Once they cleared the southern coast of Georgia, a course was directed toward island Cuba.

Filibustering was a strange word to Felix Casandro, but not to the crew, who'd traversed this watery course many times during the past year. Aboard the *Black Swan* were arms, ammunition, quinine and other medical equipment which, if they arrived safely, would be turned over to Cuban insurgents. They did arrive safely, and in succeeding voyages Casandro was to learn that American cruisers and gunboats stationed in the harbors along the coast from New York to New Orleans rarely carried out their interception orders. But Spanish ships did, and with a vengeance.

One day, back at Port Brunswick, new orders were handed to Felix Casandro by a man wearing a Panama hat and a white summery suit. An agent for the Cuban Junta had brought them to a waterfront cafe, where Casandro was filled in on his new mission.

"Go . . . where?"

"Colorado. Does that seem so strange, Felix?"

"*Si,* I speak English, but how could I possibly help our cause way out there . . ."

"Out there one does not know the difference between a Mexican and a Cuban. You are a superb horseman, we've learned, among other things. You will be in charge of five others."

"For what *expresar* purpose?"

"Here, Felix, some more rum."

That bottle of rum, and another, went down slowly as to Felix Casandro was laid out a plot involving many people, both Westerners and U.S. Army personnel. Money, he was also told, would be transferred to several Denver banks. "So, Felix, you must first contact a man named Radford, a rancher. Afterwards a plan must be worked out to see that these weapons you purchase can be smuggled down to the Gulf of Mexico."

"If I agree to this."

"And?"

Felix Casandro, just entering his thirty-first year, let images of his family penetrate into the small cafe, as the musky stench of the waterfront was doing, the muted sounds of a foghorn, and in a voice tinged with sadness he said, "Do I have any other choice?"

"Do any of us?"

That had been six months ago, a period of time in which he'd isolated his mind from any thoughts about his dead family. With the help of the Junta agent and others, Casandro had put together a working plan of operation. The five other Cubans, he'd found as he set about training them, were men with lesser educations but each had suffered equally at the hands of the Spanish rulers of Cuba. One thing of an encouraging note were the few letters Casandro had received from this Colorado rancher, the gist of each that if the money was there, the Cubans could acquire a vast supply of military arms.

He found Denver much to his liking, not all that unlike Cuban cities with the mountains westerly, and it had a small Mexican population which suited Casandro's purposes. His five Cubans he had dispatched out to various ranches owned by the three main conspirators in the plot to purchase arms from the Rocky Mountain Arsenal. Of this trio, Luther Radford stood out more.

"Too greedy for my taste," Felix Casandro remarked to the sound of hammering pushing into his hotel room. He sat slumped before a table in the dingy room of a hotel a stone's throw from an abandoned army post, paperwork and maps strewn before him. He was tired, beginning to be anxious about the thrust of his responsibilities. He imagined, as he picked up the chipped glass holding a little rum, this room had seen many a whore coupling with many a blue-assed soldier, as he referred to them. Some of the wallpaper hung in neglectful shreds, as faded out as the bedding. Hallway floorboards creaked; a cocked ear took in footsteps heading for the staircase.

"Probably someone vacating this cockroach ravaged hostel."

His voice hung there for a moment, the words he'd spoken in Spanish forgotten in his worries of the here and now, which included not only ranchers Radford, Wade, and Tillman, but it seemed a host of others. They were committing criminal acts for riches to be gained. Any one of them could, and just might, try to *destruir* this attempt to ship arms out of there in exchange for more money. It was all a calculated risk, one fraught with uncertainties and no guarantees of success.

One thing troubling Felix Casandro was that he had not seen the American gunsmith, Catlin, for some time. His inquiry about this to rancher Luther Radford had brought about the vague response that Jarvis Catlin was off someplace. The riddle had been solved only the other night when he'd come across the obituary about the gunsmith in a Denver newspaper. He had liked Catlin's unreserved smile and friendly manner. The suspicions now in Casandro were that the gunsmith had been murdered for one reason or another.

"To the maps," he told himself wearily. Before him, in somewhat disheveled shape after so much handling, were maps he'd acquired of Western states and railway systems. Other maps took in the routes trains used to head out from the Midwestern states to Colorado and on to Denver, one of the larger railroad hubs. He'd discounted using wagons to carry these arms down through the Great Plains and hopefully on to Cuba.

He knew that Rocky Mountain Arsenal often shipped arms out on the Denver, Rio Grande & Western railroad to scattered army forts, a bit of news he'd picked up from Major George Devlin. It was a shortline concentrating most of its railway system into Colorado, and to use it would mean having to transfer his valuable cargo to another line. As for Major Devlin, there was something about the man which threw further worry into Casandro. Could he trust Devlin once money had been exchanged for weaponry? It seemed, sighed the Cuban Felix Casandro, he had no other choice than to try and find someone else to buy arms from.

Wearily he lifted his eyes from the table to a window grimed with dust as pushing in through the panes was a splash of reflected light, and he realized another long day had passed. He must get out, if only to get something to eat. In the neighborhood was a Mexican cantina, or should he head up to Federal Avenue and try his luck at the casinos? Rising, he stretched to rid his lower back of some pain and to uncramp his left leg. "My *compadres* out at the ranches, they must think I've deserted them. But in two weeks, according to Major Devlin, the first shipment of arms arrives. *Asi*, at least I have that to look forward to."

Emptying his glass of rum, he reached to a rickety dresser for the shoulder holster holding his .32 Smith & Wesson, letting come to him now a certain woman he had seen at that Mexican cantina. Mostly, he needed someone to talk to, and later on, if the woman was willing, a room could be found someplace.

"After that I will think about *Cuba Libre.*"

Further to the east at least a half-mile, the railroad yards which had occupied the Cuban's thoughts over the past few weeks were being viewed from the window of an incoming passenger car by Mexican consular officer Pedro Rodriques. For some reason he couldn't fathom, Rodriques let slip out of the shadows of his memory thoughts of his old gunsmithing friend, Jarvis Catlin. *Si*, Jarvis, he mused, had this concern about Legate Valdez? Ever since that night, consular business had kept Pedro Rodriques in St. Louis. He could think about Catlin later—tonight he had other business to tend to.

Seeming to push toward the passenger train was Union Station located in the heart of downtown Denver. Deliberately Rodriques had not fired off a telegram announcing his arrival, as he wanted a few days away from all of the diplomatic business. He planned to spend the night with a woman other than his betrothed, in fact the woman who had been with him on the night he'd gone over to the Colorado Club to see Jarvis Catlin, then in the morning take her with him to Estes Park. He saw nothing wrong with this, as it had been the custom in his family through many generations. Now with the train grinding to a halt before Union Station, he reached for a small valise and shoved to his feet with eager anticipation for what the rest of the evening would provide.

Sergeant Guy Hogue had the ability to fit in most anyplace, whether it was an army post or, where he chanced to be at the moment, idling in a saloon across the street from Union Station. He was togged out in a light brown suit and straw hat. Though he'd been tossing down drinks with other patrons involved in a game of liar's poker, by last count ten shot glasses of prime whiskey, Hogue was still clear-eyed. Every so often he'd spear a glance out through the wide plate-glass window at a Confederate lurking somewhat sulkily in a buggy. Just five minutes ago Corporal Ron Benson had ambled in to say the train bearing Pedro Rodriques was pulling in and he sure as hell could use a drink. To quiet Benson's mutterings, Sergeant Hogue had sent him back out latching onto a bottle of whiskey.

Shaping a farewell grin for his drinking companions, Hogue said, "For sure liar's poker is my game. Be back tomorrow night for more of the same. But before I leave, bardog, drinks around." A beneficial hand let a greenback flutter down onto the bar as Hogue headed out the front door.

Briefly, Sergeant Guy Hogue lingered on the sidewalk,

taking in across the narrow expanse of street Union Station, behind which the Union Pacific was disgorging its passengers. In a sense this was the end of the line, since from there those continuing on would get aboard shortline railway systems. As for Hogue's presence there tonight, it was the result of a clandestine network which had managed to track down consular officer Pedro Rodriques. He went on, to bend into the buggy, where he inquired of the corporal, "Any sign of the Mexican?"

"He hasn't shown all week. Why should he show now, Sarge?"

"Keep your eyes peeled," said Hogue, "and put that bottle away." He gazed studiously across the street at the people starting to pour out of the station. To make certain that Pedro Rodriques had somehow arrived back in Denver without his being aware of it, Hogue had played up to one of the women employed by the Mexican Consulate. Once he found Rodriques, his orders were to kill the man, and they came from Luther Radford, which gave Hogue some satisfaction. He liked the idea of bypassing Major Devlin, a man he considered something of a coward.

"That could be him?"

"It is Rodriques, getting into that hack. Let them head away from the station before we pull in behind." He hadn't disclosed to Corporal Benson the reasons they were looking for the Mexican simply because Benson, when liquored up, got to saying things he shouldn't. Benson was a records clerk at the arsenal and, like a lot of enlisted men, fantasized about the day his enlistment was up so he could go out and try his hand at making a fortune. Only it never worked out that way; most simply re-upped. The corporal was one of several other enlisted men he'd brought into this gun-smuggling operation. When they took his money, Sergeant Guy Hogue had carefully explained to them they were in this thing for its duration, no matter how long it took.

Silently Hogue muttered, "I hope them Spaniards never

pull out of Cuba. We can sell arms to the Cuban Junta until hell freezes over."

"You told me, Sarge, he had quarters over on Alameda?"

"Appears Rodriques is headin' over to see that whore he's been sacking up with. Keep tailing them." Slipping a hand under his coat, he pulled out a box of Redeye snuff. He added a pinch to the snuff already in his mouth, gumming it as he eyed some whores peddling their fleshy wares on a street corner. The neighborhood was getting seedier, with street lights spaced further apart, which suited Hogue's purposes.

Guy Hogue, with nineteen years of service and a veteran of the Indian Wars, had seen and done his share of killing. Many a time he wished they were still engaged in fighting the Plains Indians. Be it squaw or papoose, his guns had sounded. There were a couple of other instances involving the killing of white men, one a cheating gambler, the other case an enlisted man owing Hogue some money. Yup, he chided himself, as Corporal Benson swung around another dark corner, don't forget that gunsmith. That one was like taking out a steer in a packinghouse, no challenge to it.

"He's coming in on where that whore lives, so pull over."

"We goin' in there to roust that Mex a little . . ."

"Some folks, including you, Benson, shouldn't live in high altitude country . . . their brains don't get enough oxygen. Just stay tight here." Easing out of the buggy, Hogue hesitated, but then thought better of telling the corporal to lay off the bottle, as Benson would lie about it afterwards anyway. Then Hogue strode away over a cobbled street containing potholes and badly in need of repair. He'd seen neighborhoods like this back in Philadelphia, slums really; he'd been a product of one. He prided himself that he'd gotten out and made something of his life, and had absolutely no sympathy for anyone stupid enough to hang on here.

Nimbly he found a recessed doorway, when the carriage which had brought the Mexican here began to turn around. Hawking out tobacco juice, he held in there, checking out the loads in his service revolver, wanting to let Rodriques get settled in with his woman before he went in to do the job. Every so often in the days since Rodriques had been gone, Hogue had checked out where the whore lived and found that she entertained at least three customers a night. Her name was Maybelle something-or-other, a displaced southern belle, or so the story went. Stuck in a leather sheath attached to Hogue's belt was a hunting knife, which he'd honed razor-sharp on an emery wheel, and with it he could split a hair damned near lengthwise. Back out on the Great Plains, Hogue had used that same knife to peel the hide from a Northern Cheyenne brave, a highlight he liked to brag on back in the barracks.

"By now," he groused, "they should be down to the business of ripping each other's clothes off." But before pushing out of the doorway, he took the precaution of planting his eyes both ways along the dark and narrow street. Movement came from the horse tied to his buggy as the horse thudded down a shod hoof before passing gas, the sound of it rippling over to Hogue, who smiled. "At least that hoss knows what it's doing, as that corporal sure don't."

Sauntering along the sidewalk as if he were part of the neighborhood, he passed three old brick houses and a clapboard standing further back. Here he went up the brick steps of an aging two-story brick building which had once been a fancy hotel and was now a rooming house for transients and girls of the demimonde. It was early enough in the evening so that most of the whores would be out trying to sell their wares and, as Hogue expected, the front lobby was deserted. Quickly he took the staircase while craning his head upward to see if anybody was coming down where the stairs cut back the opposite way. The sound of a second-floor door closing riffled down to him, making him pause, the sound of footsteps receding toward the back stairway.

On the second floor, he cut to the left, but didn't bother pulling out his revolver. He'd decided to use the knife, to spring the door lock first, then to plunge it into Rodriques before turning it on the whore, to cut her up a little, maybe detach one of those ponderous breasts the Mex might be sucking on right about then. A sadistic grin spread Guy Hogue's thin cheekbones. Why was it the Mex or Negros had to have a go with a white woman? Hogue figured the halfbloods which often came out of the unions were no good to nobody.

As he expected, the door was locked. He crouched and placed his eye against the keyhole, grimacing, for all he could see was part of a sofa and a lighted lamp by a front window. It seemed to be a two-room apartment, that door further off to his left probably leading into the bedroom. Straightening up, he noticed that above him the transom was open, then he heard her trilling laughter and the Mex crooning something to her in Spanish, followed by the creak of bedsprings.

"Keep at it," Hogue muttered, as he brought the blade of his hunting knife in through the doorjamb and wiggled the knob, which promptly turned in his hand, and he slipped into the room.

When he did, it was to suddenly be confronted by the woman wiggling out of the bedroom for a bottle of whiskey perched on an end table. She froze when she spotted the intruder, whose reaction was to fling his knife from an underhanded position, the blade hilting into her plump belly, cutting away her scream as she crumbled down. "Damn," Hogue cursed as he pawed out his service revolver and plunged on toward the bedroom.

In there, Pedro Rodriques had sprung up from the bed. Naked, he was trying to find the revolver he knew the whore kept in a dresser drawer, as his own gun was stowed in one of his valises. Frantically he kept on searching, with his back to the bedroom door. When he glimpsed the intruder's reflection in the dresser mirror he spun around, only to have Sergeant Guy Hogue's gun bark out his death sentence. The slug which struck Rodriques directly in the chest killed him instantly. But even as he was falling, Hogue fired again as a sort of insurance policy just in case the Mex was still alive, the bullet punching on through the arm and lodging in a wall studding.

Knowing the sound of his gun would bring questing eyes, Hogue jammed the revolver back into his holster and turned to reach down and pluck his knife out of the dead woman's stomach, wiping the blood away on her filmy red negligee. Then he was bolting out of the room and making for the back staircase.

At least five minutes went by before the building caretaker, trailed by a handful of others, dared to enter the room. The caretaker took in the woman's body, and could make out another, one of her customers he surmised, sprawled on the bedroom floor. "Stay back," he called out craftily.

Out here murders were commonplace, less so the appearance of a man of obvious wealth, for he'd seen the Mexican come in, and now the caretaker hurried on to go into the bedroom, where he pawed through the man's clothing until he found a thick black leather wallet. One glance inside told him he'd judged rightly. He stuffed the wallet inside his baggy shirt as he hurried back to the hallway to tell what had happened.

"I'll try to find a policeman. But ... who could have done this? Don't touch anything until the cops are here or they'll blame us ..."

Three

Now the Catlin family plot out at Sunnyvale Cemetery was marked by another headstone. *It shouldn't be this way,* Josh Catlin felt through his grief. At any moment he expected to hear his father's voice come singing out through the screening trees. His train had pulled in this morning, where he had exchanged greetings with his uncle, Dr. Paul Catlin, who naturally expected his only nephew to stay with him. Josh had agreed to this, at least temporarily, before they came out here.

"Before, you seemed to evade my question . . ."

"About how your father died," said Dr. Catlin. He had never married, though he had many lady friends, and was seven years older than Josh's father, dead now at the early age of forty-three. He was gruff of manner, blocky of build, and had no interests other than his medical career, which included being Denver County Coroner, and to dabble in local politics. Greying muttonchops pushing upon his collar made it appear he had no neck, and a smile, for Dr. Catlin, was a rare event indeed. He knew the inquisitive mind of his nephew, that the question of his father's death would be poised. Better to get this over now, he knew.

Evasively he said, "Josh, are you sure you want to hear the truth—"

His eyes blinking questioningly, Josh said, "The truth . . . about what? About . . ."

"Yes, Josh, about how your father died." He turned away from the fresh gravesite and dug a briar pipe out of a coat pocket as he headed for his carriage. "I grieve as much for Jarvis as you do, Josh. Though we had different viewpoints, besides you he was my only living relative. Yes, yes, I know, get to the point. Josh, they say your father, my brother, committed suicide."

Josh Catlin pulled up short, his mind reeling, shocked by what he'd just been told. *Not this, not my father!* If he'd been told that Jarvis Catlin had robbed a bank, had squared off in a gunfight, those were believable, but to take his own life—Never! His father always awoke every morning as if it would be the best day of his life. Certainly, after Josh's mother passed away there were bad times. But he'd rebounded, shown that old vitality, even over in England.

"Son, it happened at the Colorado Club. They found him in his room, grasping his own gun—you know, that special presentation revolver."

Josh nodded through the disbelief of what he was hearing from his uncle. He listened as Dr. Paul Catlin told of how others at the Colorado Club had verified the violent act that had ended Jarvis Catlin's life. "There is one other thing, Josh. It seems your father had taken out a life insurance policy . . . with you as sole beneficiary. Which now, it seems, isn't worth the paper it's written on. But Jarvis did leave some money for you . . . and all that he owns . . ."

"Okay," Josh said as he inhaled deeply in an attempt to chase away his anger. "Okay. I know, you're just passing on some bad news. My dad . . . he was the best. Especially after Mother passed away."

"Yes, I agree. And he passed on his gunsmithing skills to you."

"Among other things." Josh found himself settling into the carriage, and found that he could think more clearly. He knew his uncle, that Paul Catlin didn't entirely believe that it was suicide. So, where did that leave him? Among other things, he would go over to the Colorado Club, for settling into Josh's mind with a solid assurance was an unsettling notion that something was terribly, terribly wrong. What had his father said once . . . yes, when they were camped out in the Colorado wilderness, that if you want to track something down, you'd best start at the roots of the problem. Or, in this case, the place where his father had died.

"Unc, you have an opinion about this?"

Grasping the reins, and with his teeth clamped onto his briar pipe, Dr. Catlin glanced over at his nephew. "Politicians cannot afford to have or voice opinions. Appears, son, you've got that bone in your mouth. What you're asking me is, do I believe if Jarvis killed himself. As county coroner I'm in a damned-if-I-do or damned-if-I-don't situation. Meaning that those belonging to the Colorado Club carry big political sticks in these parts. If, Mr. Catlin, you can show me hard evidence otherwise, then what?"

"It will help my father rest easier in his grave."

"So you have become a gunsmith."

"Yes, Sergeant Muldowny," said Josh Catlin.

"I heard you were in London. Your father"—Muldowny gestured at his holstered revolver—"fixed this gun and did work for other policemen. Hard to believe he's gone." He was a large, ruddy-faced Irishman sitting at ease behind his desk. "Josh, I wish I could say otherwise. But it happened just as I've recorded in my report."

Josh dropped his eyes to the open file. The report was brief, and he reread what it contained. Hiding his disappointment behind a smile as he rose, Josh said, "I'm sorry I troubled you, Sergeant Muldowny."

"No, I enjoyed seeing you again, Josh. I called the manager of the Colorado Club on your behalf. Some of your father's belongings are still there, and I expect you'll want them."

Once he was out on the street in front of the Twelfth Precinct stationhouse, Josh decided to walk the short distance to the Colorado Club. Ever since coming back, Denver seemed to have lost some of its allure, to be a less friendly place. Thinking back, it struck Josh now that his father had been his best friend, that he'd not only learned the craft of gunsmithing from him, but so many other things. Always his father had preached at him that he must be his own man, figure things out for himself, rather than accepting as cold fact the opinions of others. The report he'd just read about his father's death had been coldly clinical, as had Sergeant Muldowny's firm opinion that it was indeed suicide. Inwardly Josh knew differently.

Josh came around a street corner to be confronted across the broad street by the familiar facade of the Colorado Club and closer, an urchin of about twelve hawking newspapers. "One nickel, mister, buys you one copy of the *Denver Post*. Thank you kindly."

Tucking the folded newspaper under his arm, Josh began angling across the street. He stepped onto the sidewalk under a canopy running toward the front door, only to be intercepted by a doorman moving away from a departing carriage. "You're not a member here. Say now, you're . . . yes, Mr. Catlin's son. My condolences to you." He held the door open for Josh, who passed on into the club.

Waiting for him in the front hallway was club manager Foley, a somewhat dour man, Josh recalled, and not all that prone to small talk. Foley held out a soft hand, which Josh shook briefly as his eyes flicked to a valet lingering in the background. Foley said, "Thomas here will take you up to our attic storeroom. There isn't much left, just a couple of valises." He spun on his heels and moved quickly away in search of more interesting things to occupy his time.

"Now if your pappy," said the valet, "had been one of them rich cattle kings, Foley'd been fawnin' all over ya, suh. I'm Mason Thomas, but folks jus' call me Mas." He shuffled along with Josh toward the staircase, which they began climbing.

"Josh Catlin."

"Sure, I remember you, son. Troubles me, what hap-

pened to your pappy. Just nevah seemed the kind to . . .
take his own life, nossuh."

"Could I see my father's rooms?" He stepped onto the
third-floor landing, while the valet moved on by, saying,
"Yup, Mistah Catlin's rooms are thisaway. Funny thing
about that night . . ."

Josh hurried up as Mas Thomas broke stride and gazed
studiously at Josh through somber dark brown eyes. "It
was all so neat and propah. I was the first one to enter
your pappy's rooms after we heard the shot. He was just
lying there, lying there dead on the sofa. Holding onto his
gun. The police came . . . an' it wasn't long a'fore they left.
After the body was removed, Mr. Foley was hot an' heavy
that I clean up your pappy's rooms . . . an' that we
shouldn't talk about this to nobody." Pulling out a ring of
keys, he moved over and unlocked a door, and opened it
and went in ahead of Josh.

"As you can see, Josh, all of your pappy's belongings
have been removed. Rooms have been vacant evah since
that night. Yes, that night, as I was jabberin' on about.
Don't even seem important now. But one of the pillows
was missin' from Mistah Catlin's bed. I know the police
didn't cart it away. Strange about that."

Slowly Josh pulled out of Mas Thomas, a portly Negro
with coal-black hair and a courtly smile, the events which
had taken place in the Colorado Club the night his father
had died. He learned about the poker game, the names of
its participants and, from where he stood, the layout of the
small living room. Stepping into the bedroom, he took in
the big fluffy pillows on the bed and came back to stare
down at the smaller round pillows resting on the sofa.
"Were any windows left open that night?"

"Not that I noticed. Nope, as I recollect they were all
closed."

"The report stated my father sustained a bullet wound
to his forehead. Mas, if I were to point my own gun at my

head, in this manner, I would most certainly press the barrel until it touched my forehead."

"I expect so, Mistah Catlin . . ."

"At this close range, Mas, there'd be some powder burns. Did you notice any?"

"Come to think on it . . ." He moved around Josh and stood there staring thoughtfully down at the sofa. "I remember comin' up about here . . . and there your pappy was. With that bullet hole in his forehead, seeping out a little blood . . . but as I recollect there was no powder burns."

Suppressing his growing excitement, Josh merely nodded. The lack of powder burns by itself did not point to murder. If his father had killed himself, he could have held his revolver away a little, but Josh knew now that it hadn't been that way at all. The murderer had used the pillow he'd taken from the bed to muffle the sound of his own weapon. When he'd left, he'd taken the pillow with him and discarded it someplace.

He held in the room as Mas Thomas left to go up into the attic and bring down Jarvis Catlin's valises. Josh went over the rest of what happened in his mind. The killer had taken his father's gun and fired it out a window, closing the window before coming back to place the gun in his father's hand. Then the killer had gotten away by using the upper balcony. Murder, here in the midst of wealth and splendor. He turned when he heard footsteps, and went out into the hallway.

"You said, Mas, my father was playing poker. Was there an argument? A disagreement, perhaps, with anyone? Or did he have any visitors . . ."

"Why, Mistah Catlin, I forgot about that. Someone did some to see your pappy that night. I let in some others too, gennulmen come to see, Mr. Radford, I believe. Your pappy now . . . the man come to see him . . . yessuh, a dark-haired man, a Mr. Rodriques. He didn't stay all that long though."

"Thank you, Mas, and for retrieving my father's belongings." He took the larger valise from the valet as they headed for the staircase. Earlier he had been told by his uncle that Jarvis Catlin's personal sidearm had been given to him by the police, and to his uncle he would go now. Josh knew, in his role as county coroner, he had examined the body. He had come here to the Colorado Club with only a gut feeling. He was leaving with hard facts pointing out murder had indeed been done.

Down near the front door, Josh shook the valet's hand and said, "Is it possible, Mas, that you could get me a list of the names of all members?"

Without hesitating Mas thomas said, "I reckon so. I liked your pappy, he was a kind man."

"You could mail the list to me in care of my uncle." He gave Thomas his uncle's name and address. "This will be between us. I don't want repercussions to come your way."

"You believe your father was murdered?"

"I do, Mas."

"What I've been feelin' all along, Mistah Catlin. Some of these ranchers, they've got a lot of skeletons in their broom closets. You take care now."

The next stop in Josh Catlin's quest to find out why his father had been murdered was a South Portland Street address—the house where he had grown up. Along the way he'd asked the driver of his hack to stop at an open-air stand where a farmer was peddling some of his produce. As they continued, Josh tossed an apple he'd taken out of his sack to the driver, then he took out another apple and bit into it as he unfolded the newspaper and read the front page columns.

Somewhat disinterestedly he turned the page to scan it quickly, and his eyes froze on a lower page article. ". . . Pedro Rodriques . . . and woman killed in robbery . . ."

That couldn't possibly be the same Rodriques who'd dropped over at the Colorado Club to see his father. But the name stirred memory chords. When they'd lived in Mexico

City for a short while, there'd been this man, and as it came back to him, Pedro Rodriques worked for the Mexican consular service. The difficulty was that his father had had many friends, in many places. In Denver there was a Mexican Consulate office, and it was entirely possible that Rodriques had been transferred there. Reading on, Josh saw, other than the report about the robbery and subsequent murders, the article contained no helpful information.

"You said Portland Street?"

"Yup," responded Josh, as unfolding around him was a neat tier of streets and houses he'd known quite intimately. Some of his old schoolmates still lived there, but at the moment he felt detached from them, as if he were intruding, for both of his parents were dead. His father had sold the house about a year after his mother had passed away, though he'd leased from the present owner the use of a shed which had been turned into a gunsmithing shop. It was there that Josh was going, in search of something tangible that would give him a clue to why his father had been killed. *Groping for straws,* he mused wearily.

His request that the driver head his hack up the alley brought it there and up alongside the back wall of a square log-walled building with a tapering roof. Easing out, Josh paid the driver, then he reached back for his luggage and trudged around to pull out of a coat pocket a small ring of keys. When he entered the shed hefting the two valises, the sight of equipment and other old paraphernalia brought memories flooding back.

Perched up on wooden wall pegs were a row of saddles, one of them his old McClellan, and a Texas rig and four others, all covered with a light film of dust. On a shelf built onto the south wall lay an assortment of pack saddles and harness outfits, all strewn together in centipede fashion. There were old tarps, a canvas horse cover, and some rusting horseshoes. The rest of the shed contained his father's gunsmithing equipment and tools, and a rolltop desk, where Josh turned as he set the valises down.

Easing onto a swivel chair, he lifted some papers aside until he found a thick logbook with a hard green cover. Every gun that his father had worked on, Josh knew, would be listed in there, the kind of repairs made, and who owned that particular gun. He found that the first entry in the book was dated back seven years, to 1881. Thumbing through the pages, he found that some of the names were familiar, most of them hailing from Colorado ranches or cow towns, with some entries jotted in where his father had gone into Kansas and Oklahoma, and up into Wyoming on occasion. Springtime would find him eagerly waiting for that last day of school, which never seemed to come. Then when it finally did, off he'd go with his gunsmithing father. Jarvis Catlin had a habit of hitting places way off the beaten track, which was appreciated by lonely ranchers or cowpokes and small town folk.

"Benton Wade," he read. "Dad fixed an old Henry for Wade ... can't believe it was six years ago, with me taggin' along."

He went on to other entries, not really knowing what he was searching for. Perhaps a name or some location. He came to 1886, the year his mother had passed away, with a name pushing away his uncertainty. "The Colorado Club ... Dad joined it in mid-summer." A starting point, as it was the place, he pondered, where his father had been murdered.

As he turned the pages of the thick ledger book, certain names kept showing up, most of them the names of the bigger ranchers. Radford ... Keller ... Devlin ... Wade, and Radford again, with the details of the work done on the guns.

Now he turned to another page, his finger jabbing at a name.

"Rodriques? ... Pedro Rodriques ..." He reached over to where he'd placed the newspaper by the valises. He found the article about Rodriques, thinking that all of it was more than coincidence. "But what now?"

The what now, Josh Catlin realized, was that he had to convince his doctor uncle that Jarvis Catlin did not commit suicide. For that he would need the ledger book and this newspaper. Whatever involved his father involved Mexican Consulate officer Rodriques, and members of the Colorado Club.

Four

Oftentimes Yardmaster Ralph Perrone had to put up with the peculiarities of the military, which not only involved a mess of government rules and regulations, but freight that could come in at any hour of the night. It was a half-hour shy of midnight when a phone call from Major George Devlin yanked him out of a warm feather bed. But he hadn't minded all that much, because of the deal he'd worked out with the major. Like tonight, Devlin would fork over enough money to line Ralph Perrone's pocket, with enough left over to take care of Perrone's yard crew.

Further to the south lights came from Union Station, though no passenger trains were standing at the west platform. Around Perrone, of Sicilian stock and a large man with a wide, swarthy face, the large railroad yard was alive with the rumbling of switch engines shuttling rolling stock onto side tracks. The headlight from an engine picked out his black felt hat and the jacket he'd put on over his rumpled suit. The engine rolled slowly past Perrone, cutting across tracks to a freight train which had arrived within the hour. At Yardmaster Perrone's orders, nobody had tackled the task of uncoupling the string of box and flat cars. He carried a coal-oil lantern, which was unlighted, and from around the front of the engine at Perrone's approach appeared three men.

Lights from downtown Denver seemed to shy away from the vast reaches of Perrone's domain of iron rails and engines. From nearby came the chain-effect sound of boxcars punching against couplings as the foreman in charge of his yard crew set his engine into motion—and under Perrone's heavy work boot the rail he stepped on vibrated into sound. Once again the soldier boys, he mused sarcastically, are garbed in mail-order suits, and again they'd brought the Mexican along.

Without preamble he said, "You bring the money, Devlin?"

"Yessir, Perrone, it's all there." He held out an envelope, which Perrone stuffed into a coat pocket. He led the way along the line of cars. The crew which had brought the freight train in from St. Louis had, at Perrone's orders, left.

As Major George Devlin fell into step with him, Perrone said, "Three boxcars, according to the freight manifest . . ."

"We're just concerned with one of them."

It was of little concern to Ralph Perrone if the major was involved in a little black-marketing. He'd suspected as much when Devlin had first come to him, learning that Devlin knew his way around a railroad yard. The way Devlin had explained it, both of them would be covered if something went wrong. Perrone had to agree, since boxcars, whether they were home cars or foreign cars owned by other lines, often got misplaced up to two or three years. To make sure, they'd shunt the boxcar off to a side line tonight, and the one already there and loaded with military hardware, Perrone suspected, would stay lost. This would be accomplished by Perrone destroying the "junction card" which arrived with a boxcar. It meant for all intents and purposes the boxcar had never arrived in Denver, and could that very minute be floating around in any major city.

The other part of the deal with Devlin was that of forming the lost boxcars into a train, which would head for some location the major had failed to disclose. But Perrone knew it had to be southerly, which accounted for the Mex being there. Now the yardmaster veered in closer to a boxcar, where he brought light to his lantern, and which he held up as Major Devlin unlocked the sliding door and pushed the cumbersome door back. The other soldier came to stand by Perrone as Devlin and the Mex hopped up into the boxcar.

"Like I said, Senor Casandro, a boxcar full of Gatling guns and ammo, and other explosives. Artillery shells, too."

"Your army authorities, they will not suspect anything, Major?"

"Relax," said Devlin. "A shipment of arms has to arrive at its destination point for myself or Mulcahan to assume responsibility for it, something the yardmaster is handling."

"Perhaps I do worry too much," responded Casandro. "We now have rifles and other small arms in the other car—and this. What worries me, Major Devlin, is the time this is taking."

"The only way this'll work," snapped Devlin. "Slow and easy or it'll all come apart. Or you can leave."

Coldly they regarded one another in the vague light streaming in through the open car door. "*Si*, I can," said Felix Casandro. "With the two cars. But I suspect the men you have sold your soul to, Major Devlin, would disapprove. Fortunately, they are greedy, far greedier than you. As long as I have money to pay for these arms, Radford and his *compadres* will drop down at the trough and gorge themselves. It is why men like Radford become rich—they buy men's souls. Now you know how it is, Major—"

Stung by the Cuban's words cutting so deeply into the heart of it, Major George Devlin, though angered to the point of striking out, managed to reply only with a gritting of teeth. Doubling his hand into a fist, he slammed it down on a crate top, and then he laughed softly. "Gambling got me into this. As for the army, a lazy man's way to survive, I suppose. You know, you're right about Radford. That night at the Colorado Club ... well, what the hell, why go into that. I suppose you Cuban Junta people have a lot of ready cash ... and like you say about those ranchers."

"Major, we are both trapped in a web of international intrigue, just pawns to be moved about. Though yours is the lesser risk. *Asi*, you want to live on. While I will willingly embrace *muerte*. Tomorrow at the usual place?"

After dropping off the Cuban on a downtown street corner, Major George Devlin had to put up with the presence of Sergeant Hogue in his transom hack. This was an ordeal he would have to endure, at least for the moment. Before the incident at the Colorado Club, he had Guy Hogue figured out as just another opportunist, but to have the sergeant emerge as a cold-blooded killer ... Hogue's service record would have told him that. Damn, Devlin cursed inwardly, adding this damn to all the others he'd uttered ever since the night the gunsmith had been murdered. Coupled with this was his own reluctance to bloody his hands, and Hogue's presence.

Then there was rancher Luther Radford, a man as cold as Hogue but far, far deadlier. Where Hogue could use only veiled threats, the rancher could and would use his money power to destroy anyone. Devlin got to wondering how much money there was in the envelope Sergeant Hogue had found in the gunsmith's room. By rights he was entitled to half of it, but he'd let it ride. It wasn't that he considered himself a coward, for he had done his share of duty at outflung Western posts. But in Denver lay a higher standard of living, where men sat down to discuss things without resorting to violence.

Wistful thinking, he told himself.

"Major, you've got that dark scowl on your face again.

I thought things were handled pretty good back there with the yardmaster."

"They were," he agreed. "Maybe it's that I don't like the idea of just having those boxcars sit there. On the other hand, Perrone can handle that."

"And that Cuban is payin' through the nose. We've got everything covered, and besides, if there are a few slip-ups, those ranchers will smooth it out."

"There is one thing, Hogue. That night when we met with Radford, I felt that Radford could at least have reasoned with the gunsmith. Or if he should have been killed, it should have been done elsewhere."

"What you're saying, Major," Hogue said testily, "is that I overstepped my authority. Made you look bad."

"I was the one the ranchers came to first. Not that it matters now, as we're both a part of what happens."

"Shitfire, Major, I know my place in the military scheme of things. We gotta have someone delegate authority when it comes time for that. I reckon I might as well tell you someone besides me did overstep your authority." He spat tobacco juice out the open window as they came under the spreading glow of a street light. "Radford, to be exact." He let this sink in, let Major George Devlin sit there, the man's eyes registering glittering suspicions, silent fears and uncertainties. "You can read about it in the papers."

"Spit it out, Hogue."

"Sure, Major. Like I said, it was Radford again. The gunsmith Catlin had a visitor the night we was there, if you recollect. Someone from the Mexican Consulate, it turns out. Man named Rodriques, who I killed last night . . . him and some whore. So if you've got any argument with that, have it out with them money men."

"No," Devlin finally said. "No. Simply because the amount of money we stand to make out of this is staggering. Murder, one or two, makes no difference now, I suppose." Their carriage began angling toward the sidewalk and the beckoning lights of a Forest Avenue saloon.

"So tomorrow," said Hogue, as the carriage pulled up in front of the saloon, "the Cuban is gonna fork over more money." Opening the door, he regarded the major through a smile. "So, paymaster, just so me and my men get our fair share. See you back at the arsenal." He hopped out and strode into the saloon.

His carriage moving on without Hogue's somewhat menacing presence, Major Devlin felt the tension easing away. Hogue would do his job, of that there was no question. As would Yardmaster Perrone, and the ranchers, and the arsenal manager, Mulcahan. The only weakness in this was his agreeing to send along an armed escort for the Cuban's train once it pulled out of Denver. He could put Hogue in charge of that detail . . . a delightful thought. Then as he'd been planning to do ever since the weight of his debts had hammered down on him, he could hand in his resignation and simply disappear. If the Cubans needed more military arms, Hogue and the others could handle it.

"Sir," the driver called back, "you said the Golden Nugget Casino?"

"There, or the Alhambra."

Five

Shortly before dusk, Josh Catlin eagerly took in his uncle's large fieldstone mansion pushing over a guarding row of quivering aspens. Doctor Catlin's country estate lay southwest of Denver some five miles, in an area of rolling prairie and cathedral-shaped buttes which grew larger westerly, where they pushed toward the mountains. One of the other buildings was a smaller brick house in which lived a housekeeper and her gardener husband. Lights beaming out of a lower window told Josh that Doctor Paul Catlin was in his study.

Barely had the hack pulled up than Josh was scrambling out with ledger book and newspaper in hand. For him it had been a long and revealing day. But instead of fatigue dogging his mind, he was strangely exhilarated. Instead of using the front door, he cut across the lawn and onto a cobbled walkway which brought him around to the kitchen door. Through its glass panes he took in Maria Juarez presiding over the large four-burner range, and her husband, Carlos, peeling potatoes over by the sink. He hadn't appreciated it at the time, his father's insistence that he learn to speak Spanish. Or for that matter, he mused sadly, other things his father had passed on to him.

He entered with a smile. *"Buenas noches, Senora Juarez."*

"Ah, Josh, you are back." Her English was passable

though stilted, and she was a comely woman, in her late forties, with braided black hair.

Carlos Juarez merely nodded as he kept on peeling a potato.

"We will eat in another hour. Your uncle asked about you . . ." She laid a scolding smile upon Josh as she nodded to a basket of fruit resting on a table. "Carlos just picked the apples."

The Juarezes had worked for his uncle as long as he could remember, which prompted him to ask, "When was the last time you saw my father, Maria?" Selecting an apple, he used a paring knife to cut it in half and cut out the rind.

"The last *tiempo* . . ." Like her husband, she would sometimes lapse into Spanish when problems arose, which she read in Josh's question. "Carlos, wasn't it . . . a month ago . . . ?"

"*Sí*, thereabouts?"

"Did he act any differently? Like perhaps something was troubling him?"

"Your father," Maria said lightly, "always wore a smile. Where"—her eyes rolled—"his brother is so somber. Some of your father's things were put in the room he used when he came here. Perhaps there—" Wiping her hands on the apron she wore, she came over and placed a comforting hand on Josh's cheek. "It is so sad, what happened."

He placed his hand over hers as he said, "Do you believe he took his own life?"

Without hesitating she said, "Not your father—never."

"At least I have you in my corner. With these"—he nodded at the items he'd placed on the table—"I hope to convince Doc Catlin that my father was killed . . . and I wish I knew why."

He left the kitchen burdened down with the newspaper and ledger book, and churning notions of how best to approach his uncle. They'd never truly been close, since it seemed Doc Catlin wanted it that way. Probably the reason Paul Catlin never married was that it was hard for him to show emotion, or to express his true feelings. Even on hunting forays into the mountains after elk or Bighorn sheep, just him and his uncle and father huddled in around a campfire, a wall of reserve held Doc Paul Catlin captive. On the other hand, Josh knew that in his role as county coroner Paul Catlin was open-minded.

The door to the study stood open, but his uncle had heard Josh's footsteps and gave a beckoning wave of his hand. Removing the briar pipe from his mouth, he said, "At last you're home. What have we here, one of Jarvis' ledgers?"

"One that he used to record the make of gun he worked on and who owned it."

"I remember how he used to religiously record everything he did. Took as many pains with the guns he worked on."

"Paul," Josh said exploringly, "then perhaps you remember a man named Pedro Rodriques?"

"Sure, as a matter of fact Jarvis brought Rodriques over for dinner, one night last summer. A Mexican diplomat, as I recall."

"Rodriques was at the Colorado Club that night."

"The night your father died . . ." Doc Catlin leaned back thoughtfully in his wicker chair as he clamped down on the stem of his pipe. He knew this was leading someplace, that Josh simply couldn't accept the truth. Puffing away, he added, "Well, go on, I'll hear you out."

Tapping a finger against the ledger he'd placed on a coffee table, Josh said, "Jarvis worked on one of Rodriques' guns about a month ago. And here, this article from today's paper tells about a Pedro Rodriques getting killed."

"What you're saying is that this Rodriques, and the one listed in Jarvis' ledger, are the same man. Josh, this newspaper article gives the address where the murder occurred—a savory part of town. Hardly the place where a man of Rodriques' stature would venture."

He dragged his chair closer to the coffee table, grimacing as he rubbed the nape of his neck. "I assume you went over to the Colorado Club?"

"Where among other things I learned that Rodriques had been there. I will be receiving a list of the club's members."

"This prying, Josh, could get you into trouble. Son, I arrived at the club about an hour after your father died. I saw nothing amiss other than to believe that Jarvis killed himself with his own gun. If you ever suggested it was anything other than suicide . . ."

"Which is exactly what I am suggesting. From a source at the club I was told a pillow was missing from Jarvis' bed."

"A . . . pillow?" Catlin folded his arms across his chest, frowning.

Quickly Josh detailed his theory of why the pillow was missing, and that instead of suicide it was murder. "That club has some very influential people as members. People not only with considerable wealth but political power. You know Jarvis, how everyone confided in him, knowing he'd never violate a trust."

"You have a point there, but . . ."

"But as you said, Paul, there were no witnesses. Other than those involved in the poker game." Now he cross-examined, saying, "Did you find the bullet after it exited from Jarvis Catlin's head?"

Puzzlement squinted the doctor's eyes as he inhaled pipe smoke and the question. "As a matter of fact, there was no exit wound."

"Then, Doctor Catlin, we have our witness."

"Josh, once fired, that bullet was bent all out of shape. Just a hunk of useless lead now."

"Over in London I worked with Colt's people on a new development in firearms called the Metford System of Rifling. I—"

"Heard of it, of course. Other systems of putting lands

and grooves in gun barrels' exits too, Josh. None of which can be introduced as evidence." Doc Catlin's words were tinged with naked skepticism.

"We test-fired all manner of weapons using the Metford system," Josh plunged on. "To discover that every bullet we fired retained individual characteristics alien to any other bullet. Again and again, until I'm convinced beyond any reasonable doubt that . . ."

"Yes, yes, Josh, I know what this is leading up to. You want me to have Jarvis' body exhumed."

"Once we have that bullet, Paul, I can use my microscopic equipment to examine it. Then if it came from my father's gun—"

Flintily Paul Catlin said, "I'll need a court order."

"You're county coroner."

"The news of which will, I know, be leaked to members of the Colorado Club. I sense some danger in this for you, Josh. But if Jarvis didn't kill himself?"

They became aware of the housekeeper filling the doorway, and then Maria Juarez informed them that Doctor Catlin had a visitor. "A Mr. Valdez?"

"Some peddler?"

"He told me he is from the Mexican Consulate."

Doctor Catlin went out to escort Legate Arsenio Valdez into his study, where he introduced the legate to Josh. Said Valdez, "Pardon me for this *invasion* of your home. It has to do with your brother, Doctor Catlin."

"Jarvis? Please, sit down."

"Sadly I must tell you that one of my people was murdered, just last night."

Glancing at his uncle and back at Valdez, Josh said, "That would be Pedro Rodriques." He held out the newspaper containing the article about the murder.

"*Si*, it was Rodriques. I found in Rodriques' desk some mention of Jarvis Catlin . . . this note, as a matter of fact."

"My father, as you know, is dead."

"Is that so?" questioned Legate Arsenio Valdez.

"Yes," said Doctor Catlin. "It was on the same night your Mr. Rodriques came over to the Colorado Club to see Jarvis. But that was some time ago, going on two months now."

"Thank you," said Valdez upon rising. "My condolences to you gentlemen. If ... if you come up with anything, please contact me."

"Senor Valdez, officially Jarvis' death is listed as suicide."

Out by the front door, Valdez said, "Do you think otherwise?"

"Until tonight my mind was set in concrete about how Jarvis had died. Now things are unraveling."

"But what evidence do you have, Doctor Catlin, to the contrary?"

"Josh here is about all, and his suspicions. He's a gunsmith same as his father was. Perhaps more. Legate Valdez, I certainly will"—he shook the Mexican's hand—"get back to you." He held by the open door until Valdez's carriage was rolling away.

"It is time to eat," Maria called out from the living room.

"Well?" Paul Catlin looked at his nephew and said, "Meaning do we chow down or take the necessary steps to exhume Jarvis Catlin's body? What I mean, Josh, is that we're not going through the jurisprudence of my office as county coroner. Whatever your father stumbled upon involves the Mexicans in some way or other. Was Jarvis murdered? Tonight, son, we're going to find out!"

Down a little, where cedar trees guarded a hollow, Doctor Paul Catlin left his buggy. Beyond the hollow lay one of the gravel lanes wending through Sunnyvale Cemetery, which eventually went out through a gate in a wrought-iron fence. The cemetery took in several acres of rolling land south of the city. Distantly, off to the southwest, an occasional lightning bolt lanced groundward. But the storm, at least from Doc Catlin's experience, was of no concern to them, for it would push out into the plains.

Of immediate concern was a light in the caretaker's cottage off toward the northern edge of the cemetery. Josh had been sent over there to keep watch lest the caretaker came out to look over his domain of gravestones. He'd returned to report that the caretaker had fallen asleep in his rocking chair, to which Doc Catlin had remarked, "Name's Farragut. Not all that ambitious, or imaginative."

Digging alongside Josh was Carlos Juarez, and it was going well because the dirt hadn't sodded firmly. The grave was on a slight rolling hill, surrounded by mowed grass and trees, and up a little sat Doc Catlin puffing on his pipe with one knee propped up. By his side lay his medical bag, and in the doctor internal questions were pushing through his mind.

"You boys are doing pretty good," he said.

"Sí," said Carlos as he paused to lean on his shovel handle. "But, Senor Catlin, I never expected to be digging in such a place . . ."

"For a fact the pair of you'd make damned fine grave robbers. You might consider that, Josh, instead of gunsmithing." He said it in a jocular way, to take Josh's thoughts off the job at hand. Got a lot of fortitude, he mused, to be able to come out here and do this. "Or, Josh, you could become a police detective, as you sure were right about Pedro Rodriques." Coming erect, he came down to relieve Carlos.

"We should be getting close," Josh grunted as he dug his shovel in deep to lift away heavy marled clay. "Think that storm'll hit?"

"Nope," said his uncle. "Echoing Carlos' words, I never thought I'd be an accomplice to a crime. Beneath my dignity, too." His white shirt was streaked with sweat and clay, and a blister had broken on his left hand, but he kept on digging, wanting to get it over with. "That list you spoke about, Josh . . ."

"Of names from the Colorado Club?"

"Could be dangerous going around asking those boys irritating questions."

"Won't have to if I'm wrong about this."

The doctor's shovel struck into the wooden coffin and he said, "Won't be long either, before we find out. Doggonit, Carlos, go fetch that lantern from the buggy. At the same time, detour by the caretaker's cottage first, just to be safe." Dropping the heavy shovelful on the pile above his head, he put a bracing hand against his lower back and stood there, breathing heavily. He looked at Josh still plying away with his shovel, naked from the waist up to show the corded chest and arm muscles, and envy stirred in Paul Catlin. To be a young man again, to do things differently, like getting married . . .

He said, "Just a little more and I'll open her up. When I do, son, I want you to keep watch up there. You and Carlos. I want you to remember your father as he was . . ."

"Sure, Paul, but I'll tell you, this is getting to me. Figured I could handle anything."

"Sure, son, just shake most of what you feel from your mind now. I don't like it much either. But in my job as county coroner I got used to it. Farragut still dead to the world, Carlos?"

"Si," nodded the Mexican. "I brought the lantern, and here is your bag too, Senor Catlin."

With a helping hand from Carlos, Josh Catlin came out of the grave. He stood there, watching as the lantern was passed down to the doctor, along with a wooden match which Doc Catlin used to light the lantern. After Carlos had dropped down, he handed the lantern to Carlos. As his uncle leaned down preparatory to opening the casket, Josh spun away and trudged up to view the cottage and the lights of the city beyond that. He didn't feel all that tired, though there was still the task of refilling the grave.

Rather it was the deep expectancy, the anguish that if the bullet that was removed from his father's skull came from his own gun, all of this would have been in vain. But Rodriques' death told him otherwise.

Strangely to him now came Lanai Meling's melodious voice, as if she were speaking from the elm standing guard near Josh. She had often been in his thoughts. Regretfully Lanai had decided to hold on in London, though she'd promised to write. Though he knew it was the slight wind playing impish night tricks, Josh still felt her comforting presence. His father had liked Lanai, had never been troubled at all that she was a Eurasian. It was another thing he liked about Jarvis Catlin, the man's lack of racial prejudice. A man for all the world—yet tragedy had overcome his father.

"Peace," he murmured consolingly, "peace." His eyes stabbed again toward the cottage, flicked back to the tree and his private dreams returned.

Down in the grave, Doctor Paul Catlin had sent Carlos back to the buggy to keep watch and see that nothing startled the horse. He'd braced the lantern in some loose soil and was gripping a forceps in his left hand, his right gripping a long, slender probing instrument he'd worked down through the bullet hole in Jarvis Catlin's forehead. It would be a straight penetrating wound, he wagered, knowing the sight of his brother's face, though he was inured to this kind of work, would be disturbing. Stubbornly he kept probing deeper, opening the wound wider inside the skull. Then it was there, an object he knew was the spent bullet.

Removing the probing instrument, he dropped it into his bag and came at his brother's forehead with the forceps, muttering, "A hell of a thing to do to you, Jarvis, but after all that's happened I want to know the truth of it too." Forcing the forceps into the wound opening, he went in search of the leaden slug, then he had it gripped by the forceps and out it came. When it did, Doc Catlin found that his hand was shaking.

From his bag he fished out a small piece of cloth, into which he dropped the leaden slug, which he placed with the forceps back into his bag. Wearily he closed the lid of the casket, and held there on his knees for a moment before calling out to Josh.

"Okay, son, it's over. Get over here and help me climb out so we can start filling in this grave."

"What did it look like to you?" Josh inquired anxiously.

"A doggone bullet, son." He'd doused the lantern, and now he handed it and his medical bag up to Josh, who set them aside and turned back to help Paul Catlin climb out. "A bullet, but judging from its weight, doubtful it came from Jarvis' gun, a Colt .31 caliber as I recollect. But no time now for speculation. So grab a shovel while I go get Carlos. Then the three of us can get to filling in this grave and vamoose."

For the first time in his life Doc Catlin was denied access to his house, with Maria Juarez ordering the three of them out to the main storage shed. Grimy, and reeking of a musty stench, they had no choice but to troop after Carlos into the shed, where washbasins and hot water awaited them. Up on wall hooks hung clean attire. When they finally did gain entry to the kitchen, Maria had awaiting them hot food and hotter chicory coffee. Even, they realized, something so important as proving Jarvis Catlin hadn't committed suicide took second fiddle to the whims of Maria Juarez, and quietly they settled in around the table.

Josh, however, left for his room. He came back bearing a black case containing his microscope and another large valise. The ticking wall clock caught his eye; coming onto five o'clock. He drained a glass of water first, and began nibbling at the food as Doc Catlin said, "I'm just as anxious as you, Josh. Maybe more so. Pass those eggs over here, Carlos. Gravedigging can sure work up a man's appetite. But look at these blisters—a man sure pays for it."

"*Si,*" agreed Carlos, as he stroked his thick drooping mustache.

"Well," Catlin said to his nephew, "you're chomping at the bit, so get to it. Set your stuff up on the chopping block. And Maria, we'll need some more light in here."

Quickly Josh got the microscope set up on the chopping block, and from the other container some of the gunsmithing equipment he'd brought back from London. Included in this were sample bullets both fired and unfired, tagged to identify their caliber and weight. One of the objects was a hand scale, on which he placed somewhat gingerly the bullet Doc Catlin had removed from his brother's body. Anxiously everyone watched as Josh adjusted the scale.

Then in a calm, detached voice to conceal his excitement, Josh said rather matter-of-factly, "The weight of this bullet indicates without a doubt . . . it was fired from a .45 caliber weapon . . ."

"And not Jarvis' gun," Paul Catlin solemnly agreed.

Over by the sink Maria Juarez brought the hem of her apron up to wipe a tear away from her eye. To her and everyone else it sank in ominously that Josh's father had been murdered as he claimed.

"So, it seems we have our witness," intoned Josh. He lifted the leaden slug from the scale and selected another as he added, "This sample bullet was fired from a Colt .45. See, it weighs the same as this one."

"Carlos," said Doc Catlin, "if you and Maria will excuse us, there's something I have to discuss with my nephew, tired as I am." He motioned Josh back to the kitchen table, where both of them settled in as the others left the room.

"Coffee?"

Josh declined with a shake of his head as he speared a piece of ham with his fork, and put more pepper on his cooling fried potatoes.

"The way of it, Josh is that when we violated the sanctity of your father's grave without benefit of a writ of disinterment we flat out broke the law. Let me define this a bit more clearly"—picking up his briar pipe, he struck the tip of a sulphur against a table leg and brought the flame up—"if either of us takes this bullet into police headquarters ... and tell 'em where we found this bullet ..."

"I get your drift. They'll never believe you performed night surgery out at a cemetery, Doc. So, where does that leave us?"

"With the truth, so far. Which is damned plenty, if you ask me. Suicide has a nasty ring to it. Like someone in the family is carrying yellow fever ... or has leprosy. We will clear Jarvis' name, somehow."

Munching at his food, Josh said pensively, "Murder, done by someone at the Colorado Club. Could Rodriques have been witness to it?"

"Digging up one grave is enough for this aging county coroner. But there is a connection." He yawned and pushed his cup away. "I am retiring for perhaps all day to rest these aching bones. I know, you'll be questioning your silent witness. I just hope that bullet can produce some answers. So g'morning, Josh."

With the departure of his uncle, Josh went over to the chopping block. Under the light of three surrounding lamps placed there by Maria, he examined the leaden slug. It had retained most of its killing shape, and the rifling marks stamped into it from its exit from the barrel of a revolver stood out clearly. Frowning, he studied the slug some more, then Josh reached over and selected a slug of equal weight. He placed both of them under the lens of his microscope.

What Josh found after minutes of scrutiny were similar characteristics, and he murmured, "Both of these slugs are .45 caliber English government boxer cartridges." Meaning, to Josh Catlin, that both slugs were U.S. Army issue bullets. A picture of an army issue .450 bore breechloading central-fire Colt revolver formed in his mind. He could see someone thumbing the hammer back, with the weapon aimed squarely at his father. He willed the terrible vision away, to have other thoughts leap to attention.

His father had often done consulting work for military installations strewn around Colorado. Words sprung forward, commanding attention, a poetic phrase of his father's—something about the business of war. Yes, from the Duke of Wellington.

". . . All the business of war, and all the business of life . . ."

The rest of it was a jumble of words to Josh. But his father had always considered weaponing an army to be business, in a sense. Or, this army nonsense, was he jumping to conclusions? Weapons were stolen. Those departing from military service oftentimes smuggled out weapons. Suddenly the frustration of it all brought him stepping away from the chopping block in mute disgust, with a stabbing glance revealing that another day had dawned in Denver.

But with this revelation Josh also discovered that he didn't need sleep. He took stock of his equipment, and of what to do that day. Still mulling it over, he picked up the silent witness, the leaden slug, and placed it carefully in a doeskin sack. In his mind he'd cleared his father of any wrongdoing. But not so Mexican diplomat Pedro Rodriques. So he would go, once he'd changed into the proper attire, to the Mexican Consulate to pay his respects to Legate Arsenio Valdez.

"Perhaps . . . just perhaps, the Mexicans have involved my father in something? And my father, well, he always honored old friendships . . ."

Six

A little colony of banking institutions occupied a two-block stretch of Federal Boulevard in downtown Denver. At that hour of the morning the boulevard was filled with two-way vehicular traffic. The crosswalks and sidewalks were filled with bank employees pushing into either one large brick building or another. Just to the east on Colfax Avenue was located the U.S. Mint, with the gold dome of the state capital building looming on Broadway.

It was as if, Felix Casandro pondered with some amusement, the banks were shouldered together, the better to keep an eye on one another. He'd known bankers back in Cuba, pasty-faced and cold-eyed men armed with their weapons of collateral and high interest for the money they so reluctantly loaned. Here they smiled more and postured less, but they were all cut from the same bolt of unending greed.

Today he had papers identifying him as one Reymundo Aguilar, an agent for an import-export firm out of New Orleans. He had other names, which he'd used to get at money scattered about in several Denver banks. Casandro's suit, dark grey with a black vest, was one of three he'd had tailored over at a little haberdashery on Sixth Avenue. There was the owner, an aging tailor, a fellow Cuban who claimed to be from Puerto Rico, and the man's plump, middle-aged daughter. The tailor was part of the Cuban

Junta network and any day now, according to a recent telegram, two more Cubans would arrive to help Felix Casandro ship the military weapons out of the country. When they
arrived, he would have to escort them down to Reese Tillman's ranch.

As for Casandro, it would be good to get out of the city
and away from all the intrigue. He doubted that in his absence Major Devlin would do anything foolish, like finding
another buyer for the weaponry. Today, once he'd with-
drawn fifty thousand dollars from the Western Mercantile
Bank, they'd meet for lunch. He began crossing over to the
bank hogging most of the block on the western side of the
boulevard. He carried a large valise and in a shoulder holster a .32 Smith & Wesson. It would be good someday,
came a melancholy thought, not to have to pack a
weapon. And now when he thought wistfully about island
Cuba, there were also memories of his dead family.

"At least they are no longer at the mercy of the
Spanish—"

He followed others entering the Western Mercantile
Bank, the eyes of a rather attractive woman going seduc-
tively over the nattily attired Casandro. His eyes flicked
disinterestedly past hers as he detoured across the wide expanse of marble-floored lobby. He'd been there once before to withdraw some money, and the desk he sought was
not occupied by vice-president Spalding but by a comely
woman with soft auburn hair. Doffing his felt hat, he introduced himself.

"Yes, Senor Aguilar," she said as color touched her high
cheekbones. "I'm Annie Wyatt." She managed to break
her eyes away to study the papers he'd laid on the desk before he folded onto a chair. "Fifty thousand—I will have to
clear this. But I foresee no problem." She rose in a swirl of
shirts and left a smile behind for Felix Casandro.

"Ah, Senorita Wyatt, *un momento.*" So far in Denver he
had refrained from getting involved with any woman. But
through the loneliness that had set in, Casandro wanted

desperately to simply meet someone he could talk to, over lunch perhaps. At the silent inquiry in her eyes, he added, "My job keeps me far, far from my home. One gets lonely to see a smile in a lovely woman's eyes, or just to enjoy a woman's company over lunch."

"You are asking me to lunch, Senor Aguilar. I don't know, I . . ."

"Just up the street at the Broadmoor. *Si, si,* perchance you have other plans . . ."

"No . . . I, I'll think about it."

"If you're there," shrugged Casandro.

Ten minutes later he was on his way to another bank, careful to stow in the valise along with the money the papers identifying him as Aguilar, who he would have to be if Senorita Wyatt showed up at the Broadmoor. Now at a second bank across the street he withdrew another fifty thousand dollars. From there he walked the short distance to Sixth Avenue and called upon the tailor, who upon shaking Casandro's hand announced that two more Cuban *compadres* had arrived. "They are upstairs, Felix, in my living quarters. My daughter is up there keeping them company."

Casandro patted the graying tailor on the shoulder and said, "Yours is the hardest job of all, Senor Ponce. Staying here when you long for Cuba."

"So many years," he agreed, "and how much longer before we can truly say, *'Cuba Libre.'* Two things I have gotten, Felix, all this grey hair . . . and patience. And a daughter I cannot marry off—for all she cares to do is to stuff herself. The cross I bear is not only for Cuba, I'm afraid." Chuckling, he shook his head as Casandro found the inner staircase.

Passing through the open living room door, Felix Casandro exchanged glances with two men sitting apart from one another, while the tailor's daughter rattled pots and pans in the back kitchen. One of the Cubans, a squat, broad-shouldered man, dipped a hand into a coat pocket;

a precautionary measure. Both of them had on rumpled clothing and needed haircuts, while stubble covered their swarthy faces.

In Spanish Casandro said, "Which one of you is Blancas?"

It was the other one, the thin one with the broken nose, who responded. "That is I, and you must be Casandro." For one so wiry he had a deep and pleasant voice. "How was my English?"

"Not bad," grinned Casandro as they shook hands.

"They call me Dionicio," volunteered the other Cuban. He did not bother to rise from the chair. "So, we are here—"

"This is a waiting game," they were told by Casandro, as the daughter appeared with a tray holding some cups and a coffee pot. He nodded at her as she went about filling the cups and passing them out, but Casandro waved his cup away. "You will be safe here. Until I come back to take you away." He waited until the tailor's daughter had gone back into the kitchen. "To join the others."

"They told us little back in Tampa, Casandro."

Down the line Felix Casandro sensed he would have trouble with this Dionicio. He began questioning the man, hoping to find out more, only to receive for the most part noncommittal nods, though Dionicio did reveal, with sour reluctance, that he came from Baracoa, which Casandro knew was in the province of Oriente, and that he was a fisherman. Even over at Baracoa, a small city way off in western Cuba, Havana's long and bloody arm reached to enslave his people. Only in the mountains could the insurgent Cuban armies exercise some freedom, since the Spaniards kept away from these rocky heights. "It pleases me," said Casandro, "that you are here. I have given your host, Senor Ponce, some money which he will pass on to you to buy a few things and some new clothing . . . western garb."

"I am a fisherman, not some *vaquero.*"

He returned Dionicio's sullen glare and said, "I could

arrange passage for you back to Tampa, my friend. But you are needed here. The choice is yours."

Blancas laughed and said, "It has been a hard journey for both of us. I see you are impatient to leave, Senor Casandro. Don't worry, it is Dionicio's way."

After leaving the haberdashery and walking eastward along Sixth Avenue, the sight of the Broadmoor Hotel picked up his gait. It was his habit to arrive early for any meeting, and today he would be early, by a good half-hour. The presence of the American lady banker, if she chanced to show up, would no doubt antagonize Major Devlin, a man who often saw shadows when there weren't any. The truth of it was that the major was merely bagman for rancher Luther Radford. As for the rancher, two of Casandro's men were out at Radford's ranch posing as Mexican cowhands, the three others at Tillman's Ox-Bow Ranch further out in the plains of eastern Colorado. Many Mexicans worked for the ranchers of Colorado, and dirt cheap, he knew.

He went in the Monaco Street entrance of the stately, five-story hotel, and avoided the lobby by taking a hallway which led past one of the barrooms, out of which came piano music. Further along he waited in line with others there to have lunch in the Calumet Room, where he'd dined before. The major wasn't among the few people already in the dining room, he noticed, as the maitre d'hotel escorted him to a table set for four.

"There you are, sir. And if the lady shows, you'll want a bottle of Chardonnay . . ."

The Cuban nodded as he placed the valise in close to his chair and settled onto it, a glance out the wide pane of window giving him a clear view of the street. Opening the valise, he took out the papers he'd used earlier, leaving only the money in the black leather valise. A waiter arrived and Casandro ordered coffee, as once again he checked out the people floating by on the sidewalk hoping to catch a glimpse of Annie Wyatt, only to spot Major George Devlin alighting from a transom hack holding onto a valise identical to Casandro's.

In a moment the army officer, in civvies and sporting a smile, was seated across the table. He seemed more relaxed today, mused Casandro, as Devlin said, "Won a bundle at poker last night. So, how have you been?"

"Getting by, I suppose," he said laconically. "You surprised me, Major, by not inquiring about the money first."

"You haven't disappointed me yet. I brought along a shopping list, Casandro. In the valise. Lists some interesting weaponry." Major Devlin eased his valise under the table, where it was exchanged with the one containing the money. "Sorry to say, but it'll be at least two weeks before another arms shipment is scheduled in. A rather large one this time."

"Good," said Casandro. "Have you given any thought to a possible route from here down into Texas? By the way, I took the liberty of inviting a lady to have lunch with us. She knows me as Rey Aguilar."

"Humm," frowned Devlin, "does she speak English?"

"Here she comes now," said Casandro around a smile. "Perhaps you could ask her yourself, Major." They rose, and he bowed slightly as Annie Wyatt came up to lay hesitant eyes upon Major Devlin.

"I hope I'm not intruding?"

"Not at all," he reassured her, as he pulled a chair away and she sat down. "Senorita Wyatt, this is an old friend of mine, Major George Devlin. We were discussing a business matter."

"Go right ahead," she said.

"About buying land down in southern Texas, or around New Orleans. Wasn't that right, Major?"

"Yes, ah, Rey, I believe so. I do have some other matters to tend to. Miss Wyatt, a pleasure meeting you. Keep in touch, Rey."

Alone with the woman, Felix Casandro gestured away Devlin's leaving before they had dined. He kept on smiling at Annie Wyatt, intrigued a little by her, because generally a woman became a bank teller and nothing more. She was thirtyish, he guessed, and quite charming, he found, as they conversed. The waiter came up and she ordered a chef's salad, Casandro the lamb, and a bottle of wine. "I really shouldn't have any," she said.

"It isn't every day I enjoy the company of a lady." More talk continued from there, with Felix Casandro conscious after a while of the comparisons he was making between the American woman and the woman he'd married, although the memories of how Juanita had been were fading a little. The inevitable question came, and he responded with a pensive smile.

"Once, *si*, to a wonderful woman. But, things happen." He left it there, not wanting to cloud his mind and the noon encounter with the past. She revealed, though he didn't pry, that she had been divorced some five years ago.

Too soon for him their luncheon was over, and suddenly they were moving out of the lobby onto the sidewalk, where to his surprise she said, "Rey, if you're not doing anything tonight, please drop over for coffee."

"Why, that would be nice. *Si*, on Davidson Street, *si*, I think I can find it. Until then, *hasta luego*." He held, watching her hurry away, making a mental note that it would be Reymundo Aguilar calling on Senorita Wyatt. "So many names I have to use in this risky affair—but it will be Rey Aguilar calling on her tonight."

After tonight he would leave to guide the new men down into Colorado. That made seven, but even that wouldn't be enough if something went wrong. Hefting the valise, he caught the eye of a cabdriver. He would go back to his hotel room and look over the papers given him by Major Devlin, while for the first time in weeks he wasn't dreading the coming of nightfall.

* * *

It was after sundown before Major George Devlin had completed making his rounds, but with one more delivery to make, the Powder River Saloon looming in false-fronted splendor upstreet. First he'd headed over to Union Station and given Yardmaster Perrone some money, then out to Rocky Mountain Arsenal to do the same and chiefly to confer with Mulcahan. The rest of the money, around seventy thousand dollars, was still in the valise. Some of it was earmarked for Sergeant Hogue, so the sergeant could take care of his men. Hogue hadn't been out at the arsenal today, had been absent a lot lately, and this worried Devlin.

"Needs disciplining," he spat out. "Just got a damned nasty attitude. As if he's commanding this thing." Pride aside, Devlin knew that it could prove dangerous to brace Sergeant Guy Hogue. Man was renegade enough to pull a gun, just arrogant enough to gun him down. As he reined up in front of the saloon, there was just the slightest feeling of fear, and he shrugged this away. "Just because Hogue gunned down that gunsmith, nope, he won't bully me."

He'd found out the Powder River Saloon, though run by an old-time cowpuncher named Ace Riddell, was actually owned by Luther Radford. It was there he went to pass along the ranchers' cut of the money they'd gotten from the Cubans. The saloon was in the southern sector of the city, in a neighborhood of old houses close to some shipping pens strung along a spur line. It was strictly a cowboy bar, replete with a stage on which dancing girls and musicians performed. Riddell was a big strapping man, tipping the scales at over three hundred pounds, but inclined to be peaceable unless someone got to feeling ornery.

Reining his buggy to a halt across the street from the saloon and behind some horses idling at a hitchrack, he opened the valise and counted out the money he would give to Sergeant Hogue. Devlin had already gotten his cut, but even so he counted out another ten thousand dollars, which he thrust into an envelope. By doing so, he was short-changing Radford and his rancher conspirators. "Blame it on that Cuban," he muttered righteously.

At the moment in another part of Denver, the Cuban Felix Casandro was handing his hat to Annie Wyatt, along with a single red rose. That she was pleased shone in her eyes as she went ahead of him through the modest living room. To his surprise he saw in the adjoining room a table set for two. "I hope you haven't eaten, Mr. Aguilar."

There, as he'd noticed in the living room, the walls were covered with framed paintings, the furniture was Old English, and the hardwood floor was gleaming, with woven round rugs strewn about. The house seemed to reach out and throw comforting arms around Casandro, and he felt more at ease. "I . . . really, Senorita Wyatt, I was hoping to ask you out for dinner."

"I'll bet eating out is old hat to you. I grew up cooking for a threshing crew of my brothers and sisters on our Kansas farm. Had to after my mother passed away. It's just sort of a lasagna hot dish I threw together—complemented with some wine."

"It will be delightful. You painted this—"

"They're supposed to be elk grazing in a mountain meadow. I go up there sometimes to, to get away . . ."

Casandro turned and reached for her hand. "I'm finding you are a woman of many talents. While I . . . well, I can sing a little." The next moment she was moving into Felix Casandro's arms. They exchanged a tentative kiss, and just as quickly moved apart, still not sure about one another but keenly aware that something had happened.

"Please, Mr. Aguilar, sit down . . . tell me about yourself . . ."

"It is Rey—and I'll call you Annie. And really there isn't much to tell . . ."

Seven

The Mexican Consulate building lay south of the capital building and fronted onto Broadway. In the office of Legate Arsenio Valdez, a woman secretary had just delivered a folder thick with papers. In leaving, the young woman's eyes strayed over Josh Catlin seated next to his uncle, Doctor Paul Catlin, who'd been pleased to find the legate was also a pipe smoker.

"These are the last pieces of correspondence worked on and received by Pedro Rodriques," said Valdez as he peered across his desk at them through a pair of reading glasses. "I have gone over them again and again." He lifted a hand over and picked up a wrinkled piece of paper. "Except for this note, there is no other letter from your father, Josh. Though there is no evidence, I feel as you do, gentlemen—there is a connection. Now to this bullet, Doctor Catlin, you removed from Senor Catlin's body . . ."

"It was Josh who convinced me it wasn't suicide. As I said, Senor Valdez, we went like thieves at night into that cemetery. I did it"—he inhaled deeply of tobacco smoke—"this way because I sense danger, in all of this. We cannot now go to the police to present this bullet as evidence. But we wanted you to know, Senor Valdez, that your man Rodriques could have been a victim of circumstances."

"We want no scandal attached to this," said Valdez,

"but the truth of all this must come out. Your father, Josh, mingled with many socially acceptable people, I shall say."

"Certainly everyone belonging to the Colorado Club was in the chips," said Josh. "Not only ranchers, but the city's uppercrust belonged. My father did gunwork for most of them, though the gist of his work was done out at ranches and in cowtowns. He just liked to get out there, not so much for the money either."

"You, as you said, are leaving?"

"Taking my gunsmithing tools and such along. Mostly as a dodge to check on some ranchers, who I found out were playing poker with Jarvis Catlin the night he was killed."

"And you will take along your silent witness—"

Doc Catlin spoke up. "While I stick here and do some snooping. There's a certain police captain I trust. I suggest, Senor Valdez, we get together with him."

"It would have to be done with *discrecion.*"

"Out where Rodriques was killed, there's bound to be witnesses. I just might head out there myself in my position as county coroner. You know, Josh was expounding last night about how Jarvis got along with people, as sort of a father confessor to many folks. My guess is he heard something out of the ordinary, maybe some businessmen belonging to the club lining up some big crooked deal. Or some ranchers."

"This police captain," ventured Valdez, "it would be his responsibility to look into this. *Sí*, we must see this man. And, Senor Josh, when do you leave?"

"Soon's, Senor Valdez, I get back and get saddled up."

For Josh Catlin the trail around mid-afternoon pointed due south, one that he knew well from having gone with his father so many times. He had a packhorse trailing in close behind, and was astride a rangy black marked by white at its fetlocks and a white star on its forehead. The horses hadn't been on the trail for some time and they were frisky, jerking about under their rigging, but otherwise by Josh's reined command holding to an easy lope. Scattered clouds passed overhead. Meadowlarks sounded their tink-a-link-link, and red-breasted blackbirds flitted through sparse prairie grass.

The horses were part of Jarvis Catlin's estate, and Josh had stumbled upon some musky old railroad bonds stuffed up in a gunnysack in the shed; right now his uncle was checking on their present value. Of greater value to Josh was the gunsmithing equipment he'd inherited. It was all he really needed to get to the chore of making an honest living.

Under the guise of a gunsmith Josh hoped to gain closer access to ranchers Radford, Wade, and Tillman. The other night the valet from the Colorado Club had hand-delivered the names of those belonging to the club. Afterwards, Mas Thomas had lingered over coffee as he detailed what he knew about the relationship between the trio of ranchers and their connection to Josh's father. Doc Catlin was there too, asking gentle probing questions that brought out a lot more. Part of it was that the two men who'd come to see Luther Radford that night had shown up before, going back a couple of months, according to Mas Thomas. Once they'd brought along another man—to which the valet was able to attach a name, Kevin Mulcahan.

Pushing along the main stagecoach road, which would eventually reach into Castle Rock, then Colorado Springs and beyond, Josh knew that his uncle would try to find out more about Mulcahan and the others. He had to leave it behind, the bitterness towards those responsible for his father's death, and even lingering thoughts of Lanai Meling. From the roster of names given to him by Mas Thomas, he had consigned to memory the names of six poker players. Four of them had been ranchers, the other two lived in Denver. Perhaps none of them were involved, but Josh felt he had to make those names his starting point.

Nightfall came and it wasn't long before a full moon hung way out easterly in the High Plains, keeping Josh saddlebound. A couple of hours before he'd veered away from the main road and begun angling southeasterly in the direction of Reese Tillman's Ox-Bow holdings, a large spread of over two hundred thousand acres pushing as far as Big Arroyo, one of a half-dozen cow towns strung along Sandy Creek.

His remembrance of Tillman was that the rancher had taken to breeding purebred cattle and he had two sons, both around ten years older than Josh. Tillman, though fair, ruled his sons and waddies with an iron grip, and Tillman liked to party, even coming into his seventies. As for his politics, Reese Tillman was a big contributor to Colorado's Republican Party. Among other things, Josh had packed along his microscope, stowing the bullet taken from his father in the same case.

"Next I've got to get my hands on Tillman's personal sidearm," he muttered to the whickering horse, and Josh knew his horse had smelled water up ahead by a treeline. The exhilaration of heading out into the plains had worn away and some of his muscles had tightened up. Now moonlight guided him into a narrow creek, where he swung down onto a wide swath of prairie grass. The moon was still as big as he'd ever seen it out there, which helped when he gathered wood for his campfire.

It seemed the moon was still there when Josh awoke, only to find it was coming onto first light. He didn't bother with restoking the campfire but got his horses ready to go and pulled out within a half-hour of rising. He would breakfast at Kuhn's Crossing, and maybe pick up on some local gossip. One precaution he'd taken that morning was to buckle on his gunbelt. For a while it seemed a heavy burden at his right hip, then he forgot it was even there.

Like other places taken to selling supplies in lonely places, Kuhn's Crossing and the ramshackle store there had the same weary and decrepit look. Junk was strewn around the main building, rusty tin cans, bottles, discarded bridles and a saddle with the silver conches gouged out, and a rusting horse-drawn mower. Back by the twin privies, one marked heifers, the other missing its door, a tethered mule was chomping on high weeds. A clothesline had on it three pairs of red flannel underwear and assorted clothing, among which was a petticoat about as big as a bedsheet, and Josh knew this belonged to Toby Kuhn's wife. He'd forgotten her name, or maybe she had it tattooed on her body someplace, for his recollection was she'd once traveled with a circus. He liked pulling in here since Kuhn's Crossing, in his opinion, had character. Would they remember him?

"Well tarnation, Catlin, sure I remember you. 'Specially that time you was here with your pa and this halfblood Comanche wanted to cut your carrot off 'cause you used yer slingshot on him. You still a wild, reckless kid?"

"That was way back when," Josh grinned. "Now I'm gunsmithing by my lonesome."

"Well . . . so how's yer pa—"

"He's dead, Mr. Kuhn."

"Dead? Old Jarvis? That does sadden my mind." Toby Kuhn was big all over, with a shaggy head of snarly hair held in place by a grimy black bowler. For a shirt he had on red flannels, and baggy pants and scuffed boots. His wife, Orphie, Josh now recalled, loomed in a curtained doorway behind the counter where Kuhn stood. She was even bigger than her husband, round-faced, and with eyes that rarely missed anything. There was a purplish welt up by her right temple, and Josh got to wondering if they'd tussled again, a regular ringside event with the Kuhns. Sometimes cowhands would come in just to get things going between the storekeeper and his wife, and sometimes it would backfire; when Orphie was riled up she didn't give a damn who she took out, with either hand.

"This is Old Jarvis' kid . . . Josh . . ."

Sullenly Orphie Kuhn said, "You come here to buy somethin' or to stand there shootin' the shit with Toby?"

"Ain't she the refined one."

"Shut the hell up, Toby, or so help me . . ."

"To eat, Mrs. Kuhn." Josh couldn't keep from grinning. He moved over to where two tables had been set end to end, and where three booths hugged a wall riddled with old posters and notices tacked up there by locals, a community bulletin board for everyone within fifty miles.

"Riders comin' in," said the storekeeper, swatting at a bottle fly. "Damned things, they bite you, you swell up some." Moving around the counter, he squinted out the door for a better look. "Ox-Bow hands. Probably snuck off to come in here and plug into a bottle of rotgut. What's that, Orphie?"

Her voice cut out of the kitchen again, but octaves louder. "I expect they'll be wantin' to be fed too, so roust yer ass, Toby, out back to the henhouse for some eggs."

Leaving a muttered word for Josh to take over, the storekeeper and erstwhile hog-house proprietor found the back door, which slammed crookedly to a close. A dog bayed, one of a pack of blue ticks holding out back in shade as they were too lazy to check out the new customers. Josh went back of the counter when the cowhands began swinging down out front, using their hats to slap the dust from their clothing, and joking about something as they did. They were young, rip-cord lean, packing side-arms, and coming on in.

"Hey, Tobe," called out the first man through the door, blinking to let his eyes adjust to the dimmer interior of the large cluttered room. "You ain't Tobe."

"Went out back to get some eggs. I'm just watching things, I reckon. Mrs. Kuhn is out back though." Josh nodded at the cowpoke's companions.

"He keeps the whiskey under the counter. Just pass over a bottle is all. Ain't I seen you before?"

"Probably have, or my father, Jarvis Catlin."

"Yup, the gunsmith. You're Josh then." He pulled the cork out with his teeth, spat it away, and began guzzling down whiskey. "Whoa, that cut clear to my testicles, I reckon." He handed the bottle to another hand, who ambled back to the tables. "Hey, Orphie, it's me, Cadie Morgan, an' Price an' Webster. Come to sample some of your prime vittles."

"Bullshit, Cadie!" Orphie Kuhn roared out. "You've always bitched about my cookin'. But I'll let you boys chow down, you got hard cash. Dammit, Toby, where's them asshole eggs!"

Something rattled in the back kitchen, and everyone out front exchanged pleasant smiles. Cadie Morgan, as he reached for the makings, said to Josh, "Been a spell since you or your pa've been out to Ox-Bow." A blue bandana was tied around his neck and the long end of it spilled down over his checked black and gray shirt. The gloves he'd peeled away bulged out a back Levi's pocket. One of his upper front teeth was chipped away, and here and there a few small scars pitted his lean face. The other waddies had about the same appearance, but with different colored hair and ways of talking.

Josh was about to say that his father was dead, then the storekeeper appeared and took over the conversation. "Damned fox musta raided my henhouse, but I managed to salvage enough eggs to feed you trampy waddies. You pay for that bottle, Cadie?"

"Not yet," he said truthfully. "Will after we've 'et."

"Orphie," Kuhn yelled back, "they's gonna eat too."

"Collect the dinero first, dammit, Toby!" Now she came up front bearing a large platter heaved with piping hot food. "You, kid, set and begin slopping it down. Want more, call back." She had a scowl for the waddies while picking at her nose as she returned to her stove followed by her husband, who came back holding a blackened coffee pot.

Over at the table, he filled Josh's cup as he said to Cadie

Morgan, "I sure can't figure out Reese Tillman hirin' on some greasers. He stopped by here, Tillman did, on his way back from Denver, him an' three of them greasers. Lordy, Cadie, you know he ain't got no truck for them kind."

"To tell you the truth, Tobe, they ain't cowhands as they don't know a cow's rump from its horns. And I got my suspicions they ain't Mex greasers either."

Cowpoke Hap Price drawled, "Sure somethin' strange about 'em. I speak a little Spanish . . ."

The other waddy, Webster, muttered through a grin, "He got the clap from a high-fangled Spanish senora down at Turtle Springs."

"Anyway," scowled Price, "I asked these *hombres*, well about old Mexico and like Webster here, they don't know hoss-shit. Mostly these *hombres* hang around the bunkhouse."

"Yup," affirmed Cadie Morgan, "they're different, somehow. Sneak off at times to check out all those guns they carry. But Ol' Reese Tillman says to leave 'em alone."

If they were Mexicans, pondered Josh Catlin, could they be connected to the Mexican Consulate and to Pedro Rodriques? But one thing he knew, that he was on the right track, had made the right decision by coming out here, for with absolute certainty the owner of Ox-Bow Ranch was involved in some conspiracy. What really did happen that night at the Colorado Club? According to Mas Thomas it was just another high-stakes poker game, until a gun sounded and—

Josh let the rest of it die away as he listened to the cowhands and Toby Kuhn drone on about the lack of rain and how dusty it was. Once he got to the Ox-Bow, he was sure to pick up something. Pushing his plate and his cup away, he pulled out a silver dollar as he rose. He said to Cadie Morgan, "I'm heading out to see Mr. Tillman."

"Don't tell Reese you saw us," said Morgan.

"Keep the change," said Josh as he flipped the silver

dollar at the storekeeper, who'd claimed a chair at the table.

Out of the kitchen came Kuhn's wife, carrying a large tray. She said to Josh, "You leaving, kid? You paid Tobe I expect."

"A silver dollar, Orphie," said her husband. "Which I'm pocketing."

The way he said it, around a cocky grin, caused something to come unsprung in Orphie Kuhn's mind. She slammed the tray down on the table scattering food out of the plates. Then she hammered her husband alongside his left ear with a sneak right hand and he sagged out of the chair, cursing through his pain. It was then Cadie Morgan made a drastic mistake by giggling his pleasure. Reaching across the table through her anger, she latched onto his pretty blue bandana and brought Morgan strangling up from his chair. Josh, observing this bit of action from just outside the front door, grimaced when Orphie let go a walloping right hand that struck the waddy flush in the face.

Then Orphie Kuhn shouted, "There, take that you grinnin' ape!"

From back of the building came the satisfied chorusing of the blue ticks, their baying pushing after Josh Catlin as he climbed aboard his horse and reined away. Back of him, Josh heard the storekeeper's voice raised in strangled fury. The next moment one of the cowpokes, it appeared to be Hap Price, came sailing through a grimy front window.

"Yup," smiled Josh as he urged his horses down into the shallow creek waters, "no question but Kuhn's Crossing has a lot of character."

Eight

By late morning Josh Catlin was riding across the northern reaches of the Ox-Bow Ranch. He swung his eyes westerly to Pikes Peak and lesser mountains stretching on far beyond the limits of his vision. Around him much of the grass was still tawny due to lack of rain, but a few prairie flowers were blooming. Cattle were becoming more plentiful, and when he came over an elevation he saw about a mile ahead of him cowhands hazing along a small herd. This was open range, the only barriers creeks leafing out from rivers like the Arkansas and Purgotaire. Where other ranchers had put up fences, aging Reese Tillman still went at it the old way, though even back when Josh was younger he could remember Tillman's sons wanting to put up barbed wire.

All the way down from Kuhn's Crossing he couldn't stop thinking about those Mexicans that Tillman had brought out to his ranch. And though Josh could speak Mex lingo, he wouldn't reveal that fact until he had no other choice. Coming onto some wetlands, a pair of teals went clacking by overhead as if not liking the intrusion into their watery domain. Less than a mile, he knew, from there to the home buildings screened by cottonwoods and brush lining a creek and pine trees Reese Tillman had planted.

More cowhands appeared as he got in closer. Two of

them had their lassos wrapped around the horns of a Longhorn bull they were trying to move along, and dust was rising around the commotion of cowpokes trying to get the bull to move out to the herd ground, the bull swinging back and forth in an attempt to hook their horses. It appeared they weren't having much success, and Josh recognized Art Tillman, the older son in his late thirties, watching from a safe distance. As he recalled, Art didn't cotton so much to ranch work as to hitting into town to gamble.

The wave he threw Tillman drew the same response, and Josh reined up his horses and said, "How you been, Art?"

He was beefy through the chest, Tillman was, with a round, jowled face. He wore expensive range clothes and fancy red-topped boots inside his trousers. The cuffs of his shirt were tucked inside leather wristbands inlaid with the O-B brand underscored by a rocker. He was unarmed, but carried a scabbarded Winchester. "Reese told me about your pa, Josh. That packhorse—you taking over his gunsmithing chores?"

"Hope to, Art. Got to make a living."

"I've got a couple of guns need fixing. Along with Reese and some of the hands. Let's head where it's a heap cooler. You, Winters, make sure that herd yonder drifts over to Coulee Creek." To Josh he muttered as he swung his horse around, "Hard to get a good working hand anymore."

There were at least fifteen buildings making up ranch headquarters, and several corrals and some holding pens. Some pigs were rooting about amongst the pine trees growing in a wide circle around the entire set-up, and back of that were cottonwoods. Further away rose a low butte, others showing further out in the plains. To Josh it had always been a comfortable place to come.

A hand, at their approach, came out of a hip-roofed barn, to tend to Tillman's horse. Somewhat gingerly Josh dismounted, then he led his horses into the barn where he got them into a back stall. Looking back, he saw that Art Tillman was trudging away toward the main house, which was typical of the man, and Josh shrugged this away.

"I'm Ernie Bivans, out of Pueblo."

"Josh Catlin. I see Art hasn't changed any."

"Mostly he's pissed 'cause he can't talk his pa into a rockin' chair. Wants to take over damned bad, where his brother Mel is just content the way it is." He brought over a wooden bucket full of a mixture of oats and sweet feed and moved up past Josh, unstrapping the pack saddle from his horse to sprinkle the contents of the bucket over hay the horses were chomping at.

"I heard up at Kuhn's Crossing that Reese has taken on some Mexicans . . ."

"They're here, and not doin' a lick of work. Tobe Kuhn still as ornery as ever?"

Josh smiled at what had happened up there. "I reckon he is."

"You some kind of carpetbagger?"

"I fix guns. But not as good as my father."

When Josh was finished with his horses, he came out of the barn to find all of the Tillmans, with the exception of Art, gathered on the front porch. He picked up his gait a mite, the hard ground drumming hollowly under his boot soles. Reese Tillman still looked the same, though Mel, his son of forty, was sporting grey sideburns. Their wives were there too, and it was Reese's wife who spoke for all of them.

"Landsakes, Josh Catlin, you're a man now." She embraced him and patted him on the arm. "And you've been all the way over in England."

"Howdy, Mel, Mr. Tillman."

"I'm so sorry to hear about your father," said Reese's wife.

"Now, Nellie," scolded Reese Tillman, "don't be carrying on now. We all miss Jarvis. Can't tell you, Josh, how much."

"We always enjoyed coming here," said Josh. "As I told Art, if you need any guns worked on . . ."

"We sure have," said Mel Tillman. "All this dust sure plays heck with any kind of gun you pack along. You remember Nancy. So, let's go in and get comfortable, and you can tell us, Josh, all about these English dandies—"

"Yup," snorted Reese Tillman. Entering behind Josh, he placed a comradely hand on Josh's shoulder. "I hear London ain't all that tame when it comes to fillies and such." Just for a moment a speculating glint steeled the rancher's eyes. Surely all the boy was there for was to do some gun work. What had happened to Jarvis Catlin back in Denver, well, he still wasn't over it. Just like that, Luther Radford had arranged the murder, acting on his own as if him and Benton Wade were Radford's hired hands. He was determined to brace Radford about it, but in good time. For his present worry were those three Cubans he'd palmed off to everyone as Mex cowpunchers. But for all those gold dineros he planned to garner out of it, he'd send them packing.

After a couple of days everyone got used to having Josh Catlin around, and they turned their efforts to the routine of the ranch. Josh, having set up shop in a space cleared for him in the granary, found he was up to his elbows in gunsmithing. He had declined the offer of a room in the main house in favor of the bunkhouse, chiefly to find out just why the somber-faced Mexicans, if they were that, were hanging out at Ox-Bow.

Most of the cowhands were out, either riding fence or watching over scattered herds of cattle. Three hands were working there and sleeping in the bunkhouse, as was the cook. Josh had found that the Mexicans, when in the bunkhouse, kept off by themselves. He hadn't let on to anyone he spoke Spanish, and though he would pick up a few words, Josh still hadn't determined why the Mexicans were there.

Then into the granary had ambled Reese Tillman with a couple of rifles and a holstered gun that needed adjustment. Josh knew it was the revolver the rancher liked to pack around, and it was a .45 caliber Colt, the same caliber as his silent witness bullet. After Tillman had left the granary, Josh had taken the Colt with him back of one of the sheds where wood sawed into short lengths and used for the fireplace was piled. He'd fired a couple of bullets from the Colt into the end of a piece of wood. That was where he came to test-fire other weapons, and nobody came over to inquire about the shots. Hefting the short piece of wood, he brought it back to his workshop in the granary, to begin the laborious task of digging out the bullets. That particular length came from a cottonwood, and it was a softer wood than oak or mesquite, so Josh knew both slugs shouldn't have been damaged all that much.

Though late afternoon sunlight was coming in through a small window and the door stood ajar, he lighted a lantern and set it next to his microscope on his makeshift workbench. One of the slugs he'd pried from the wood he put under the microscope stage next to another slug marked with a small X and the one which had killed his father. He turned the coarse-adjustment gear as he placed his eye over the eyepiece, and fiddled with the gear again until both slugs came into sharp focus. In a moment Josh's anticipation died in an explosion of expelled air.

"Like two snowflakes," he muttered in wry disappointment, "their markings are dissimilar. But at least Reese Tillman isn't the murderer." Though, he suspected, Tillman knew who the killer was. The slugs he'd fired from the rancher's gun he tossed into a nearby trash barrel. Sacking the silent witness bullet, he placed it back in the black microscope case.

You shouldn't take it so hard, Josh chided himself, for tracking the killer down could take months, even a year or two. Brushing a fly away from his forearm, he bent to the task of checking out the action in Tillman's Colt. Josh knew he would have to repair every weapon brought to him, or arouse the curious suspicions of Reese Tillman. One point in Josh's favor was that perhaps Tillman considered him too young to be much of a worry or threat to whatever Tillman was involved in. Another thing were the Mexicans. For as that cowpoke had stated back at Kuhn's Crossing, and was common knowledge in those parts, Reese Tillman had never before had a Mex on his payroll, except for a cook one time.

The echoing sound of a horse's slow chop passing by the granary drew Josh's attention away from his work. He caught a glimpse of a rider's back, and then two more riders pushed on past the door, and Josh slid off the high stool and moved over to hone in on who they were. The last two, he found, were Mexicans and judging from their dusty garb, cowhands, as they had riatas tied to their saddles.

Now Josh's dismissing glance went to the man out front. The *hombre* rode as if he were somebody, and sat stiffly erect in the saddle of his horse coming in on the main house. His saddle and clothing were more expensive, and as his horse went to sidestepping, Josh caught a glimpse of dark, handsome features. Knowing that Reese Tillman welcomed Mex cowhands out to his place the same as a plague of locusts, Josh wondered what the rancher's reaction would be to this invasion as the rancher shouldered out of the front door. They were about fifty yards away from the granary, upwind, but clear to Josh came Tillman's washed-out voice.

"Howdy, Senor Casandro. I see you brought some more of your *compadres.*"

"They will be going on with me, Senor Tillman, to the ranch of our mutual friend. It has been a hot and dusty ride."

"Reckon it has, way the weather's been." Reese Tillman

beckoned to a cowhand mending one of the corrals. "Linder, see these men get situated in the bunkhouse. You'll have to tell me, Senor Casandro, just where we're at with this . . ."

"Why I'm here, senor." Felix Casandro retained the smile as the dour-faced rancher swung about and went back into the house. He couldn't afford to let it bother him, Tillman's abrupt and discourteous treatment, of not only today but during their earlier meetings. Some men weren't even aware they were racist by nature, and probably Tillman was that way. He must, Casandro realized, keep his personal feelings at arm's length, especially when they were about to acquire more weapons. Something made him turn toward the granary, where he encountered the pondering eyes of the young man standing just inside the doorway. Then Casandro was reining his horse after the others heading for the bunkhouse, to where three of his countrymen were coming on foot out from under shading trees.

Having stayed there before, Josh knew the main house had at least fifteen bedrooms tucked on both floors, and indoor bathrooms. Two large chimneys rose at either end of the large oak-beamed house, with fireplaces at both ends and one fireplace upstairs in the billiard room. Once Josh had accompanied his father here to Ox-Bow at the same time the governor of Colorado and his entourage had arrived to do some hunting.

After Josh had called it quits for the day, heading over to the bunkhouse, Mel Tillman had dropped by to ask Josh up for supper at the main house. Generally Josh would eat with the Ox-Bow hands and the Mexicans back at the cook house. They weren't friendly meals, as the air was filled with tension, and Josh would welcome the change. More so, since Mel Tillman's parting words to Josh were that Mexican Legate Arsenio Valdez was the guest of honor.

At the moment, Josh stood by the front porch steps gazing through the open front door and down a short hallway. He was still trying to puzzle the thing out, standing there as tenderfooting notions about what to do pushed through him. Plain as a blacksmith tonging an iron shoe into shape, he'd heard Tillman call the man Senor Casandro. Was it possible the real Mexican legate up in Denver was involved in this? That Arsenio Valdez was just stringing them along? For Valdez to be involved, the man had to be a consummate actor. After all, came Josh's wavering thought, he was an experienced diplomat. There was the night when he'd confronted Doc Paul Catlin, and shortly afterwards Legate Valdez had arrived. Had it been to find out what Josh and his uncle knew regarding Jarvis Catlin's death?

"This thing," he said wonderingly, "has more twists and turns and sudden moves than a horse bucking to get a burr out from under its saddle . . ."

"Buenas noches, Senor Catlin."

He hadn't heard the Mexican come up from behind, and Josh managed to checkrein his look of surprise. He said, "Evening," hoping it sounded casual.

"Permiter me to introduce myself. I am Arsenio Valdez." With an elegant sweep of his arm he removed his hat and held out his other hand, which Josh shook tentatively. "I hear you are a gunsmith."

"Of sorts," he replied. "I gather you're from the Mexican Consulate at Denver."

"Si, and here at the behest of Senor Tillman. My country is interested in these cattle he is crossbreeding. Such a lovely evening." A disarming smile in his eyes took in the wide sweep of star-studded sky.

A man came out onto the porch, and Josh looked to see that it was Reese Tillman puffing on a cigar. He'd changed from his usual garb of old range clothing into a cattleman's suit that shone dully through light pushing out of the door and windows. "I reckon you gents would like some before meal picker-uppers, which I've got plenty of. I have to say that Josh here lost his pa recently. Damn, I miss ol' Jarvis, as he could make a gun damned near talk. I expect, Josh, you feel the same way."

"Yes, it's different without him around." Josh knew the cagey old rancher was just testing the wind as to his mood and feelings, along with probing for any chinks in his armor. The gist of it was, Josh realized, that he'd stumbled upon something out here, and one misstep could see him occupying a shallow grave, one with no head marker. But he would rather be no other place tonight. Even back in London cow-mooning after Lanai Meling.

"Come on in you two," drawled Tillman over his shoulder.

Rancher Reese Tillman stood there leaning on his cue as one of the white ivory balls on the billiard table struck a third rail and nudged against the other two balls. Tillman shook his head in silent appreciation. "Where the hell, Casandro, did you learn to play billiards like that?"

They were alone except for the fire crackling out sparks in the fieldstone fireplace and their own grudging appraisal of one another. The head of a moose with a massive set of antlers put up on the south wall seemed to be staring across at another one of the rancher's trophy kills, the head of a large bison. There were elk heads, mule and white deer, and a mountain lion. Casandro had been in other rooms like it, but there the trophies had been South American or African game animals. The men possessing those things were all the same, except for a certain Spanish general in Cuba who had put up the severed head of an insurgent leader. Soon afterwards the Spaniard had been assassinated.

He had briefed Reese Tillman as to the current situation

in Denver, and to his impatience in having to wait for more weapons to arrive. As yet, he hadn't discussed with Tillman the death of the gunsmith. Casandro knew that instead of suicide it was cold-blooded murder. Chalking his cue, he regarded the rancher across the table. "So far you people have been lucky . . ."

"What do you mean, lucky?"

"That you were able to explain away Jarvis Catlin's death."

"Now dammit, Casandro, that was suicide."

"As you say. What about the other one, Rodriques—"

"Who in tarnation is he?"

"He was a Mexican diplomat, an old friend of Catlin's. The luck of the draw that Pedro Rodriques came to the Colorado Club that night. He did see the gunsmith, I've found out. Now the pair of them are dead."

"It's news to me, Casandro. I want this thing to work just as much as you do. Both of us stand to get what we want out of it. You know Radford could have ordered this done."

"Then I suggest you and Radford and Benton Wade get together. Or are you afraid of Radford?"

Ominously Tillman said, "I'll forget you said that, *hombre*. I wrested this land from the Comanche and Arapahoe, killed others when they tried to crowd me out." He laughed as he turned toward the bar and refilled his glass with brandy. Eyeing Casandro again, he added in a more friendly way, "You're right, we've given Radford too much slack. Sometimes Luther gets carried away with his own ego."

"Is it just *coincidencia*, the gunsmith's son coming here?"

This gave Reese Tillman pause. He watched as the Cuban missed a shot, then Tillman studied the options of how to make the shot open to him. Before shooting he straightened up from the table and said, "Josh was close to his pa. Traveled a lot together. But when this happened, Josh was over in England. So all he's got is suspicions to go on. I'll tell you, my hands are clean in that killing. And that includes the Mexican. But right now, Casandro, I'll have to back Radford up, to the hilt. I guess I expected that some would get hurt along the way . . ."

"There is always a price," Casandro said heavily. "Josh Catlin did say he was going to leave tomorrow some time."

"What about you?"

"*Sí*, it is important I leave quickly. For Luther Radford's ranch. Where I'll give the men I sent there some new instructions . . . and to reassure them all is well."

"You know, Casandro, if you're so concerned about Josh knowing more'n he should, he'll be alone out there. As I don't believe in happenstance either."

"You mean . . . kill Josh Catlin?" Here we have a man, Felix Casandro pondered bitterly, who had watched the gunsmith's son grow into manhood, a man who was just saying his hands were clean. As if with a clean conscience the Sunday tithe the rancher dropped into the offering came from his ranch earnings, while the money he was making out of this gun-smuggling operation went into bank accounts. This separation of good and evil, this salving of Reese Tillman's conscience, was probably the reason Tillman had survived to become a cattle baron, meaning the rancher had buried deep within himself the ghosts of his past.

"Kill Josh? No, I hardly think that's necessary at this point. He'll get over what happened to his father, turn out to be a damned fine gunsmith." Reese Tillman, as he sent a ball spinning around the billiard table, felt something tugging at the dark edges of his memory, and it had to do with Josh Catlin. But probably nothing of any importance, he shrugged. But it was that Josh was fluent in Spanish, and the voice of the Cuban came at him with a question.

"Then you'll be coming to Denver within a week . . ."

"Yup, just to keep tabs on Radford, as he plans to be there too. You also spoke about Major Devlin, that the major has to be watched."

"To a certain degree, Senor Tillman. He spends too much time at the gaming tables for a man, as I've been told, with money problems. People could start to talk."

"We've got no other choice than puttin' up with Devlin. When you pull out of Denver, I expect there'll be more wantin' to buy weapons. Or maybe you Cubans will be back for more. The money we're gettin' overrides the risks. Don't worry, we'll straighten Devlin out. But if we can't, Luther Radford spoke highly of this sergeant ... ah ..."

"Sergeant Guy Hogue—whom I suspect killed both the gunsmith and the Mexican. Who you people kill is no concern of mine, unless what I've come to acquire is threatened."

"That, Casandro, is awful dangerous talk."

"Every day my people die, and part of me dies with them. *Buenas noches,* Senor Tillman."

With the sudden departure of the Cuban, Reese Tillman stood by the billiard table gazing studiously at the green felt cloth as it took to wavering some, bringing him back into the past, and the killings he'd done. Certain faces came to mind, Indian and white and Mex, with the lines hardening in his weathered face and his eyes going steely. He hadn't shed one tear then, and he'd be damned if he would shed any now.

"Casandro ... he won't upset the apple cart. But the man's right, we've got to take care of some loose ends. Got to control Radford for damned sure. And Jarvis' kid, just grasping at straws." He knew that suicide was an awful stigma to attach to a family name. And he mused further, this Cuban worries too much, as Josh Catlin is headin' away from Denver where he would be less of a threat to all of them. "Patriots like Casandro claims to be, damned if they don't turn into meddlesome zealots. The money— take it and run."

* * *

Oftentimes the Cubans would meander out of the bunkhouse to go down by the creek coursing past the northern edge of the treeline and sit there around a campfire. The waddies sharing the bunkhouse had, after a while, lost interest in this and would sack for the night. Their jokes about the bogus Mexicans had paled a lot too, had turned their mindbends to hazing Josh Catlin.

Tonight for the Cubans there was no campfire, gathered where they were further west along the creek and talking softly. With the coming of mid-summer they didn't need coats, and a full moon threw down all the light they needed. Tonight they were there by order of Felix Casandro. At their leader's quiet order, one of them stood watch in case anyone but Casandro should slink over to pick up on what was being talked about.

Dionicio, one of the recent arrivals, was recanting the tale of how he'd fled from Cuba and wound up here, a story matched by the others. What made their stay out there bearable was its short duration. Despite that, they were cautiously wary around the Ox-Bow cowhands. They'd discussed with some worry Josh Catlin's arrival, as he certainly was no cowhand, and carried himself like a man with authority. It was Blancas who suggested they kill the gunsmith, to have once again Dionicio speak out that to do so would bring down upon them the wrath of Felix Casandro, and the local law.

"So, Martinez, you spent more time with Casandro than any of us," said Dionicio. "What do you think, about our *oportunidads* of pulling this off?"

"Excellent, I'd say." His teeth flashed white against the dark olive skin shadowed by nightfall. "As we are not dealing with renegade blackmarketeers . . . but with an American Army officer. When our train pulls out, as Casandro told me, it will be under official orders. Of course, there is always the *peligro* of . . ."

"Of betrayal," Blancas spat out. "I will kill if necessary.

Even an American. For I feel they should have sent their armies to Cuba long before this."

"So do I!"

They hunkered down under sleeping cottonwoods and swiveled their heads to take in a blackened silhouette emerging from the deeper recess of the pine trees. Felix Casandro had just received a sombreroed nod of recognition from the lone sentinel, and what he'd overheard chiseled his smile away.

"There will be no more talk of killing," he said. *"Asi,* I agree that American intervention should have come long before this. But the gravity of the situation is that we insurgents must not expect help from outside quarters."

"How goes it in Denver?"

"It will not be long now, a week, two. We have been promised uniforms to wear aboard the train. As for our route, that is still open for *discussion."*

Dionicio fluttered a hand. "As long as we are heading south."

As the talk of the Cubans went on, the thrust of their purpose for being there carried over to the low thickets to the east and into Josh Catlin's ears. The talk of a train, and being supplied with uniforms and official orders, could only mean the U.S. Army was somehow involved. Beyond a doubt they were Cubans, come to acquire military equipment. He was glad he'd risked coming out there, but what he'd learned so far was sketchy at best. Several military posts were scattered around Denver, and just to go to one and say one of its officers was selling arms to some Cuban insurgents . . .

He was laying belly-down, and had strapped on his gunbelt. Around him there were stirrings in the higher tree branches, birds fluttering nervously about. In close, crickets were click-clicking, away a little came the croaking of frogs, and the voices of the Cubans were low-pitched, as of men used to speaking in guarded monotones. They most certainly, he deliberated, had nothing to do with his father's death, or perhaps the death of Pedro Rodriques. Josh felt they couldn't involve themselves in open gunplay, which was why this Casandro had brought them away down there.

Silently he murmured, "I sympathize with these men . . . and with those Cubans still fighting the Spanish . . . but not with men like Luther Radford . . . Tillman, and the like . . ."

These ranchers, he thought hot and angrily, were making fortunes out of this, since the Cubans had mentioned a trainload of stolen military hardware. His father had often been asked to check weapons at army posts in and around Denver, as part of his regular clientele. Sometimes Josh would tag along, more to see the soldiers drill than anything else. Could it be that Jarvis Catlin knew the army officer, had set up this thing with the ranchers? In his mind, had he whitewashed his father of any involvement whatsoever? Shaking this away, he honed in on Casandro's melodious baritone voice.

The Cuban said, "We leave tomorrow, Dionicio and Blancas and I, for the *hacienda* of Senor Radford." Their presence had lifted the spirits of the three Cubans who would remain behind. Casandro saw no need to tell them any more details, such as receiving a letter from the Cuban Junta, telling of how other Cubans had filtered into New Orleans and into other port cities close to the Texas-Mexico border. An idea was forming in Felix Casandro's agile mind, and he was grateful that all of the men he'd selected were former railroad hands. Despite their knowledge of that, and of ships, their luck would have to hold.

Earlier, Felix Casandro had voiced his desire to stay in the bunkhouse, and he moved now alongside Dionicio back through the trees, as Dionicio said quietly, "We have all Cubans behind us. Despite what Blancas said, the Americans will help us. But the way it is now, their hands are tied."

"*Si,*" Casandro agreed, as he passed through a thicket a

few feet from where Josh Catlin was hiding. "Tonight I will pray to sweet Jesus for all of his help. When we get to Senor Radford's ranch, I suspect this gunsmith, Catlin, might come there too. This still troubles me, what happened to Senor Jarvis Catlin, as he was of great help to our cause. A needless death, I'm sorry to say, Dionicio."

"You were not involved in it?"

"I knew nothing about it until there it was in the newspaper. I thought, did the ranchers have a falling out? But . . . whatever, the past cannot be brought to life." Flooding into Casandro were the voices of his family and others killed by the Spanish, and sadness squinted his eyes as he came in on the bunkhouse.

Back in the trees, Josh Catlin felt a sense of relief, having overheard most of the exchange between the pair of Cubans. He could see that Casandro was a man of honor, and extremely intelligent. The man had a monumental task before him. And so did he, Josh reckoned—to find his father's killer.

Nine

Doctor Paul Catlin had never gotten used to the mad
hatter angling of streets in downtown Denver. On a city
map it appeared as if an underground earth fault had
heaved one section of streets butting into another, creating
small off-shoot plazas and courts which were difficult to
find even for longtime residents. Only official business ever
brought him into the confusing labyrinth of buildings and
streets.

But today his thoughts were centered far from that, as
he stood out front of the city and county building waiting
for Detective Mike Garrison. The building had an unique
M shape, the center wing crowned with a turreted dome.
His office lay deep in a buried corner and to the rear so he
had to use a back entrance when coming to work. Parked
out on Bannock Street was his carriage, where his driver
was chatting with some cabbies waiting for fares. Across
the street a park took up a city block.

Tamping fresh tobacco into his pipe, Doc Catlin's impatient eyes fixed in on Garrison pushing outside and discussing something with a couple of lawyers. Then Garrison
was clattering down the steps, and he fell into step with
Doc Catlin, who said, "I hope this isn't another wasted
day."

"Wish you weren't so impatient, Doc," Garrison retorted, as they climbed into the back seat of the buggy. He

had dark Irish features and at five-eleven weighed a solid
two hundred pounds. Garrison was on unofficial loan from
the Twelfth Precinct, while Doc Catlin's driver was one of
his mortuary assistants.

On two separate occasions they'd gone over to the Colorado Club to question the club manager and his staff.
Like discarded corn huskings, all they'd encountered were
dead ends, although rancher Benton Wade, one of those
who'd played poker that night with Jarvis Catlin, was in
residence. Wade had since departed for his southern Colorado ranch, and he had added little to what they already
knew.

Often he thought about how Josh was faring out there,
hoping no harm would come to his nephew. He hadn't
pulled any punches with Detective Mike Garrison, stating
emphatically how they had acquired the bullet which had
killed Jarvis Catlin, and of his going over to lay his suspicions on Legate Arsenio Valdez that both murders were
connected. Since that time Garrison had gone out by his
lonesome to question those whose names had been given
to him by the county coroner. What both of them were
seeking, and which still elusively avoided them, was a mo-
tive. Politics, business, and money oftentimes became bed
partners.

Garrison's clipped words cut away Doc Catlin's train of
thought. "There's this Mexican place, El Jaro's, up ahead.
I'll spring for breakfast."

"Hot spicy food this early?" questioned Paul Catlin.
"You've got something?"

"We can talk in there." When they were seated in the
small Mexican cafe, Garrison, after ordering a tamale omelet, told the others he'd located the mysterious Kevin
Mulcahan.

"Rocky Mountain Arsenal—"

"Yup, Doc, Mulcahan's run that place for three, four
years now. The way I figure it, we've stirred things up over
at the Colorado Club. If Mulcahan was in any way con-

nected with your brother's murder, someone at the club would have contacted him. The pot's boiling . . . and it'll really boil over when we call upon Mulcahan."

"You have a devious mind, Mike," said Catlin as the waitress came back with their orders, for him and his assistant, Hank Young, plates of ham and eggs, and an omelet which the detective was lacing with Tabasco sauce and catsup. "And a cast-iron stomach. Getting back to Mulcahan and the arsenal, I know that Jarvis often did work out there."

"So you told me before," said Garrison. "That is one big son'bitch place. Besides civilian workers, army ordinance has troops out there."

"Tedious work, this seeking the truth."

"You've been at it, Doc, long as I have, and it don't get any easier." Sprinkling some more Tabasco sauce over his omelet, he smiled across the booth at his companions. "Damn, you oughta try this sometime."

"I do," intoned Doc Catlin, "and I'll die an agonizing death. Waitress, a glass of milk if you please."

The young woman with the flowing black hair had just alighted from a passenger train and moved out of Union Station to gaze at the transom hacks lined up along Wazee Street, a narrow, cobbled thoroughfare lined opposite by business places. Why she was there still mystified Lanai Meling. How could she possibly have left cosmopolitan London to venture across the Atlantic and come here, after spending endless days on trains? She waved a cabdriver over with a stunning smile.

"Where to, lady?"

"I have the address in my purse."

"Along with a lotta luggage. Yeah, I know where that place is, way the hell . . . out aways."

Passing through the downtown sector, Lanai Meling took in the sights and sounds of Denver, inwardly releasing

private thoughts. Back in London she had been weighing
more carefully what the future held. To continue on working as a dancer, or to succumb to an English lord who so
desperately wanted to marry her? Always there'd been
musings about Josh Catlin, and more and more the worried notion that he was lost to her forever. Then one chilly
and foggy day it was as if a dam had burst inside, and Lanai knew that she loved the young American gunsmith.
From there she simply let the dictation of her heart guide
her.

The ride to Doctor Paul Catlin's outflung home took
over an hour. Along the way the cabdriver kept throwing
back curious glances at his passenger. Then he was pulling
into a long driveway, and it was Lanai Meling experienc-
ing self-doubts. What if Josh had stopped loving her, and
in fact had an American girlfriend?

Out by one of the circular flower beds placed by a corner of the large house worked Carlos Juarez, who had
ceased his toil when the carriage swung into the driveway.
He came forward as the carriage pulled up before the front
porch, and then to his relief, as he spoke little English, his
wife came out of the house.

Maria Juarez had a tentative smile for the young woman
turning away from the carriage, although questions danced
in the housekeeper's eyes. Here was someone of exceptional beauty and obviously of some wealth. "*Si*, how can
I help you?"

"This is Doctor Paul Catlin's house—" Receiving an af-
firming nod from the Mexican woman, Lanai Meling
plunged on, "I am here at the invitation of his nephew,
Josh."

"I . . . I see?" questioned Maria, as she wiped her hands
on her apron. "But you see, senorita, Josh Catlin is
gone . . ."

Wavering disappointment splashed across Lanai's face.
"Gone? But he will be back, I gather?"

To Maria Juarez, the woman's English accent was a barometer that the young woman must be the one Josh had mentioned who lived over in London. He hadn't mentioned that Lanai Meling was of Eurasian ancestry. When she noticed the slight trace of fear pushing into Lanai's eyes, Maria held out a welcoming hand. "*Sí*, you are Lanai. We must not keep you out here in this wind. Carlos, and you, bring in Miss Meling's luggage." Still holding onto Lanai's hand, a comforting gesture, she walked with her into the front entryway. "Josh will be back, soon I hope. I know he will be so pleased to see you. But . . . forgive me my *maneras*. You must be hot and tired out from making such a long journey. Carlos? Carlos, put Miss Meling's luggage in the upstairs bedroom, the far one. Then heat water for her bath. That is my husband, Carlos. And I am Maria."

"Oh, thank you," said Lanai, as she unpinned her hat. "This is all so . . . unexpected. I . . . well I left England in such a hurry, I do hope Josh hasn't changed his mind . . . that he still remembers me . . ."

"But Josh does, Senorita Lanai. And tonight you will meet Doctor Catlin. Come, come, upstairs where I will show you your room—"

The sentry, a corporal dressed in a summer uniform, snapped to attention when the buggy rolled in through one of the two main entrances to Rocky Mountain Arsenal. From there Detective Garrison took charge, flashing his police badge and asking where they could find the man in charge. As they rolled on, the names of those he'd come up with in the covert investigation marched through Doc Catlin's mind, names such as Sergeant Hogue, a major named Devlin, Radford and Reese Tillman.

What he had determined with some concern was that the list of names seemed to be growing. It meant that this wasn't merely someone getting into an argument over a poker game, but a wide-sweeping clandestine plot of some sort. That these people, if in fact more than one person was involved in the murders, could kill a foreign diplomat . . . to Doc Catlin this meant men of considerable influence were involved. The bottom line, he groused inwardly, was that somebody was buying something from somebody else, with a lot of money exchanging hands.

"Obviously," he said to Mike Garrison, "the military is involved in this."

"Not necessarily, Paul," said Garrison. "This place has quite a few civilian employees. These people aren't getting rich working out here either. Look how big this arsenal is—covers a lot of acreage. The storehouse for most of the western military posts. Do it the right way, you could move an awful lot of equipment out of here without any questions being asked. But, black-marketing guns, could it be that?"

Following in the general direction pointed out to them by the sentry, Hank Young, a lean, slat-faced man in his mid-twenties, reined his horse around a corner, where they headed toward a neat complex of red brick buildings. He was excited about being involved in this, and it had surprised him, since Doc Catlin kept his distance. At least it got him out of the morgue. Reining in closer to the sidewalk fronting a long, two-story building, he kept to his seat as the others scissored out just as a civilian and some army officers came out onto the walkway.

One of the officers inquired of Doc Catlin, "Can I help you, sir?"

"Yes, thank you. I'm looking for Mr. Mulcahan."

"I'm Mulcahan," responded the civilian, a wiry, pleasant-faced man wearing rimless glasses. "Is this important, as I'm . . ."

"Yes, you're busy, sir. I'm Jarvis Catlin's brother, if you remember him."

"Then you're Doctor Catlin," Mulcahan said quickly. "He told me about you. Except for the major, these gentlemen are in charge of an I-G inspection team. And I'm happy to say they found everything in order."

"No missing guns . . ."

Mulcahan looked sharply at Detective Garrison, gauging the intent of the statement. "Of course not. Major Devlin, will you escort the doctor and his friend into my office while I finish my business with Colonel Baxter?"

Then Doc Paul Catlin had to mask a look of surprise. The man walking ahead of him toward the open door had been there, according to witnesses, on the night Jarvis was murdered. He realized also that little word-slide by Mulcahan about everything being in tiptop shape out here was for his benefit. That brief view of Kevin Mulcahan told of his being an ass-kisser, a word that was sometimes bandied about at City Hall. It was a breed he detested, more'n a bad batch of smoking tobacco. Anyway, he mused, Garrison had tracked Mulcahan out here to Rocky Mountain Arsenal, so he'd just follow along with the man's line of digging out the truth. But even as he followed the major into a large office, Doc Catlin knew the men would be artful dodgers when it came to that.

Mike Garrison was a chain-smoker, the butt of one cigarillo barely leaving his mouth before another was gritted between his teeth. Even before the major could gesture for them to be seated, Garrison went to the attack. "Would that be Major George Devlin?"

"Why, yes—"

Nodding sagely, Detective Garrison said sharply, "You have under your command one Sergeant Guy Hogue."

Hesitation wormed across the major's face. "Why are you asking?"

"This is asking?"

Devlin took in the detective shield pinned to Garrison's worn leather wallet. He managed to find his voice. "Is this part of some official inquiry . . . and I didn't catch your name . . ."

Doc Catlin said, "Sorry, this is Detective Mike Garrison.

And as you're probably aware, and even if you aren't, Major, I'm Denver County Coroner."

"Yes, of course." Major George Devlin wasn't all that certain where this was leading, and it was with a sense of relief that support for him came with the appearance of Mulcahan, the man still wearing that cattish smile. "Ah, Kevin, Detective Garrison here is asking some very pointed questions."

On the verge of easing down behind his desk, Mulcahan kept standing as the smile slipped away. "And what is it you gentlemen want to know?"

"Simply," went on Garrison, "to know if Sergeant Guy Hogue is under the direct command of the major."

"He is," Devlin said quickly. "Has he . . . has he committed some crime?"

Mike Garrison ignored the question as he tapped ashes somewhat carelessly from his cigarillo toward the ashtray on Mulcahan's desk. Some of the ashes spilled onto paperwork, producing a scowl from Kevin Mulcahan, but he retained a tight-lipped silence. An unexpected smile lifted Garrison's mouth, the sort of expression on his face that of a person about to share a secret. "Sir, Major Devlin, you were at the Colorado Club the very night Doc Catlin's brother expired. Was the sergeant with you that night?"

"Hogue?"

"Sergeant Guy Aloysius Hogue?"

Where he stood, occupying the outer part of the circular rug with the Great Seal of the United States woven into it, Doc Catlin could just as well have been in another room. The eyes of the major and Mulcahan were centered on Detective Garrison. Smoke curling up from Doc Catlin's pipe hid the amused glitter in his eyes. They looked like a pair of mongrels caught sucking henhouse eggs, but through the spat of humor there was also in him a muted anger.

"I must tell you, Major Devlin, we have a witness as to what transpired that night."

"Yes, Hogue went with me . . . to the Colorado Club. I must tell you it wasn't the first time either. I know people there. I believe Mr. Mulcahan has also been there, on numerous occasions."

"But not the night," inquired Garrison, "that Jarvis Catlin was murdered."

"No," snapped Kevin Mulcahan, "I was at my home, some friends will verify that. I don't see . . ." He paused, threw a surprised glance at Major Devlin. "You said . . . murdered?"

"Foul, foul murder."

"No, you, sir,"—Major Devlin stabbed a hand at Doc Catlin—"were there in your official capacity as county coroner. According to newspaper accounts you said it was suicide."

"I don't see," Mulcahan said acidly, "what this has to do with me or Major Devlin. I knew Jarvis Catlin, as a fine upstanding citizen. But to come here with your accusations—"

"Gentlemen," Detective Garrison said softly, lightly, but through probing eyes, "I'm here only because both of you were acquainted with Jarvis Catlin. I have worn the soles of my brogans thin checking out others who chanced to be at the Colorado Club that night." Again he chucked ashes from his cigarillo in the general direction of the ashtray. "Now why do I feel that Doc Catlin's brother was murdered?"

"Well, why?" Major Devlin shot out nervously.

Mike Garrison had built up to this moment. In that room he was taking in a pair of men standing naked as jaybirds, according to what their body language had revealed to him. Though he hadn't laid eyes on Josh Catlin, it was as if Josh was there, the words he uttered those of a murdered man's son.

"Gentlemen, we have a silent witness to the murder of

Jarvis Catlin!" Trailing cigarillo smoke, Garrison and Doc Catlin took their departure.

Once the arsenal had fallen behind, Doc Paul Catlin surveyed the man occupying the back seat of the buggy with him for the longest time, and through admiring eyes. Then he summed up his feelings in one crisp sentence, borrowing some of the Irishman's words in doing so. "Garrison, you are one devious son'bitch."

Savoring the moment, Detective Mike Garrison muttered soberly, "You might feel the repercussions of their wrath. They're guilty as sin of murder, but of what else?"

"How convenient for them that Inspector General team was there to give them a clean bill of health. Dammit, Mike, we're back to square one."

"Not entirely, as our fellow conspirators don't know that. Are you boys hungry?"

"Sure am," their driver said brightly.

Nodding in agreement, Doc Catlin said, "A silent witness? Both the major and Mr. Mulcahan will want to find out the person who's betrayed them."

"And all we have to do is come in and pick up the body parts."

"You're reading my mind, Mike. Two murders are just the start of whatever Major Devlin and the others are involved in. I just hope my nephew Josh is still alive."

Later than he had come home in a long time, Doc Paul Catlin found himself driving his buggy around the last bend in the road. Still astir in him were the events of a day that had revealed some of the truth he sought. He had tarried too long with Detective Mike Garrison in an Irish pub hard on Denver's North side. But, in his own estimation, he was reasonably sober, and surprised too that he'd matched Garrison drink for drink.

The sombering side of it all was that he had abused the powers of his office. They, his political enemies, would love dearly to use the epitaph "grave robber" against him. Well, let them, for at that moment, he felt the grief of losing his brother overwhelm him. The gelding took over from there, pushing up the driveway to where Carlos Juarez was waiting. Spearing Carlos with an inquiring eye, he said, "The house is lighted up like a Christmas tree."

"You have a *huesped*, Senor Catlin."

"A what?"

"A senorita . . . from . . . from . . ."

"I reckon Senora Juarez will tell me from . . . wherever . . ." And when Doc Catlin went into his house, he was informed by Maria Juarez that he had a house guest. Following his housekeeper into the front dining room, he stopped in silent wonderment.

"This is," said his housekeeper, "a friend of Josh's, come all the way from England. This is Senorita Lanai Meling."

"Do I recall," groped Doc Catlin, "Josh's speaking about you? Yes, but he's gone, ah, Miss Meling. Gathering my thought processes, you lived in England?"

"Yes, Doctor Catlin, I did. I knew both Josh and his father. It saddens me when I think of what happened, I . . ."

"What happened isn't exactly the truth of it, Lanai, if I may call you that. Come all this way to see Josh, huh?" He smiled at her sudden loss of composure. "I see guns isn't the only thing my nephew worked on over in England." He shot a mock glare at Maria Juarez. "I could fit my chops around a nice T-bone steak."

"You could," she glared back.

"Be fitting, Maria," he said tiredly, "that I tell both of you, I reckon, just what happened today."

Ten

That unpleasant encounter with the detective and Doc Catlin was the least of Major George Devlin's problems. Soon afterwards a man came out to the arsenal with a message that Luther Radford wanted to see the major over at the Powder River Saloon. He'd left soon after, accompanied by Kevin Mulcahan, not to head directly to the saloon, but to try and find Sergeant Guy Hogue, who they'd found out with some dismay had taken off again.

They shared a carriage, and to calm himself down some, Major Devlin had brought along a bottle of whiskey. He'd checked the loads in his service revolver with uncertain hands. Drumming through his mind, and Mulcahan's, was the identity of this secret witness. Snapped out Devlin, "It was just me and Hogue, and Radford?"

"Perhaps?" Kevin Mulcahan said through jaundiced eyes. He didn't like the way Devlin was attacking the whiskey bottle, but to say something would rile him even more. Devlin, he was beginning to realize, disliked confrontations. In a way, he welcomed their running into Sergeant Hogue tonight. Too many accusing words from Devlin would see the sergeant putting another notch on his service revolver, of that Mulcahan had no doubt.

It took a moment for Major Devlin to remember the name of their driver, a corporal and one of Sergeant

Hogue's hand-picked men. "You, Corporal Latner, there's this bar up ahead ... we'll check it out."

Knowing the habits of Luther Radford, Mulcahan figured Radford would be hunkered in at a poker table. Arapahoe, a downtown street, wasn't as busy as during the day, with their horse pushing along at a clippy canter. To come here trying to find Hogue could take the early shank of the evening. If they showed up late, it would only add fuel to the rancher's suspicions. As for his own, Mulcahan had it figured that Major Devlin, in his role as paymaster for the plot involving the Cubans, was shortchanging the lot of them. If that proved out, Sergeant Hogue was the least of the major's worries. He'd killed the sonofabitch himself. He forged a smile for Devlin.

"What if you look around for Hogue," he said, "while I head over to see Radford?"

The look Major Devlin cast at Mulcahan was as though somebody had dashed cold water in his face. The palm of his hand punching the cork back into the whiskey bottle, Devlin let it sink in as he dropped the bottle by his feet. Right then, it struck him, Sergeant Hogue was the least of his worries. If he didn't show up at the Powder River Saloon, there was no telling what kind of plot Mulcahan and Radford would hatch, and he just might find himself out in the cold. Or worse, Radford ordering him killed.

"Dammit, I guess Hogue can wait. Tell me, does it trouble you, these ranchers getting the shank of the money while we do their dirty work? Well, it does me."

"Sure it isn't right, George. But chew on this—these cattlemen can cover things up if anything goes wrong. So far all we're talking about are two boxcars packed with armament. Way I figure is these Cubans will want more weaponry than even we can supply."

"Maybe this Casandro runs into bad luck along the way—"

"We've got to make sure if that happens the Cubans don't pin the blame on us. And if it does happen, they'll find someone else to buys guns from. They're not going away. Play it right, we can make millions out of this."

"Okay, we play along with these greedy cattlemen. This silent witness that damned detective was talking about . . ."

"I doubt if it was Sergeant Hogue," said Mulcahan. "If so, he's a dead man."

On a hunch, Felix Casandro had decided to hold off making the long ride over mostly tawny-grass prairie to Luther Radford's ranch tucked in close to the Rockies. Instead, he'd struck due south in the direction of La Junta and the Arkansas River. The three of them had pulled away from Reese Tillman's Ox-Bow around noon, a half-day's ride behind Josh Tillman. That had been two days ago, and around mid-morning of the third day they were at least ten miles west of La Junta; a merchant back there had given them directions to Benton Wade's large cattle spread.

His dealings with the three ranchers from whom he was buying military equipment had revealed to Casandro that Benton Wade let his partners do most of the palavering. Wade seemed to have a mind of his own, and though mighty close-lipped, Casandro had this hunch the man might open up. He suspected that Wade was getting cold feet about the whole thing.

He liked the looks of the delta land pushing away from the Arkansas north of them; they'd crossed the river about an hour ago. All a man had to do was to shove a bunch of cattle out there to graze, and come fall round 'em up and find a stock buyer. As usual, Blancas was lagging behind, with Casandro watching a woodchuck scurry away as he said to Dionicio, "You asked me before, can we trust these cattlemen? This is why we are coming down here. I do not believe that Benton Wade knows about the death of this Mexican diplomat. We will tell him about this, just to see how Wade *reaccoinars* . . ."

"He is in too deeply, Felix, to even think about pulling out."

"*Si*, I agree. But it is wise we come here. To learn more about your allies before they become your enemies."

"You are saying . . ."

"All three of them, Radford and Tillman and Wade, are very avaricious, to the point of gluttony. Otherwise they would not have come to the Cuban Junta in the first place. They control Major Devlin. Meaning, Dionicio, they control the army in and about Denver. I feel they will try to coerce more money out of us. They . . ."

"*Hola*—it is that gunsmith!"

They had been following a vague trail lifting along the lower elevations of a long flat-crowned butte, and as Casandro reined around, he took in Blancas about to bring his rifle to bear on a horseman cantering along closer to the river. Before Blancas could fire his rifle, Felix Casandro spurred in close and grabbed the rifle away from the Cuban.

"You damned fool," he said tautly. "We cannot afford to go about killing Americans. That is for the others to do, Radford and his hirelings."

The bulky Blancas spat out, "Why is he here? He has been following us."

Dionicio, who'd pulled out his revolver, rode up and said, "Blancas, you have been a pain in the ass ever since we left Florida. I want no more of this, or I'll kill you myself. Do you comprehend, Blancas—"

"He is right," Casandro said to Blancas. "Your rogue manners could see us all getting killed. But, Blancas"—he handed the rifle back—"you are right to ask why has the gunsmith shown up now. He is so obviously going to Benton Wade's ranch. Perhaps Josh Catlin's father has plied his trade out here. That must be it."

"We know there is more," Dionicio said sagely.

"Of course," agreed Casandro. "The plot thickens. This

Josh Catlin, he has stumbled upon something, no doubt, amongst his father's personal effects."

"We had nothing to do with his father's death?"

"That is of little *consecuencia* at this point in time. Destiny has brought us together. As they say, the luck of the draw—"

"El surete de el empate," Dionicio echoed as they rode on.

With some apprehension Major George Devlin went up to a room just off the second-floor balcony. Warily he had settled down as rancher Luther Radford had handed he and Kevin Mulcahan glasses of whiskey. He'd never been able to discern the mood bends of Radford, but tension lay in the small room used as an office by the man running the saloon. Even though the door was closed, racket from the main barroom punched in through the open transom.

Devlin's anxiety increased when, or at least it seemed to him, both Mulcahan and Radford shifted their chairs and regarded him in unreadable silence, with Radford picking at something that had gotten lodged between his upper teeth. But it was Kevin Mulcahan who spoke first.

"George, I just received a telegram about some more arms shipments."

Frowning, Devlin said, "Why didn't you tell me before this?"

"Cut the crap, Devlin," said Radford. "I'm not pleased with the way you're handling things. That last payoff from the Cuban was short ten thousand dollars."

"He only gave me ninety thousand," blustered Major Devlin. "Go ask Casandro about this . . ."

"I would, but Casandro left town." Grimacing in thought, Luther Radford stared distantly at the ceiling. "Let's go over it again, about this police detective coming out to Rocky Mountain. Are you sure, the both of you, you didn't leave out anything?"

"No," frowned Mulcahan. "It was this detective and

Doc Catlin, throwing a lot of stupid questions our way. This witness ..."

"We've been trying to track down Sergeant Hogue."

"No, not Hogue," snapped Radford. "The county coroner's been snooping around the Colorado Club hoping to come up with some dirty linen. Out at the ranch when a dog gets to sucking at hen eggs we kill the damned cur. Same thing about Catlin, he's sucking around ... only thing is, the sorry damned fool broke the law." Radford let whiskey gurgle into his glass, a malicious smile creasing across his face.

The rancher let the tension push at the pair of them, before he said, "Doc Catlin disinterred his brother's body."

Devlin almost leaped up from the chair. "He what?"

"Found this out through police sources. 'Course, we can't prove it as there were no witnesses. But it happened, and why, dammit?"

"This doesn't make any sense," speculated Mulcahan. "Everyone's accepted it as suicide."

"I'll tell you why. It was because Jarvis Catlin's son, this Josh, is back." Radford hammered a fist down on the table as he half-rose, a dangerous light glinting out of his squinting eyes picking at both of them. "Josh Catlin has been makin' a nuisance of himself over at the Colorado Club. But ..."

Major George Devlin gulped down the whiskey and made a grab for the bottle, receiving no objections from the rancher. He was as nerve-racked as he'd ever been, and willing to do most anything to get back in Radford's good graces. "We have him killed."

"Unfortunately, Major, Catlin's pulled out of town. If he hadn't he'd be dead right now, I guarantee you that. Perhaps I should have talked Jarvis Catlin into pulling out of here for Europe or Hawaii. But second-guessing after a man's dead is like lookin' up a dead burro's asshole. Major, you get word to Sergeant Hogue that I want to see him, that we're going to settle this thing. And now to business—"

"Yes," said Mulcahan, "the arms that are coming in. We're getting a lot more this time. Enough, I wager, to see the Cuban pulling out of here on a special train. Major Devlin and his men will be aboard that train just to make sure things go right."

"Are you up to it, Devlin?"

"Certainly," he said to the rancher.

"Make no mistake about it, Devlin," Radford said hotly. "It's your responsibility to see that this train reaches the Gulf Coast without incident. From there, whatever. Now get out there and look for Sergeant Hogue. And for damn sure, lay off anymore whiskey and gambling. Now, get out." His glaring eyes and contemptuous words followed the major out of the room, then the door thudded shut.

"You're too hard on Devlin," said Mulcahan.

"The man's a thief as well as a coward."

"Maybe so. I know Devlin. Push him too hard and he'll crack."

"We could put the sergeant in charge of this military detail—".

"Won't look right, Mr. Radford. Devlin'll come around, I'll see to that. Right now I want to get over to the railroad yard and talk to Yardmaster Perrone."

"Does Perrone know about me an' my rancher friends?"

"Not through me. And to give the major credit, he will definitely not reveal anything, as he knows what the consequences would be. Getting back to Josh Catlin, it could be entirely possible his father left papers behind."

"Yup, anything's possible. But if Jarvis Catlin had done so, this police detective would have asked a lot more questions. I've been a poker player long enough to know when someone's bluffing. As for Catlin's son—what the hell, Mulcahan, an accident can be arranged."

Eleven

Cattleman Benton Wade had really laid out the welcome mat for the son of recently demised gunsmith Jarvis Catlin. Among Wade's recollections was one of how Josh Catlin had had a crush on one of his daughters, and other anecdotes came to mind for the elderly rancher. This had all been after the initial shock of recognizing the rider coming in trailing a packhorse.

No sooner had he gotten Josh Catlin settled in the main house than one of the rancher's cowhands was there to tell Wade that more riders were coming in. Mex greasers from the looks of them, the cowhand had retorted. Passing outside, Benton Wade was surprised, and mildly worried, to hone his eyes in on Felix Casandro. The others, he reckoned, were also Cubans.

The fact was, he liked Casandro. Perhaps he'd change his mind if this deal went sour. But it was there, and the man was fighting for his country, which in Benton Wade's opinion didn't have a Chinaman's chance against those Spanish Inquistitors. Walking with Casandro toward a corral, Wade drawled, "I thought the deal was your men would bunk at either Radford's place, or Tillman's?"

"We were at Ox-Bow," said Casandro in a pleasant tone of voice. "And on our way toward Radford's, then I decided to detour down here."

"Any particular reason . . ."

"For one thing, the man who just pulled in, Catlin."

"Shitfire, Casandro, I've known Josh since he was damned near in swaddling clothes. Came with his pa so often out here I thought he was one of my sons. Told me he was into gunsmithing. So I gave him some of my guns to paw over . . . an' if he's as good as his pa it'll improve my shootin' when I go huntin'."

"*Si*, I agree a man has to make a living. But I find it *extrano* that Senor Catlin's only other stop was Ox-Bow, to see Reese Tillman."

He stood there chewing on this as Casandro began unsaddling his bronc. Try as he might, Benton Wade couldn't make out Josh Catlin as any kind of threat. Hadn't Josh been over in England when that unsorry incident had taken place at the Colorado Club? Reaching to his shoulder to get at an itch, Wade said, "You got anything solid against Josh, or is this all spooky suspicions?"

"Call it gut feeling, senor."

"What I figured. Got to tell you, Luther Radford came in over last weekend, and pulled out yesterday for Denver. We agreed it was best he stay up there to make sure this thing goes right. I'll put you up at the main house. Your men can camp out in the bunkhouse."

"I am obliged," smiled the Cuban, as his bronc trotted into the corral. "What you have here, this marvelous ranch, a man can do no better."

"I hear Cuba has a lot goin' for it. Would have more if the Spaniards get rousted out of there. So I figure there's not a helluva lot wrong with helpin' you Cubans get some guns, somethin' to fight with."

If compassion for my people were Benton Wade's only concern, Casandro mused bitterly, the rancher would shower upon us all of those riches he has rotting away in Colorado banks. He cautioned himself not to get melodramatic. For as a shark can pick up on the scent of blood miles away, any weakness he revealed would only add to Benton Wade's arsenal of callousness. There was also the cold reality of it, in that he and his *compadres* were expendable, that if they failed, were killed, they would occupy unmarked graves someplace out there on the High Plains.

"You were there the night Jarvis Catlin killed himself—"

"You mean at the Colorado Club? Reckon I was. Catlin was sittin' in with us."

"Senor Catlin had a visitor that night, someone from the Mexican Consulate."

"Wasn't aware of that," said the rancher. "Funny Luther Radford never brought this up. But it don't change Catlin bein' dead. What are you drivin' at, Casandro?"

"Just that this Mexican diplomat was killed, about two weeks ago." He could see the flare of surprise creasing Benton Wade's forehead, which told him that Wade's only role was as silent money partner to Luther Radford. How blindly the cattle barons sided with one another, no matter what the crime, it seemed.

"Back at Ox-Bow," Casandro went on, "I was introduced to Josh Catlin as Mexican Legate Valdez, a deception we must continue now that Catlin is here."

"Yup, sure, Casandro. Could it be the Mexicans have stumbled onto something . . ."

"It isn't the Mexicans I'm worried about," he replied around an evasive smile. He swung sideways to look at the waiting Cubans. He did not bother introducing them to Benton Wade, who said, "Once you get your men settled in at the bunkhouse, come on up for a drink." Wade headed away in that stiff-legged stride of his.

"We leave in the morning, for Radford's place."

"The gunsmith . . . what about him?"

"What he does will determine our course of action."

From the sanctity of the tack house Josh Catlin had watched the Cubans ride in boldly. Josh knew the brief conversation between the Cuban named Casandro and Benton Wade would include concern over why he had shown up. That had been a couple of hours ago, and already Josh had determined none of the three revolvers he was checking over, those belonging to Wade, had contained the bullet which had killed his father. He wasn't all that disappointed, as he liked Benton Wade. Only now he was seeing the man through different eyes.

"Perhaps Benton doesn't know who killed my father . . . but he's part of it . . ."

Josh put his tools away before dousing the lamp. He liked the leathery smell wafting about the small log building, the saddles hung up on pegs peering down like old friends. And right now he sure could use some friendly advice, a thought he consigned to the wind whistling in through an open window. He knew he wouldn't get anything worthwhile out of Wade, one of the wiliest horsetraders in those parts, so it had to be the Cubans, in particular the one passing himself off as a Mexican diplomat. When the lamp was out, all of a sudden it seemed a lot darker outside, and lonelier in there.

As it had always been, the evening meal at Benton Wade's consumed a heap of good food and the early shank of night. To push away his bitter anger, Josh had gone on with wild stories of night life in London, some of them imaginary concoctions. He was surprised to learn, though he shouldn't have been, that Legate Arsenio Valdez was intimately familiar with the English way of it.

"I remember at Trafalgar Square," went on Casandro, "encountering this bewitching lady, of the night we shall say. Only as it turned out, the lady was shilling for a pickpocket."

"By the way, Josh, you did a fine job on my guns. Especially the Bisley model .32."

"The problem was the mainspring, Mr. Wade," said Josh. Through the exchange of smiles, in Josh was a buildup of tension. Earlier in the course of their conversation he'd learned that Luther Radford was probably up in Denver by now, and that the man sitting across the table,

Casandro, was leaving in the morning. But not before he braced the bogus Mexican. "Now, if you'll excuse me, I reckon I'll head over to the tack house and finish repairing this Winchester . . ."

Once he was clear of the main house, instead of heading directly for the tack house he found the corral holding his horses. Bracing Casandro, Josh knew, would bring the wrath of Benton Wade down on him, which was why he'd decided to pack up his gear and be ready to move out. His saddle horse whickered over at Josh's soft summoning whistle, but he had to slip in through about a dozen horses shying to the far side of the corral in order to cast a looped rope over the neck of his packhorse. Quietly he brought both horses out of the corral and behind some haystacks reeking of musky alfalfa. He stopped suddenly when a cowhand pushed out of the back door of the bunkhouse and stood there framed in yellow light, rolling a cigarette into shape. Before he'd finished, someone called out that it was the cowhand's turn to deal, and he swung about and went back in.

Without further incident Josh went around to the darker side of the tack house, where he tied up his horses. Easing away some of his building anxiety was a helpful cloud pushing in front of the moon. During the day a buffeting wind had kicked up a lot of ground dust, and though the wind was still there, it was a dying wind not strong enough anymore to lift dust or even ruffle a man's hat. He slipped into the tack house and reached for one of the packs holding some of his gunsmithing equipment. He hadn't seen anything wrong in lying to Wade that he was going to hold in there for a few more days, and that he'd already packed everything he'd brought along.

First he got everything aboard his packhorse. After cinching his saddle into place, Josh stole away to an elm tree which was planted on an intercepting course between the main house and the bunkhouse. Pulling out his revolver, he spun the cylinder as he gazed southerly, to find lights were being doused in the dining room.

Thoughts came, of how to handle it, that even though Benton Wade hadn't actually killed his father, Wade was just as guilty. And Casandro, a gunman of sorts, with both Casandro and Wade quite capable of killing him if they felt threatened in any way. Both men had probably killed before, but Josh hadn't, and that fact held in him as a man came out and down the front porch steps, the moon clearing impishly to show him it was Casandro. He could feel tension firming his grip on the revolver as he brought it down low to his side, pushing more behind the tree. The soft whistling sounds of some Spanish song told Josh the Cuban was a few yards away.

Josh stepped out quickly, the clacking noise of the hammer on his Colt being thumbed back halting the Cuban, who recognized his assailant. "*Senor, que quiere decir esto?*"

"This means," Josh answered in Spanish, "I want the truth out of you, Senor Casandro."

"Casandro? *Si*, that is my name. And you probably know I'm Cuban." He'd lifted his arms, but now he smiled. "The truth—if I told you that, Josh, both of us would be killed."

"You're clever with words," Josh said tautly. "I know that Tillman's involved, and Benton Wade, and so is Luther Radford in the death of my father."

"*Si*, that is the truth. My people and I were not involved in this. You can believe that or not. I can tell you this, I came out here at the instigation of the Cuban Junta."

"Yup, back at Ox-Bow I was listening to you Cubans talk about *Cuba Libre* and all that . . . and my guess is you're out here for one reason, Casandro, to buy guns. Way I figure it, them ranchers and some renegade soldiers have gotten together to give you what you want."

"An educated guess that could cost you dearly," said the Cuban.

"You used my father, or the ranchers did, to gain entry

to a military installation. You were there posing as a Mexican diplomat. Then something went wrong—"

"No, Dionicio, do not shoot!"

At the sound of Casandro's voice, Josh Catlin threw himself into the protecting branches of the tree, and as he did a gun barked. He felt a stabbing pain and ignored it as he broke running into deeper shadows. There were three of them, he gasped silently, and the sound of that gun will rouse Benton Wade and his men.

Even as Josh was coming in on the tack house in a stumbling run, Felix Casandro had hurried over to place a restraining hand on the arm of Dionicio. "Hold your fire."

"But he was going to kill you!"

"Not at all," said Casandro, as lights came on in the main house. Now men were exploding out of the bunkhouse.

"What the hell's going on?"

Casandro said to a cowhand, "Dionicio tried to kill a coyote that was slinking around back of that barn."

"Yup, damned coyotes are awful bold."

"But," hissed Dionicio, "the gunsmith, he's getting away—"

"Listen to me, quickly now," said Casandro. "If Catlin were a killer he would have gunned down both Tillman and Wade after making them tell him who the real killer of his father is. I believe only by accident will Josh Catlin stumble upon the truth of all this. As to why I let him live, his is a holy purpose. Where the men we deal with, Dionicio, they have no souls."

"*Asi*, I tried to kill a coyote. Here comes the rancher."

Turning that way, Casandro began walking Benton Wade, who'd grabbed a rifle, back toward the main house, explaining as they went what had happened. Finally Wade drawled out, "A lot more of them critters this summer. Hope your man killed that mangy coyote. D'ya hear that, sounded like hosses . . ."

"Probably some of your horses shying away from this

coyote. *Buenas noches* again, Senor Wade." He swung around and made for the bunkhouse, and for Dionicio and now Blancas waiting in the shadowy recesses of the log building. It was Casandro's guess that Josh Catlin would return to Denver. How badly Catlin had been wounded he didn't know, so it was a possibility too that come tomorrow morning, out on the trail, they'd stumble across the gun-smith's body. That saddened Felix Casandro.

Why had he let Catlin get away? Especially when his escape could endanger everything. It came to Casandro, the why of it, all having to do with his own family, and how they had been murdered by the Spanish rulers of Cuba. So he knew what Josh Catlin was going through, the days of wondering agony and self-torture, the never-ending thoughts of revenge. Between them, came further revelation, was this bond of suffering. Where it would lead to he did not know, but he would encounter Josh Catlin again, of that he was absolutely certain.

Twelve

Far away in the sultry, wavering haze distorting the horizon, a mirage of a moving freight train caused a weary smile to split Josh Catlin's heat-fevered lips. He was certain the temperature was pushing near the hundred mark, and there wasn't a cloud marring the sky, except for a raggedy bit of grey holding way to the south over a distant peak. Water hadn't been a problem, as he'd been heading due west along the Arkansas River.

Pikes Peak was looming a lot closer and, unlike mountains more to the north, it wasn't crowned with snow. Pueblo was within his grasp now, and there he'd find a railhead, and a train that would carry him back up to Denver. If he got that far, not only as a result of the nagging wound to his left side, but through the worry of just surviving. He knew those Cubans and Benton Wade were hot on his backtrail. His imaginings told Josh that, as there'd been no tangible clues, such as dust pushing up from horsemen, and when using his field glass he had scoped in on nobody.

Wrapped around his midriff in torn remnants was one of his shirts. Though the bullet had punched out through an exit wound, the wound itself wasn't all that deep, but it still radiated a lot of pain. That other Cuban; he was still puzzling over why the man hadn't fired again, as Josh remembered that he'd been out in the open and desperately trying to reach the tack house. That ride of two nights ago was as hard as it had ever been for him. Tracking his eyes to the Big Dipper, and to the connecting North Star, he had guided on the star as best he could. There were long spans of time when he had ridden headlong down into sunken reaches of prairie to lose sight of the mountains westerly. For all he knew he could have blundered around in a big sweeping circle and encountered his pursuers. But here he was now, picking up on the faint but welcome sound of a train whistle.

By the sun he reckoned it was late afternoon, and still hot enough to fry eggs on a flat rock. He had eaten spar-'ingly, sometimes throwing up what he'd partaken of, while the horses went calmly about their business of chomping at short prairie grass. Beckoning cottonwoods caused Josh to rein his bronc closer to the river. Uncorking his canteen, he reached up and lifted away his hat, then he let warm water cascade onto his head and shoulders. He went in closer and swung down, as both horses went out into deeper sucking mud to slake their thirst.

He knew enough about gunshot wounds, and he'd cleansed the wound with some medicine that he had packed along. It would probably need stitching, but that could wait and be done by his county coroner uncle. As the horses stood there drinking and otherwise swinging their heads to ward away swarming flies, Josh went through a pack in search of a clean shirt and one of his bandanas. He's shucked his sweat-stained shirt, the sun striking down at his bare torso.

"Radford, the man's left for Denver," he pondered out loud, just for the sake of hearing his own voice in an attempt to ward away a lonely feeling. "By now Benton Wade's prob-ably fired off a telegram up there . . . filling in Radford on what happened . . ." Or, as Josh resettled his thoughts on a closer locale, both of them might have confederates in Pueblo. One more killing wouldn't faze them any.

Gingerly he put on the clean shirt and the bandana, and

he felt a little better about himself. Once he was saddle-bound, Josh left the lower reaches of the floodplain to take the main road. Not all that far ahead he could make out some higher buildings in Pueblo, one of a bunch of larger towns strung up and down the railroad line hugging close to the eastern reaches of the Rockies. Every so often he would take a gander over his shoulder, and once he'd spotted a dust plume which turned out to be a stagecoach.

The haze of night was settled around him when the hardpacked road carried Josh into Pueblo. Slowly he brought his horses through a maze of rails making up a railroad yard, and off a little he picked out cattle milling about in holding pens. A vibrating sound told him a train was coming in, and then his jogging bronc was taking Josh up a street composed of old houses and business places. Bypassing the first livery stable, which seemed to have fallen on sorry times, he chose one that was splashed with a fresh coat of red paint and white trim. An aging Russian wolfhound came wagging out to sniff around the horses as, with some effort, Josh Catlin swung down from the saddle.

The hostler coming out turned out to be a middle-aged woman puffing away on a corncob pipe. "Plenty of empty stalls, mister." She went back into the hip-roofed building followed by Josh, who got his horses settled in separate stalls.

"What are you, a peddler?"

Hefting his saddle, he turned and set the saddle on a stall wall, then he said, "A gunsmith. Maybe you recall my father coming through here, Jarvis Catlin."

"Name's familiar," she grumped out. She wore a shape-less felt hat that somehow fitted her lined but friendly face.

"You interested in buying my horses?"

Thoughtfully she chewed on the stem of her pipe, and then her eyes dropped to Josh's side, taking in the dark discoloration piercing through his shirt. Lamely he said, "It's nothing . . . I got cut up coming through some thickets . . ."

"Mister Catlin," she said ponderingly, "you come in

here wantin' to sell me these horses, which could be stolen. Now, what really happened?"

"A long story better left untold," he replied as he stared back into her probing eyes. He sensed in the woman the inner strength of a person able to eke out a living, with no one daring to say otherwise. "You could tell me your name."

"Gilda Matheson, sole owner of this place and widowed goin' on . . . too damn many years."

He grinned back, drawing strength from her blunt presence. "I was shot. What you see on the packhorse is my gunsmithing equipment and such. And I've got papers attesting to my identity. Truth of the matter is, ma'am, I'm out here trying to track down the man who killed my father. Name's Josh."

"That was a mouthful. But I feel what you say is the gospel truth, Mr. Catlin." The wolfhound sidled up to begin licking at her hand. "This is Lobo, an' he'll take you next door where I live."

"But . . . that's all right, ma'am . . ."

"Hush up and let me tend to unloading your packhorse. My ma has supper on the griddle, an' we'll welcome another mouth. Over chow we can haggle over your horses. Peaked out as you look, how long have you been on the trail?"

"Couple of days is all. But it seems a heap longer, ma'am . . ."

"Gilda, call me that . . . and now get, as Lobo wants to eat too."

The house, once he was let in by the hostler's mother, a greying woman with stooped shoulders, turned out to be possessed of tidy rooms and fluffy curtains holding out the night. Lobo, after a final sniff at Josh's heel, bounded ahead into the kitchen. He was shown a place to wash up, a small room adjoining the kitchen. Lathering up with a bar of soap that smelled like liniment, suddenly he felt weak and sagged onto a convenient chair, letting the dizzy spasm claw away at him. His thoughts were that he felt safe there, at least for the moment. Closing his eyes, Josh, who had managed to snatch

only a few moments of sleep ever since fleeing from Benton
Wade's ranch, felt himself drifting away.

Sometime later he became aware of voices, that of Gilda
Matheson's, and of a man's, and he groped his eyes open
just as the hostler appeared. "Easy, Josh, you can trust Doc
Lynch not to ask any pryin' questions. Okay?"

"Howdy. Josh, is it? Ain't the first time Gilda's brought
me over to treat someone. This time though, I'm doing it
just to sample some of her ma's cooking. The front bedroom, Gilda?" He helped Josh up from the chair and they
went into a bedroom, where the hostler was pulling the
coverlets back on a high feathery bed.

Barely had Josh been able to remove his shirt than he
was stretching out on the inviting white sheets, on his right
side. He felt someone tugging his boots away from his feet,
but it seemed he didn't care as sleep claimed him.

"I tell you, Josh, when you got around to eatin' you
were hungrier than a quilled dog."

Through the smile he had for Gilda Matheson sitting at
the table with him in her kitchen, Josh showed traces of
the worry he felt. He had lingered on at Gilda's, had to because of the stitches sewing up his wound, and words of
warning from her that some of Luther Radford's hired
hands had ridden into Pueblo. The word was out they
were looking for him. Though he'd known some of the
cowhands working out at Radford's Doubletree spread,
Gilda Matheson had informed him acidly that most of
those men were gone, and coming in to work for Radford
were a scurvy lot of gunhands and such.

"They'll be looking for someone riding in with a packhorse," he said. "Not some bespectacled dude spiffed out in
a monkey suit." The suit was a loaner from Doc Lynch, and
it was equipped with a black vest and a starched white shirt
that made Josh feel awful uncomfortable. On the counter by
the sink was one of the doctor's old black bags, in which Josh

had stowed his holstered gun, a Colt .45. A smaller caliber gun he'd tucked into his belt. He had presented his horses to Gilda, despite her objections, and all of his gear was stowed in the livery stable. All he needed to do next was to put on his hat, one that had belonged to Gilda's husband, and make that trek over to the railroad depot.

Over her cup she regarded her house guest. "You still look kind of gamey."

That remark didn't make Josh feel any better, or the next barb from her.

"I've seen better lookin' trail-kill. Another day or two won't make any difference."

"You sure have a way with words, ma'am."

"But I can see"—she reached for her corncob pipe—"you're determined to go out there and get sorely hurt again. Least I can do, Mr. Catlin, is escort you over to the depot. By the way, you must have been dreamin' up a storm last night, those sounds coming out of your bedroom. Somethin' about a woman—Lanai?" The change of expression on Josh's face told her she'd just rowed into troubled waters.

It had been a bad last night for Josh, his dreams switching between his search for his father's killers and the more pleasant imagery of Lanai Meling. Why should he think of her now? By now she was probably married to some rich Englishman. "Mrs. Matheson, ma'am, I expect it's time to go. Someday I'll be back. Not so much to get my things, but to see you."

She rose as he did, and she said, "Words like that used to make me blush—all over." A smile broke out. " 'Course, I still like to hear 'em." She went ahead into a back entryway, and to Josh's concern thrust a small pistol into a pocket of the coat she slipped on. The coat was long and faded, and she had on under it washed-out Levi's and an old shirt, with her hair pinned up under her hat.

From the livery stable they went west along the narrow side street, to come out onto a wider thoroughfare. In passing along the boardwalk the woman at Josh's side received nods of recognition. Still off to the west lay the railroad right-of-way, and they began crossing over, but warily on Josh's part. He held the black bag in his left hand as he gazed further upstreet at men lounging in front of saloons. As smoke from her pipe came wind-blown at him, he remarked joshingly, "By rights you should have consumption of the lungs."

"By rights you're right ... but I enjoy my vices. You know, you're steppin' kind of fidgety, like your shoes are filled with burrs."

"This baggy old suit doesn't help any. Hear a train whistle—maybe it's the one I'm to board pulling out."

"Nope, that'll be a freight train hauling ass." She grinned at that, stabbing him with concerned eyes. "Even your mother wouldn't recognize you in that get-up. Up this next block and we reach the depot." The cowhand loping by on his horse twisted in the saddle to cast back a curious eye.

Josh made out the Doubletree brand on the horse, and he figured more of Radford's men were lurking by the train depot. Earlier that morning Gilda Matheson had gone over to purchase a one-way ticket to Denver, to report back that coming and going she'd spotted Doubletree hands roaming around Pueblo, more than usually came in during the week. That had made Josh believe they were trying to box him in, not only Radford's men, but those he assumed were pushing in from the east, such as Benton Wade and those Cubans. A sign fronting over a building in the middle of the block read it was occupied by an undertaker.

He said, "Maybe I should head in there first and size out a coffin. You know, Gilda, you oughta just turn around and let me go on alone. You've done enough. I just don't want you to get hurt."

"There's the depot," she said, as if Josh's words had been snatched away by the wind beginning to yowl amongst the buildings.

Beyond the low, dark-green frame building he could make out the back section of a passenger train. The pathway they moved onto led along the north side of the depot, where a few buggies and carriages were parked. To the south Josh noticed with some concern saddled horses tied to a long hitching rail. The cowboy loafing by the horses slid his eyes Josh's way, a man with his legs spread apart in a poise of watchful arrogance and one hand hooked under his gunbelt.

Josh said, "Could be one of Radford's hands. Look, I haven't hid behind a woman's skirt before, much less her pipe. I'd better go it alone from here." They stopped together and regarded one another.

Finally she said as the train whistle shrilled, "Okay, just hop aboard, Mister Catlin, and we'll probably see you again."

He had stowed in the black bag, along with his Colt .45, his microscope and the spent bullet Doc Catlin had removed from his father's body, and some other items. Wordlessly he went on, veering around a pair of horses hitched to a carriage, and toward the platform where some people were milling about, with others beginning to board the Atchison, Topeka & Santa Fe passenger train, which would terminate its run in Denver. A section of platform ran along the north wall of the depot, the main chunk of it westerly and fronting onto the main railway line. Hopping onto the platform, he eased up and snaked a glance around the corner of the building.

"At least three of them, and I reckon looking for me." He held there as the conductor called out for everyone to board, with the train whistle giving out a piercing wail. As the train began moving, Josh still stayed in close to the wall, figuring he would swing aboard the back caboose.

"Hey," a voice came from behind Josh Catlin, "ain't I laid eyes on you before?"

Turning quickly, Josh found himself staring back at the cowhand who'd just stepped around the back corner of the depot. He knew the man, Rip Tygee, a longtime Double-tree hand. Then Josh was spinning around and bolting for the moving train, which was beginning to pick up speed, and with people scattering out of his way. That was probably the reason Tygee and the other Doubletree hands held from firing their sixguns. A desperate lunge carried Josh sprawling onto the vestibule, where he grimaced in pain. Now he held low as one of the cowhands hammered a couple of shots his way, the bullets striking metal parts of the caboose to ricochet away.

Then he was out of handgun range, but knowing word would be sent up to Denver that he was on his way there. Picking himself up, he shouldered into the caboose and was on his way into a passenger car only to be intercepted by the conductor. Josh passed the man his ticket along with a tentative smile.

"I see by your bag you're a doctor . . ."

"Yes, ah, heading up to Denver to hang up my shingle."

"Next time you take a train be on time so's to avoid using the caboose. G'day, sir."

A couple of strides carried Josh to an empty seat, and he sank down to find that he had worked up a sweat, although his wound didn't hurt so much. He'd eluded Radford's trap to kill him. As he recalled, they'd pass through Colorado Springs and Castle Rock and then Littleton before pulling into Union Station where, he expected, he would have a reception committee. But at least for the time being he was safe.

"Doc Catlin . . . hope he's all right . . . and I'm hopin' he's come up with something tying Radford to all of this . . ."

He removed from his bag a stub of pencil and a small notepad, on which he began jotting down the names of the people he'd encountered in his search for his father's killer, a list that Josh felt would contain more names.

"But only one of them counts—"

Thirteen

Out on the western limits of railroad track known as the switchyard an engineer began backing his locomotive toward a line of cars that had been there for the last month. During the afternoon he had brought over five boxcars which had just arrived from back East, and now the Pullman car and the two passenger cars hooked to his engine would go towards making a sizable train. At a signal from his switchman, he let his engine grind to a halt, the jarring sound of the couplings ringing up to the engineer.

He took in Yardmaster Ralph Perrone lurking with four other men just this side of another row of boxcars hooked together. He knew something was in the wind just from the yardmaster's particular interest in those cars parked away by their lonesome, but he hadn't become an engineer by prying into Ralph Perrone's business. His suspicions, though, were that the U.S. Army was involved in it, as attested to by the government seals on the boxcars. Anyway, the money he was getting from Perrone was going a long way towards putting food on the table for his brood of seven children. The shift of a throttle brought his engine rolling away as his switchman, who'd scrambled up a steel ladder, came into the cab.

"That should do it for the day, Al."

"Yeah, we moved a lot of rolling stock today. One of

them's a cowman. But two others have all the earmarks of soldiers. What country we plannin' to invade now?"

"Let the yardmaster worry about that. Mine are that my missus is in the family way again."

"That'll be eight, Al. You need the extra money."

"Tell me about it. But it ain't keeping me from stopping at O'Leary's Bar before heading home. Gettin' back to those boxcars, sometimes this Mexican shows up with the yardmaster. Haven't seen him around lately."

"Got a hunch he'll show up before that train pulls out. Another kid, Al. You Catholics have it tougher'n us Baptists, that's for damned sure . . ."

With his eyes fixed to the engine pulling away in the direction of Union Station, Luther Radford's thoughts were pushing beyond the railroad yard clear to Pueblo. That damned kid of Jarvis Catlin's wasn't a kid anymore but he was proving to be a damned nuisance. All talk of the gunsmith killing himself should have been buried by now. He couldn't believe that Reese Tillman hadn't done something about Josh Catlin. Then it was Catlin showing up at Benton Wade's. Lucky Wade had hoss-sense enough to fire off a telegram to him. And once Catlin showed up in Pueblo, dammit all, his luck had run out. Still, in the rancher was a nagging premonition it hadn't gone that way at all, and he was in a foul mood.

In a whiskey-rasped voice he said, "Now if that"—he'd been about to say Cuban, but checked himself—"Mex was here we could get this train underway."

"There's enough military hardware here to start a sizable war," said Mulcahan.

"Yeah, well we'll let them greasers kill one another." Radford handed the yardmaster a thick yellow manila envelope. "Obliged for your help, Mr. Perrone. The way this set-up is, everybody profits, and damned handsomely."

"You mentioned further shipments were coming in?"

"This could be a long-haul operation, if nobody gets greedy." The last part of what Radford had said was meant for Major George Devlin, flicking ashes from his cigarillo. Right now he needed the major, more than the major needed to be involved in it. He didn't want to see Devlin put in for a transfer, for the next officer to head the military operation out at Rocky Mountain Arsenal could be an honest sonofabitch. So, and despite his misgivings, Radford knew he'd have to put up with Major Devlin, gambling, sneaky fingers and all.

All of them had set smiles for the yardmaster, striding off into late afternoon shadows angling easterly. Off a little stood Sergeant Guy Hogue, as was his way. There was no distinction in his scorning dislike for officers or thievin' businessmen, as Hogue referred to them. That was buried deep within him, and he never let it surface, nor any other part of his makeup. He was to those men simply a sergeant, the man handed the mundane tasks, a uniformed lackey. But what set Guy Hogue apart from it, a shade above them, and they knew it and feared him because of it, was that he could kill without remorseful afterthoughts. The night he'd killed the gunsmith Hogue had gone afterwards to partake of a steak supper, and later found a woman to wallow with until daybreak. Much to Hogue's chagrin he'd come down with a social disease. Her body was found, two nights ago, crammed into a trash barrel in an alley just downstreet from the Colorado Club.

"Hogue."

"Yessir, Mr. Radford?"

"And you, Devlin. The Cuban still hasn't paid us in full. But when he does, this whole thing becomes a military operation, towards which Mulcahan has put together all the necessary paperwork. One trainload of guns now, the start of a whole lot more arms being bought by the Cubans." He began walking southward along the tracks. "What I'm gettin' at is, I don't want anything to go wrong. You read me, Major Devlin—" No longer was the major paymaster for the operation, something he'd told the man in no uncertain terms, not with them expecting to get from the Cuban Junta close to a half-million dollars. With that money, Devlin could pull a vanishing act.

Radford disliked walking all that far in cowboy boots, especially picking his way over all the iron rails, and when they came to Wynkoop Street which passed in front of Union Station, it was the major and Kevin Mulcahan getting into one carriage, with Sergeant Hogue striding over to pass along the sidewalk. Back of him Luther Radford had heaved up into his waiting carriage, the reins being handled by his ranch foreman.

"How'd it go?" asked Deke Martin, a blunt-faced man with grey eyes.

"Everything's set," said Radford. "Let's pick up the sergeant. Yup, everything but that Cuban forkin' over the money." He twisted in the seat and gazed back at Mulcahan's carriage disappearing around a street corner.

Pulling to the east onto 19th Street, Martin eased to the curb, where Sergeant Guy Hogue got in back to sit alongside the rancher, who was relighting his cigar. Now that the sun had slipped behind the jagged mountain crests, the streets were darker, and it would stay that way at least for another hour, and then night would set in hard. Radford enjoyed coming to Denver, as it was a city where a man could run into a lot of crooked deals, if he was wily enough add to his fortunes. You had to outfox the fox, the rancher liked to say.

Even before the encounter with the major and Mulcahan over at the saloon he owned, the Powder River, Luther Radford had hired the sergeant to do a little work for him. It involved keeping tabs on Doc Paul Catlin and that police detective. He knew that the doctor had a house guest, some Oriental woman. He began sharing the bottle he'd brought along with Sergeant Hogue as their carriage rolled along the cobblestones.

"I'd still like to know why Doc Catlin performed that autopsy. What about this woman stayin' with him?"

"Her name's Lanai Meling. Came over from London. Found out she's interested in Catlin's nephew, Josh."

"Speakin' of that snoopin' son'bitch, what the hell is he up to? You know, Sergeant Hogue, Josh Catlin headed out of here about the same time as Felix Casandro. Maybe I made a mistake orderin' you to kill that Mex diplomat. But no sense peerin' up a dead hoss's asshole now."

"Way I figure it," said Hogue as he brought the whiskey bottle away from his mouth, "is that Josh Catlin could have stumbled across somethin' in his pa's papers or personal effects. I feel like you, that I don't want no headstrong kid spoilin' a sweet set-up like this. You ever try to live on a sergeant's pay? Sucks to high heaven, Mr. Radford."

"Knowing you, Hogue, you've come up with somethin'—"

"We want Josh Catlin occupyin' a cemetery same's his pa."

"He might be dead by now," pondered Radford. "Last I heard he was hauling ass west along the Arkansas River, and if he makes it to Pueblo my boys'll finish the job. Seems there was some gunplay out at Wade's ranch. But it wasn't until the next day they found where he'd stopped to take a breather—found blood splattered on some rocks."

"If he is dead, we'd better do the same to Doc Catlin. I could take some men out to that ranchero of his easy enough," Sergeant Hogue muttered as their carriage swung into the alley behind the Powder River Saloon.

"I'll think on it." Radford got out and threw the empty whiskey bottle toward trash littering around a rusty barrel. "The Cuban—when did the major say he'd be back?"

"Week at the most."

"Dammit Hogue, he shouldn't have left in the first place." He brought his worry over this in through the back hallway, trailed by the sergeant. The saloon was just one of many business places Luther Radford owned in Denver, along with interests in gold mines located in Colorado mining camps, some of which hadn't panned out. But he liked risking his money just in case. He figured the present deal was better than gold, though with more time it could have been managed better. But like the early days when he'd fought off Indian attacks and homesteaders, men such as that gunsmith and the Mex had to die.

To his silent pleasure, the main barroom was full, which brought his eyes and thoughts to the barmaids spreading their lissome charms among the drinkers and card players. Originally he was going to name the place Doubletree. But his church-going wife had killed that notion. A wave from Ace Riddell helping out the bartenders brought him up to the back end of the bar, where Riddell handed Luther Radford a yellow envelope.

"Delivered late this afternoon."

"Hate gettin' late afternoon telegrams," complained the rancher as he tore the end away from the envelope and pulled out its contents. Back came Radford's sour mood. "The son'bitch is trainin' up here to Denver—Catlin!" Slowly his meaty hand crumpled up the damning bit of news. A shot glass appeared before him on the polished bar top, whiskey gurgled into it, and he tossed the whiskey down to have his glass refilled. At his side, Guy Hogue had to beckon for a drink to get one.

"Over here, Hogue, we have to talk," said Radford. He went back to one of the few empty tables and sat down heavily. Realizing his cigar was out, he jammed it into a big metal ashtray and dipped a hand under his coat for another. "So he's alive, Hogue—which is where you come in?"

"Ain't all that hard to figure out. We go and latch onto this woman friend of Catlin's, this Chinese bitch or whatever. We hold her aboard that train, an' when we leave, she goes with us."

"Meanwhile Josh Catlin'll try to find her. A word from me will give him some ideas of where to look. Remember, Hogue, dead she's no good to us." Pulling out his billfold,

Radford fingered out some paper money, which he tossed casually before the sergeant. "A thousand for now. Day after tomorrow I'm meeting with the Cuban. Once he coughs up the money, I expect Casandro'll want to get his trainload of military gear headed southerly."

"What about the county coroner and this detective?"

"Blowing smoke up our asses is all, Hogue. They haven't a clue as to what happened that night at the Colorado Club."

"You said these Cubans might want to buy more armament from us . . ."

"I expect it all depends on this first shipment reaching the Gulf Coast. The major being in charge of this military detail leaves a lot to be desired. You make sure he toes the line, Hogue, and conducts this whole thing strictly as a military operation. Hell, with all the paperwork Mulcahan rigged up, nothing should go wrong. Yup, but now there's tonight and Catlin on his way back."

"By midnight I'll have her stowed on that train. It would sure simplify things if Doc Catlin is home when I get there. I'd take him out, along with his hired help."

"Don't be stupid, Hogue. I want no killings out there. That happens, the police will be swarming all over this thing. Now get, as I've got other business matters to take care of."

They'd had a choice earlier, of taking off after Sergeant Hogue ambling away from the railroad yard, or rancher Luther Radford. Instead Detective Mike Garrison had made the decision to follow Major George Devlin. Doc Catlin had gone along with it, because both of them felt Devlin was vulnerable. That night it was just the two of them, seated beside one another on the front buggy seat.

After their appearance out at Rocky Mountain Arsenal, repercussions had come down to Detective Garrison, that if he kept up the illegal and harassing investigation of respected citizens he'd be suspended from duty for an indefinite period. Then Doc Catlin had been called on the carpet by the police commissioner, who'd stormily lashed out that the county coroner's office had ruled the death of Jarvis Catlin to be suicide. Further, there was no connection in any way between the suicide of Catlin and the murder of the Mexican diplomat. Simmering down later at a downtown saloon, Mike Garrison knew to reveal the truth would probably see Doc Catlin thrown in jail, as well as himself.

"Everything that happens back in that railroad yard," said Garrison, "comes under the jurisdiction of the yardmaster. In this case, Ralph Perrone." Ahead of them rolled Devlin's carriage, and as had been the case last night, upstreet toward the Western Casino and Gaming Emporium. Downtown traffic had picked up, chiefly because heavyweight fighter John L. Sullivan was defending his world championship crown at the Denver Athletic Club.

"Perrone's tough," Garrison went on. "And he's got at his beck and call some trigger-happy railroad detectives. Over the years he's managed to misplace, shall we say, a helluva lot of rolling stock."

"At least we know where they're holding those boxcars."

"Come morning you won't be able to find them, as there's any number of sidings Perrone can move them to. Or those boxcars might be rolling out of there right now."

"At least we know the Mexicans aren't involved in this," said Doc Catlin. "Would it do any good to notify Sixth Army headquarters over at St. Louis?"

"Anything we send over there will get lost in military red tape. And if they do check back here with the Denver police, word'll get right out to Rocky Mountain Arsenal. Our best bet is Major Devlin—sooner or later he'll lead us to the people who are buying these arms. Yup, they're pulling around behind that casino. I could use a drink."

"Same here, and something to eat. Mulcahan is here too, maybe for a reason other than gambling."

* * *

On Thursday night, as she'd done ever since going to work for Doc Catlin, Maria Juarez had her husband take her over to play bingo at St. Peter's Catholic Church in the nearby community of Littleton. That night she'd talked Lanai Meling into going along, and a little after ten o'clock everyone was moving out of a hall hooked to the main church. It was Maria's only vice, as her husband called it, but it enabled her to pick up on gossip circulating through Littleton's Mexican population.

"You won, Lanai. Only one game, but enough to get your money back."

"I will share my winnings with you, Maria."

"No," Maria said, as she took in Carlos snoring away where he was stretched out in their buggy. "What I listen to all night. Come on, *los ojos* Carlos, wake up." She tugged at his arm, and he awoke slowly and looked about as if he were lost.

"Asi, this torture is over," he said.

The women settled onto the back seat, where Maria scolded, "There is a *cantina* just down the street. You could have gone there."

"Maybe I did," Carlos said, as he reined the horse into motion. Once they were away from the square of brick buildings making up the church and down a couple of blocks, with a country road opening up to him, he flicked his reins and the horse settled into a canter.

"I'm so worried about Josh."

"As I am, Lanai. He has a mind of his own, sometimes too much so. And now Doctor Catlin is also *complicado* in this, along with this policeman, this Senor Garrison. I do not know what to think, as I worry too much."

"That is so," said Carlos, "as it says in the Bible, worry is a sin—as is bingo."

They came by a long ridge stippled with pine trees and mossy rocks, passing a countryside house facing a low butte off to the west, the road curling that way toward Doc Catlin's two-story house, pushing over more pines that Carlos had planted two summers ago. By its own accord the horse swung into the long driveway, and then Carlos was reining around to the back kitchen door, where he let the women dismount, before bringing the buggy over to the carriage house.

Slowly he swung down and as he leaned to unhook the traces, a woman's scream erupted from the house. Immobilized by fear and concern, Carlos stood there, the horse whickering a warning as someone bolted out of the carriage house. Conscious of the danger, Carlos turned that way, managing to blunt the thrust of the first blow with his arm, but not a second blow that punched sickly into the side of his head, and he fell heavily to the ground. His attacker broke toward the house.

They had been waiting in Doc Catlin's study, the hope in Sergeant Guy Hogue that Catlin or his nephew would show up first to spare the women the coming ordeal. With Hogue was Corporal Wayne Latner, a thick-shouldered man with limited skills, other than a desire to drink away his monthly paycheck. They'd polished off a bottle apiece of some imported French brandy, and were sharing a third when Hogue, who'd been sitting staring out a window at the driveway, quickly doused the lamp. He had sent Norton, a confederate and supply sergeant out at the arsenal, out to the carriage house.

When Maria Juarez entered the unlighted kitchen she easily found the lamp she'd placed on a table by the back door. Lanai Meling moved on past her while untying her dark red cape, and then as the match Maria struck across the base of the lamp erupted into flame, Lanai's scream seemed to fill the kitchen.

Guy Hogue grabbed Lanai's upraised arm as Latner rushed on by to get at the Mexican woman, who recognized the danger and was breaking for the cutting block and some butcher knives lying there. But he was quicker, slamming the butt of his revolver into the woman's face, and Maria recoiled in pain. He went after her, clutching at her upper arm to spin her toward him. That time he sent a doubled fist crackling into her jawline. When she fell at his feet, he swung grinning to see how Hogue was doing.

"Hellfire, Hogue, you really hammered that Chinese bitch in the head. Hope she's still alive." Shoving his revolver into his waistband, he took in Lanai Meling lying motionless on the floor. "She's damned comely though."

Both of them took in Sergeant Norton looming in the back doorway, and Hogue said curtly to Latner, "Well, dammit, go get our carriage."

"We're not gonna wait for that sawbones?"

"Once Catlin sees what we done here," said Hogue, "he'll come lookin' for us." Crouching down, he brought Lanai into his arms and lifted her easily, and then he stepped toward the back door. "Norton, go up through the kitchen into that hallway and off to the left you'll find Doc Catlin's study and some damned fine tastin' brandy. Fetch what's left, then hustle back out here."

In a few minutes the abductors of Lanai Meling were retracing their route back into Denver. Sergeant Guy Hogue let his companions handle the bragging over how easily it had gone. He knew the men with him could be trusted, since it was a gold mine of an operation that rarely fell into the laps of enlisted men. They, and several more handpicked soldiers, would comprise the guard detail aboard that train. But before they pulled out he was looking forward to killing Jarvis Catlin's meddling son.

"Norton," he said, "you stow those extra uniforms aboard the train?"

"Yup, and enough rations for three, four weeks. Where we heading when we pull out of here, Guy?"

"Southerly, according to the Cuban. You boys now, don't be flashing all this money you've earned tonight in one place."

"Wish there was more."

"There'll be a lot more," muttered Sergeant Guy Hogue. Yup, he mused, a lot more once he figured out a way to get rid of Major Devlin. Wouldn't be so bad if the man wasn't such an out-and-out yellowbelly. "Pass that bottle back here." He sank back against the seat cushions, glancing at Lanai Meling, and he felt no pity for the unconscious woman. "Devlin . . . what to do about him . . ."

Looking back from his carriage about to roll over a hilly crest, Doc Catlin took a final look at lights filtering around Littleton, which was hooked northerly to Denver and would be the last tangle of buildings he'd see until he pulled into the driveway of his country home. With him was Detective Mike Garrison, and as it was around two in the morning, the pair of them were tired out. Back in Denver they'd left Major Devlin taking some woman he'd picked up to a hotel. The other one, Kevin Mulcahan, had left the casino earlier in the evening.

Doc Catlin had talked Garrison into coming out to tarry overnight. Mostly it had been so they could hash over the whole affair. "The evening wasn't exactly a waste of time."

"Nope," agreed Mike Garrison, "as it was the first time Luther Radford has been with them. He's damned sly, Radford. But it was just them out at the railroad yard, and not the people they're selling this military equipment to. What gets to me, Paul, is that they've got police protection. You tie that to the political clout Radford has around here and the U.S. Army in on this . . . means we're fighting an uphill battle."

"I wish we would have heard from Josh by now," said Doc Catlin. The road was covered with loose gravel and a lighter color than grassland edging off into the darker blackness of night. Stars and a quarter moon threw down enough light to drive by, and just ahead Catlin could make out the stone pillars guarding the driveway entrance. "I'll throw on some sidepork and eggs when we get there. Tomorrow I might call on Judge Foley."

"About what we're doing? Foley's kind of a rebel when it comes to being told to rule a certain way. He could throw you in jail, Paul, or the both of us. But this thing could break wide open ... and we'll need some friends ..."

"Mike, you could pull out of this. This thing started out as a simple case of Murder One. Then Pedro Rodriques was killed, turning this into an international incident. Sure, Legate Valdez has managed to keep a lid on this so far. But just like that it could explode in our faces." He reined up sharply when a horse hooked to a buggy suddenly appeared around the west side of the house to whicker its way toward them.

"Something's wrong!" said Doc Catlin. He reined up, and Garrison hopped out and went to grab the halter of the other horse. "That's the buggy Carlos uses. Tonight they went in to Littleton to play bingo, and Lanai Meling was going along."

Still holding onto the halter, Garrison walked the horse around in a circle and drew his revolver as he went ahead to come in on the west side of the house. Further to the west lay the carriage house, with other backdropping buildings to the north, and then he picked up on the shape of someone sprawled out on the ground. He let go of the halter and went to kneel down by Carlos Juarez.

"It's Carlos," he called back to Catlin, who was hopping down from his carriage.

"My God!" Paul Catlin uttered in alarm, and he broke for the kitchen door.

"He's alive," Garrison shouted after Doc Catlin vanished into the kitchen.

In the kitchen, he bent down by his housekeeper, who was moaning in pain and trying to pick herself up. Sensing someone's presence, she struck out with flailing hands, and he said, "Maria, it's me ... easy now ... easy ..." Easing away from her, he fumbled on a back table for a match to light the lamp as Mike Garrison loomed in the doorway cradling Maria's husband in his arms.

In the sudden glare of lamplight it struck Doc Paul Catlin that he'd forgotten about Lanai, and he blurted out, "Lanai Meling, either she's . . ." Hurrying up through the kitchen, he searched hurriedly through the downstairs rooms, and went upstairs to search through every room. Then he came down to find that Garrison had placed Carlos Juarez on the living room sofa and had lighted a lamp. "She's gone," announced Catlin. "Where, I don't know. But . . . for now, help me get Maria into that bedroom. Then get a fire going in the stove and heat up some water."

Briefly, Doc Catlin and Garrison gazed angrily at the lacerated side of Carlos Juarez's head. Drying blood stuck to the hair and was smeared over his face. Feeling for a pulse, he said, "A little rapid, but that wound to his head probably has a concussion. Well, let's tend to Maria."

His treatment of Maria Juarez revealed her nose had been broken, and the swelling along her jawline indicated to Doc Catlin a possible fracture. They had brought her into a separate bedroom, and she was awake, though a little groggy, and trying to tell them what had taken place earlier that evening.

"They took . . . Lanai?"

She held up two fingers and tried to mouth something, to have Garrison interrupt. "Two men came and kidnapped Lanai Meling. My guess is there were three of them, Paul. Now as I understand it, Lanai arrived here from England claiming to be a friend of Josh's." He followed Doc Catlin out of the room, where they glanced at Carlos Juarez. On they went into the kitchen, where Garrison had left some sidepork frying in a heavy black skillet, and he went there.

"I can definitely say that Lanai Meling met Josh over in

London. But to kidnap her? To come here and violate the sanctity of my house, Mike. I find that unforgivable."

"I have no doubt these men were watching your house, Paul. Perhaps Josh was their real quarry. Remember, he did stir up quite a fuss over at the Colorado Club." He lifted the coffee pot from the stove and filled two cups as Paul Catlin sat down slowly. "Instead of Josh, or you for that matter, they settled for Lanai Meling."

"They could have just taken Lanai without brutalizing Maria and Carlos. Or killed them. And we didn't find any ransom note."

"We'll hear from them," Garrison said calmly. "Here, tackle this food. Would you believe it, it's almost five. So much for any shut-eye tonight." After filling their plates, he moved over to set the skillet back on the stove, his eyes flicking a glance out the window over the sink. Tautly he barked, "Somebody's out there."

Pushing up from his chair, Doc Catlin said, "Could be they've come back to finish the job."

"One man, and he's out by the carriage house." Going to where he'd left his coat and holstered gun, Garrison picked up his gun and headed out the back door, with Doc Catlin lifting a rifle and some shells out of a gun case and then easing out the front door.

Pushing close to the back wall, Detective Mike Garrison could see the man more clearly in the lifting haze of false dawn. The man had dismounted and appeared to be taking something out of a saddlebag, which was enough for Garrison, as he broke away from the back wall and closed in quickly. "Elevate your hands, mister, where I can see them! Up, up, dammit!" He could see the man wore no gunbelt, but Garrison patted him down anyway.

Coming in with pointed rifle now was Doc Catlin, who said questioningly, "Josh, is that you?"

"Yup, and scared out of a year's growth." He turned cautiously and eyed Garrison and the revolver the man had pointed at him. Then he looked at his uncle. "Something's wrong—"

"They came here tonight," said Doc Catlin. "They . . . but of course, you wouldn't know, Josh, that she is here. Lanai Meling, she came all the way from England—and now she's gone."

"Gone? I don't understand!"

Mike Garrison said, "They kidnapped Lanai."

"Maria and Carlos, are they . . ."

"Bruised up but alive, Josh. Come, let's go inside. It appears we have a lot to talk about . . ."

Fourteen

"Not wanting to push my luck after I managed to get out of Pueblo, I vacated the train at Castle Rock, where I bought a horse and headed up here."

"So you feel, Josh," said Detective Mike Garrison, "that it's just the three of them."

"Reese Tillman and Benton Wade lend their money support to back up Radford's play. This is the way they've worked before, generally on business deals. I guess this time they caught a glimpse of the pot of gold at the end of the rainbow."

Doc Catlin said, "To murder out of hand two good men . . ."

"And kidnap Lanai."

The sun was up, striking through curtained windows in the living room. Garrison was a man who couldn't hold to a chair for long, and he prowled about the living room, cup in hand and the other holding a cigarillo. Every so often Doc Catlin would go in to check on Maria and Carlos. Josh's tale about the involvement of the Cubans cleared up the mystery of those purchasing the contraband weaponry, while Josh had been surprised that so many reputable men, as they called themselves, could let greed simply destroy their values.

"So, I see no way out of it, Doc," said Garrison. "We have no choice but to go to Judge Stanford Foley. Last time I was in his court he also jailed me for contempt . . . a little matter involving some bunco artists. But such is life as a low-paid detective. Tempting, you know, all this money the Cubans are paying to get these arms."

"That's the pity of it," said Josh. "The Cuban Junta has raised millions just to get arms for their insurgent armies. They've turned a blind eye to where these weapons come from. Would we do any different?"

"Interesting how this Casandro is going around posing as a Mexican diplomat. The question is, do you believe him, Josh, that he knew nothing about these killings?"

Josh pushed up from the cane chair and ran a tired hand across the side of his head, a faraway glitter taking him back to Benton Wade's ranch, and before that to Ox-Bow, where he'd overheard the Cubans that night along the creek. Some of the things they had said, about the suffering of their people back in Cuba, their own suffering, and of how they'd use the guns against the Spanish in battle, they were the stories not of criminals but of men wanting only freedom. They could least afford to leave dead bodies strewn from Denver down into Texas, which was where Josh and Garrison and his uncle had determined the train was heading.

"The Cubans," he finally said, "were apart from this. The killings come back to Luther Radford, in that he ordered them done."

Garrison said, "This means you still have that bullet. And now we have the reasons behind all of this. Meaning they want all three of us out of the way."

Doc Catlin came back into the living room flipping a thermometer about in his hand. "I wish you boys would get some shut-eye before you head into Denver." He held the thermometer up to his eye to comment, "No fever, which means Carlos isn't in any particular danger. But he still hasn't come out of it."

"You'll be in your office this afternoon?"

"Like you said, Mike, I doubt if they'll come back here.

Got complaints coming out of my ears I'm not doing my job as county coroner. Drop over around three, then we'll go see Judge Foley."

"Something I'm not looking forward to."

"And Josh," Doc Catlin said, "I expect one way or another we'll hear from those who abducted Lanai. Once you file a report on all of this, Mike, I expect I'll have police swarming all over the place, when by rights they should be looking for that train."

"Don't worry, Paul, I'll stick like glue to Josh. See you later."

There was something about the Pullman car that made Lanai Meling think of Singapore, the time when she'd gone with her family by train to see a Malaysian warlord, who was later beheaded in an uprising. Only that time she hadn't been gagged and tied up in a small compartment. She'd never been brutalized like this before, and to have it happen in the home of a doctor . . . They were after Josh—that had been made painfully clear to her by the hawk-faced man with the unblinking cobalt eyes, Hogue she believed his name was. She'd learned that when they'd been bouncing around in a carriage, and she had pretended to be unconscious. Even then Lanai Meling had been trussed up like a calf about to be branded.

They had arrived before dawn, and while two of them had left, oftentimes she heard the footsteps of the lone sentinel outside her compartment door. The pain of being struck was still there, but just a dull ache and a reminder these men weren't to be trifled with. Sometime before dawn the Pullman car had jarred into motion, to be moved to a different location. There was never total silence after that, for Lanai could hear other locomotives passing out beyond the Pullman car along with the familiar sound of boxcar couplings clanging together. The bedlam of continual noise spelled out plainly she was still within the confines of the railyard in Denver.

"Maria . . . and Carlos . . . are they still alive?"

All of this, she'd learned while staying at Doc Catlin's house, had to do with the murder of his brother. And why hadn't Josh come back? Their shared fear was that he could have come in harm's way. There were other pictures of Josh in his uncle's home, but her favorite was one Maria had shown her in Josh's room, which he kept on his dresser. It was of she and Josh standing in Trafalgar Square and laughing back at the cameraman as he tried to take the picture while shooing pigeons out of the way. The carefree days of London, when neither of them fully realized just how deep their love was . . . but at least that was the way it had been for Lanai Meling. By coming here she'd abandoned her past. But oh, if Josh had changed the way he felt about her . . . That was a risk she had to take, and now she was here, totally at the mercy of these killers.

A hand hammering on her compartment door caused Lanai to fight her restricting rope, then the door opened and she glared at one of her abductors. He came in holding a canteen. "Corporal Latner at your service, ma'am," he said mockingly. Lustily he took in the torn sleeve of her white blouse and the curving swell to Lanai's full body. He wore a floppy black suit and bowler hat, his smile showing some of his upper teeth were missing.

He came over and looked down at her, feeling the desire pushing at him, but recalling the words of warning from Sergeant Hogue, and silently he cursed the man. "Promise me you won't yell or nothin' an' I'll let you sate your thirst." Then he reached over and yanked the dirty bandana wrapped around her lower head out of her mouth, his hand lowering a little to play teasingly along the opening in her blouse. "Damn, you're sure some good-lookin' Chinawoman . . . an' before this is over I'm gonna sample you all over."

Her eyes widening in derision, Lanai said in controlled fury, "Kiss my Irish behind, you ugly hunk of dogmeat."

This stopped Latner, as he hadn't expected that she could even speak English, but only for a moment, as angrily he let water from the canteen trickle over her head. Then he popped her one, a hard-knuckled backhanded blow that swung Lanai's head to one side, and she went limp. "Damned Chink trash," he spat at her. His mouth worked, but he remained silent, and when Corporal Latner stalked out, he didn't bother to put the gagging bandana back into her mouth.

"She lets out a yell and I'll sink my knife into her damned belly." This was accompanied by the hard sound of the compartment door being slammed shut. "And damn you too, Sergeant Hogue, for protecting that bitch."

At three o'clock, as he'd promised, Doc Paul Catlin arrived at Stout and 20th to find waiting for him out front of the courthouse his nephew Josh and a taut-faced Detective Garrison, who said raspily, "I was just told that I quit hanging around with you, Doc, or face immediate suspension. That I'm to be reassigned out in the boonies, the 24th Precinct. Other than that how was your day?"

He returned Mike Garrison's roguish grin and said, "Just performed an autopsy on about the fattest man I've ever seen. Along with gathering my thoughts about this."

"After I filed my report, Josh and I went along with a police investigating unit back out to your house. We left it at that—that Lanai Meling had been kidnapped by parties unknown. Afterwards we came back in to look around the railroad yard. Rolling stock was being shuttled all over the place. So, let's go see the judge."

Josh, who'd brought along some of the reports he'd conducted over in London on the Metford system of rifling, had them contained in a small valise along with the incriminating bullet taken from his father's body. If anything, he was there in the official capacity of a gunsmith, and it was that role he'd play before Judge Foley, not that of avenging son. He was, though he kept this inwardly, still in a daze, not only over the kidnapping, but that Lanai was even there. If only he had stayed in England it wouldn't have happened. But it had, his father was dead, and before him this cloudy afternoon was still the difficult task of convincing a judge as to the validity of the evidence he would present. Nervously he pushed onto the second-floor landing and toward an oak-paneled door engraved with the judge's name.

With late afternoon shadows crowding into his large, oak-paneled office, incredibility had given way to a grudging acceptance of the facts presented to him by Denver County Coroner Catlin and a police detective. Still, there was in Judge Stanford Foley a marked reluctance to believe the enormity of all he'd heard. He was a tall, long-faced man with a mane of silvery hair, and with an ingrained habit of sitting stiffly erect in his high-backed chair, giving those seated before his desk the unsettling impression they were being judged rather than heard.

He said to Doc Catlin, "You not only desecrated a grave but the oath you swore to uphold. And you"—Judge Foley laid steely eyes upon Garrison—"at the very least should be drummed out of the police department. This is, by far, the most bizarre story that has ever crossed this desk. For here you have implicated not only the Denver Police Department and Army personnel, but three of the most influential ranchers in Colorado. And, gentlemen, we must not forget the international implications. So where does this leave us?"

Boldly Doc Catlin said, "For starters you should hear out Mexican Legate Arsenio Valdez."

Judge Foley raised a cautioning finger. "Those are my intentions, Doctor Catlin. Before we discuss again this matter of military weaponry and this train, I want to hear more from the son of Jarvis Catlin. Your father, Josh, repaired some of my guns. And like your father, you have gone to work for Colt's people."

"Yessir, your honor. You see, Judge Foley, guns have always been a part of my life. Before I even entered grade school it seemed I knew the workings of a Colt or a Winchester rifle. Naturally, I became a gunsmith. While in London, as I explained before, I was part of a team that conducted experiments on rifling."

Josh lowered his eyes to the bullet reposing on a doeskin pouch centered on the judge's large desk. "This is the bullet that killed Jarvis Catlin." His voice was detached, low, yet gripped with a firm intensity. "Sir, I believe you have a Prescott U.S. Navy revolver in your gun collection—"

"Why, yes, Josh, I do."

"I remember my father doing work on that gun. I believe that if you fired a thousand bullets out of that Prescott, sir, the rifling on each bullet would be exactly identical, time after time after time. So it will be with the bullet on your desk, Judge Foley. The gun barrel through which that bullet passed, a .45 Colt service revolver, would impress on every bullet fired from it thereafter the same identical markings. When I find that particular Colt, your honor, I find my father's murderer."

"Perhaps you should have been a detective instead of Mr. Garrison. You called this your silent witness. By rights I should retain this bullet as evidence to be used against both you, Mr. Catlin, and our county coroner. You have presented me, however, with a most incredible tale. And you, Garrison, you say pressure has been brought to bear on you from your superiors. Despite some misgivings, your tale is too bizarre not to have grains of truth in it. This kidnapping—a rather stupid thing to do."

"As I said before, they didn't leave a note behind. But who else could it be?"

"I will not interfere in any police investigation involving

Lanai Meling," the judge said firmly. He put the bullet back into the pouch, which he handed to Josh. "Black-marketing stolen military equipment is another matter. I will contact the Inspector General's office in Washington."

"If I may say something, your honor."

"You always manage to do so in my court, Detective Garrison."

"The shipping of military hardware out from the East Coast on trains is a tedious process at best. Records of the movement of freight cars are maintained by the car accountant, whose job it is to telegram ahead the movement of the cars to the yardmaster, in this case here in Denver, Ralph Perrone. The terminal yard he's in charge of here is filled with, I'd venture to say, from one to two thousand cars, loaded and empty. So the problem we're facing is finding one particular string of boxcars. If, your honor, we contact any of those railroad detectives requesting their help, we'll tip off Perrone. The next thing we know those cars, if it hasn't already happened, will be rolling out of here."

"I see," murmured Judge Foley, as he pushed his chair sideways and reached to a side table for the porcelain coffee warmer. Filling his cup, he dropped in two cubes of sugar and turned back to gaze studiously at Mike Garrison. "The involvement of the Cubans—this does concern me. Spain would like nothing more than to get wind of this. They in turn will blame fully the American government, as they know that sooner or later we're going to run them out of Cuba.

"So we have railroad detectives involved in this," Foley continued, "and some Denver policemen. Not directly, but taking payola money to make certain nothing goes wrong. Somewhere down the line I'm going to mandate that a grand jury be convened. But now is certainly not the time, because this is a delicate situation which I don't want spread in the newspapers. I was contemplating going on vacation—much to my sorrow I put this off. Well, Mr.

Garrison, we have had our past differences. Facing suspension, do you want to pull out of this and go back to your regular duties, or . . ."

"I know what you're saying, Judge Foley, that you can offer me no protection whatsoever if I stick in here."

"I certainly cannot issue a public proclamation stating you're working for me, Garrison. The moment word got out they would kill Lanai Meling."

"Okay," said Mike Garrison, "I'll keep stumbling along with the help of Josh and Doc Catlin. Doc, I expect they'll be more likely to try and contact you at your office."

"Yes," he agreed, "the kidnappers will want to offer some kind of deal totally to their benefit. A deal that includes you, Josh. Meet them in some secluded spot, where all of us might be killed."

"The stakes are certainly high enough to justify this," said the judge. "Garrison, stick around while we make some arrangements as to how to handle this. Doctor Catlin, though you did violate the law, as you did, Josh, in this case the means justifies the end. Don't take any unnecessary risks. Once I lay this out for the I-G boys, we should see some action."

Leaving with his uncle, Josh Catlin's feelings were that at least the judge believed them. But he was only one man, and it would take a few days at the least for Judge Foley to get a response from Washington. Out on 20th Street, he got into the back of the carriage with Paul Catlin, who was telling his driver to take him back to his downtown office at City Hall. "You know, Josh, we may never really know who killed Jarvis. But as long as we nail Luther Radford and the rest of his pack of thieves, that's all that counts. And there's Lanai . . ."

"They really wanted me," Josh said bitterly. "Maybe I should have stayed here instead of gallivanting all over the prairie in search of Dad's killer. Realistically, I have to face the cruel fact that Lanai's gone. If only these scum knew that the only physical evidence we have is this bullet. And as the judge said, it's a piece of evidence that isn't admissible in court. But we have our silent witness, Doc, and I just know they're holding Lanai out at the railroad terminal."

"My thoughts, Josh. Perhaps there won't be any ransom note, that they're hoping we show out there. If we do, they'll know we know about this deal with the Cubans. Too bad through Mike Garrison we can't lay this whole thing in the police commissioner's hands. But . . . going on supper time . . . that restaurant up ahead, Green Gables, I'll spring for the food and a drink or two."

"I would, Doc, but I've got other plans."

"I'm hoping they include Mike Garrison?"

"They do." He opened the door as their carriage pulled to the curbing in front of the restaurant, and he hopped out. "You're stopping at the office before you go home and check on the Juarezes?"

"Plan to, Josh. Just in case the kidnappers have delivered a message. You take care out there, hear?"

Leaving a smile behind, Josh hurried down the sidewalk until he crouched into an empty transom hack, and there he told the driver to head over to Detective Garrison's Logan Street apartment. He hadn't slept last night, nor had his uncle or Garrison, but at the moment the last thing he wanted to do was to crawl into bed.

Worriedly he murmured, "Lanai, I hope you're still alive . . ."

Fifteen

The task of closing out several bank accounts consumed most of the afternoon for Felix Casandro. He had arrived back in Denver late last night, but instead of going to his hotel he'd stopped by to see Annie Wyatt, who had insisted he tarry overnight. That morning Casandro had found the message from the rancher in the post office box he'd rented, telling him everything was in readiness. All that was left now for him in Denver was to meet with Luther Radford and hand over a valise heavy with money.

He would have no regrets about leaving, since in his opinion Radford had handled the whole business transaction rather badly. Facing Casandro once he was aboard the train was how to control Major George Devlin. Perhaps out in the field the major would prove to be a capable *soldado*. As for Casandro's fellow Cubans, waiting anxiously for just this moment, word the train was pulling out was on its way down to them courtesy of some of Luther Radford's cowhands waiting down in Pueblo. Why all this worry, he told himself as he got into a cab, now that you are leaving?

But he was worried, filled with the thought that Josh Catlin had somehow survived. He could have so easily let Dionicio kill the gunsmith. But he hadn't and even now, and despite all the trouble Catlin could still cause, somehow Casandro felt he had done the right thing. "Let Senor Catlin go *mano a mano* against his father's killer."

Casandro had told the cabdriver to take him over to the Powder River Saloon. That was where Radford had told him to bring the money, and he wondered at the man's callous rashness. Before he'd always given the money to Major Devlin, but he felt this was of no concern.

Packed and waiting for him in his dingy hotel room were all of his worldly possessions. Once he had dealt with the rancher, he would go back and get his things and, as he'd told the American woman, return that night. But long before sun-up he would have to leave for the railroad terminal and board the special train.

Through cigarillo smoke the Cuban said inwardly, "We have come so far—let there be no betrayals now."

The seven-man detail commanded by Sergeant Guy Hogue pushed on foot through the railroad yard. At Hogue's insistence, a dining car had been added to the night-enshrouded train they were shambling toward. Coupled ahead of it was the coal car and locomotive number 407. He was looking forward to the sound of clacking rails and getting out of Denver for a while.

By his side was Sergeant Norton, who'd handle things in the dining car. All of them wore their uniforms, responding to official orders assigning them to guard detail. Like the rest of the paperwork, the orders had been put together by Kevin Mulcahan, down to the forged signature of the general commanding the Sixth Army. "If those Cubans don't screw up," Sergeant Norton said, "this should be a piece of cake."

"You get rid of them army rations?"

"First thing I did, Hogue. Got some real fancy food stowed in the dining car—either prime steaks or seafood every night. And plenty of whiskey too."

"The whiskey we'll ration out," muttered Hogue, as he

let the others push up the vestibule into the passenger car. Coming in last, he threw at them as he passed through the car, "I want curtains covering every window. Keep it down in here tonight, nobody getting pie-eyed drunk, or he'll answer to me. I expect the yardmaster'll be showing up later tonight. He does, tell Perrone to make himself comfortable."

Sergeant Norton inquired, "You heading someplace, Guy?"

"Nothing that concerns you. Same thing for the dining room, cover all windows, Norton, and brew enough coffee to last the night. If you sleep, it'll be two at a time, as we ain't out of the woods yet."

He passed on back through the vestibule and into the Pullman car, where with some displeasure he took in Corporal Latner guzzling from a whiskey bottle. Men like the hulking Latner you chewed out at arm's length, if at all. He hadn't figured it necessary to tell the men he commanded about the woman they were holding hostage. To them this was just a simple matter of guarding some military hardware, though all of them knew every damned piece of hardware in those boxcars was earmarked for the arsenal. But Hogue figured they knew the risks and, for the money they were being paid, would take their chances.

"Latner, I told you about that."

Sullenly the corporal said, "A little whiskey never hurt nobody. Don't worry, Hogue, that Chinese bitch is doin' okay . . . had to cuff her around a little, though."

Hogue went over and pulled a window curtain down as he passed back to check on the woman. He opened the compartment door, and stirring around on the narrow bed Lanai Meling saw that it wasn't Corporal Latner but the man with the hawk-face. Closing the door, Hogue went on to enter the next compartment, where he peeled out of his uniform to put on a civilian suit. It was all part of a plan concocted with Radford over at that saloon he owned. Part of it had been the delivering of a letter to the county coroner. They would come, he knew, Doc Catlin and that meddling Josh, as instructed in the letter, out to a park north of the amphitheater. It was Hogue's job to bring the woman over there. Then one of Radford's men, a sharp-shooter, would put an end to the meddling.

The letter had been there when Doc Paul Catlin had re-turned to his City Hall office. It bore no stamp, so he knew it had been hand-delivered. Probably, he thought with some alarm, by Luther Radford's contact in the police de-partment. Of further concern to him was that none of the people working in his department had seen anyone enter his office.

The conditions in the letter, which he'd reread on his way out of the building, were that the abductors were will-ing to work out a deal if Doc Catlin and his nephew would come out to the piece of public land just north of the am-phitheater. They were to be there at 11 o'clock that night.

He knew that area quite well, the land in question part of a park system surrounded by middle-income homes. The amphitheater hugged in close to open areas used to play soccer and baseball, while to the north trees fringed along a narrow creek. The suddenness of it all, the kidnap-ping barely a night ago, and now this summons. . . . Though he smelled danger, Doc Catlin realized he had no other choice.

His carriage brought him north to Logan Street and the Randall Towers. He knew the way up to Mike Garrison's apartment, having gone there on different occasions to have a drink while poking through what they'd picked up on the characters involved in the weapons conspiracy. Only now it was to find to his utter dismay that Garrison and Josh had left. Hurrying back to his carriage, Doc Cat-lin set out in search of his nephew.

"What kind of terms," he said, lashing his reins to spur his horse into a canter, "can they possibly offer us? That we drop all of this snooping about and we'll have Lanai back?"

He began angling through the streets, figuring that perhaps Josh and Mike Garrison had staked out the apartment building where Major Devlin had taken up residence. Why out by the amphitheater, he mused. Was it cleverly set up this way to draw all of them away from the rail terminal? That must be it, that train pulling out tonight without drawing the slightest bit of attention. And there was nothing they could do to stop it happening, for to do so would endanger Lanai Meling's life, if she wasn't already dead.

"Radford, it's not only him we're bucking . . . but the army, the police . . . and with only a spent bullet to offer as evidence." He shook away the effects of not going to bed the previous night, steeling his mind to what he had to do, and offering a silent prayer that they'd be able to save Lanai Meling.

It was around eight o'clock when Felix Casandro entered the Powder River Saloon. To his surprise the main barroom wasn't all that crowded and only a few were in the big back room hunkered around card tables. Over at one table in the barroom, a half-dozen bar girls were taking their ease. The reason for the lack of customers at that time of night was pointed out by posters plastered on the walls, of the world championship fight taking place right about then at the Denver Athletic Club. Inquiring at the bar for Luther Radford, a mustachioed barkeep told him the rancher was attending the boxing matches, and displeasure scoured through the Cuban.

"Who're you bettin' on, mister, Sullivan or Jeffries?"

"Sullivan'll win," he smiled back. He was undecided about what to do, and he felt a little uneasy packing nearly four hundred thousand dollars, even though he had armed himself with a spare six-gun.

"Mr. Radford said he'd be back right after the fight. I could have one of the girls show you a good time upstairs."

"Just a bottle," Casandro grimaced, which he paid for, and took the bottle and a shot glass back to one of the tables. He resisted the temptation to get in a poker game, and he began drinking sparingly. Not only was Radford gone, but so it seemed was saloon manager Riddell, and he couldn't spot in the saloon any of the rancher's hired hands or his foreman, Deke Martin. That was the way of Luther Radford, to have around him at all times hired guns. A man, Casandro felt, who was fearful of his past catching up to him.

"Me llamo Conchita."

Startled by the woman's softly melodious voice and her unexpected presence at his table, Casandro glanced up sharply. *"Que quiere usted?"*

"Just, senor, that you might like some company."

Flickering the irritance out of his eyes, he took in this Conchita. She had on a long black dress glittering with tiny spangles and a revealing neckline. She was thin, somewhat comely, and Mexican. His gesture brought her folding delicately onto a chair across the table. She said tentatively, "I have seen you here before."

"You are barely twenty, if that."

"As the oldest *hija* it is my duty to help my family. Your name was mentioned—" She looked about guardedly. "They were speaking about guns . . . and murder . . ."

"How can I believe you?" he lashed out quietly. "I suppose you expect to be paid for this."

"It was not you, senor, they spoke of killing. It is a woman they are going to kill, and three other men. Tonight they are . . ." Her words broke away as several people flooded into the saloon. She rose, but he laid a restraining hand on her arm.

"These men, what are their names?"

"Por favor, one of them is a doctor. That is all I know."

Grabbing the money he held out, she hurried through the tables and vanished down a back hallway.

As Casandro sat there letting what she'd told him worm through his mind, more men entered the saloon, the shank of them spraying out talk about how John L. Sullivan had just knocked out his opponent. From Major George Devlin he'd been filled in on all the trouble Denver County Coroner Paul Catlin was causing, and the detective and Catlin's nephew, Josh. Killing these men, in his opinion, wasn't the right thing to do. Hadn't Luther Radford stated he had the Denver Police Department in his back pocket, that he had tentacles reaching into the governor's mansion as well? The trouble with Radford was that he had too much power, had done it his way too long. So now if anybody opposed him, the only solution was another killing. He recognized a couple of the rancher's hired hands shouldering through the batwings, then in came Radford.

It wasn't long before the rancher was beelining back to Casandro's table, and as he hunkered onto a chair a brag came out of Radford about his prizefight winnings. "Ten thousand lovely silver dollars, Casandro. The money in that bag?"

"It is, Senor Radford."

Reaching under his coat, he pulled out a long envelope, out of which he removed several folded sheets of paper. "An inventory of what you're getting. You Cubans'll be able to kill a helluva lot of Spanish ... an' there's more what that came from."

"*Si*, there are always more guns, I suppose. I don't see Riddell, or your ranch foreman ..."

"Was about to get to that," Radford said conspiringly. "In another hour I'm heading out to meet a senorita. She's this Catlin kid's girlfriend, some Chinawoman. Been holding her on the train."

"I do not like this," Casandro said tautly. "I—"

"What you like or don't like," the rancher cut in crisply, "don't matter a damn. That kid and Doc Catlin have been a burr under a saddle, stirring up a ruckus with the police. Got this detective helping them out—meaning it's time for me to do something."

"So your plan is to entice them out to the railroad yard—"

"Not out there, Casandro. I just want that train to slip nice and quiet out of here. Don't worry, I'm protectin' your investment."

"By committing murder."

Luther Radford glared at the Cuban as Casandro passed the valise to him to have Radford set it on an empty chair, and then he said, "Money, that's the only thing that matters, no matter how many get hurt, or killed. You'll be gone come morning, Senor Casandro. I'll still be here. But those meddlers won't, as they'll be dead."

"Consider this," said Casandro. "We could hold the woman hostage on the train just in case. It is a long way from here to the Gulf of Mexico, especially when you consider the capabilities of Major Devlin."

"Could," muttered the rancher. "As nothing's set in concrete. So *adios,* and *Cuba Libre.*" He held to his chair as the Cuban rose and headed for the front door.

Out on the street, it took a while for Felix Casandro to find a transom hack. As he strolled along, it was with the pleasing knowledge he would never see the likes of Luther Radford again. Now from the back seat of a hack he wondered if the seeds he'd planted in the rancher's mind would help to save the woman's life. He had allowed Josh Catlin a new leash on life, and tonight it would be taken away.

"I pray for you, Josh Catlin . . . and for Cuba . . ."

Sixteen

"Now why would I lie to a cop?"

"You'd lie to your own priest, Mrs. O'Toole," said Detective Mike Garrison as he stood glaring back at the woman in the shabby entryway of a Market Street apartment building. Halfway up the rickety staircase part of the banister was broken away. The high ceiling and walls seemed to repel the coat of old yellowed paint, the stench of the building pricking at Garrison's nostrils as he followed the woman who was laboriously making her way up the stairs. Behind them came Josh Catlin wearing the nondescript clothing of a workaday cowhand.

She paused to rest on the second floor landing, and to glare at the unwelcome visitors to her aging domain. "This key'll open the door to Sergeant Hogue's room. Don't you be stealing nothin' now, Mr. Detective."

"A plague on your snarly old head," Garrison said as he blew cigarillo smoke into her face in passing. "Look at these empty whiskey bottles and the other trash—the health department just might pay you a call."

"The health department my ass," she threw after them. "Those bastards care more about the jackasses Finnegan keeps over at his livery stable than what goes on here. And lock up after you're done."

They'd managed to pry out of Mrs. O'Toole that Sergeant Hogue had been having a lot of visitors lately, not women of the night but soldiers. That earlier tonight, she'd reluctantly admitted, a bunch of them had been here, and had left shortly after sundown. Entering the corner room, Garrison pulled up the window shade and stared out at more red brick apartment buildings. "His stuff is still here."

Josh, opening the closet door, nodded in agreement. "His duffel bag is gone ... and I don't see any valises. Probably going for a train ride." He began searching through some of the suits of clothing hanging in the closet for any papers or other bits of information, while Garrison was opening dresser drawers.

"Left this revolver behind."

Anxiously Josh asked, "What caliber is it?"

"Not the caliber you're looking for, a .32 Smith & Wesson. You really believe in this Metford system of rifling."

"More now than before, Mike." He came out of the walk-in closet. "Nothing in here."

"Same here, Josh. Most sergeants I know can't even read or write, but they're damned good when it comes to getting things done. Somehow I get the feeling we should have been keeping tabs on Sergeant Hogue more than on the major."

"I think they're about to pull out of here, Mike, aboard that train." Out in the hallway, he waited for Garrison to lock the door. "Here we have Sergeant Hogue over at the Colorado Club the night my father was murdered. Is he the murderer? He's the kind of man that Luther Radford likes to have around, not some intellectual like Major Devlin or for that matter, Mulcahan."

"Yeah, Josh, it would fit Hogue's style more to pull off this kidnapping." They hurried down the staircase, and lurking back at the door to her own apartment was Mrs. O'Toole, who blared out, "The key, Detective Garrison, and I hope for your sake you didn't lift any of the sergeant's possessions."

The key came flying by her head, and cursing she ducked, and barked at them pushing outside, "Next time you have a search warrant—or I'll go see the police commissioner!"

"A lovely lady, O'Toole," smiled Garrison, as he came down the concrete steps to stop by his buggy. Tied behind it was Josh's grey gelding, as he knew it would be virtually impossible to bring a buggy searching through the railroad yard without being spotted; a lone horseman would have a better chance.

"We have three options, Mike. Check on Radford and the major, or head out to the railroad yard."

"I'll tackle Major Devlin first. As you said, Josh, you've got a better chance of snooping around the railroad yard. Then, say, in a couple of hours, we meet over by the Powder River Saloon. It would please me mightily and piss off Radford all to hell if I bought you a drink in there. You watch yourself as those railroad dicks have about the same intelligence as a rock."

Untying the reins, Josh climbed into the saddle and said, "They have to be holding Lanai on that train. Which means it'll be guarded, I figure by Hogue and his men. See you later, Mike."

Way to the north, among the labyrinth of steel rails, Josh could see a lantern held by a switch-tender being waved back and forth. As a freight train rolled on through a switching, the light disappeared, but not lights from the city edging close to the long reaches of the railroad terminal. Josh had decided to begin his search from the south and work his way past warehouses and sidings on which stood boxcars coupled together. The gelding had become high-strung as it didn't like picking its way through protruding rails and loose gravel strewn thickly on the barren ground. One freight train had wailed in from the south, and it took all of Josh's horsemanship to hang in the saddle.

Ahead of him some distance lay Union Station, with the railroad yard extending well past that until eventually it tapered into the one main line heading up toward Wyoming. What he figured he was looking for wasn't just boxcars, but a caboose hooked to them and a passenger car. From what Garrison had told him about the operation out here a locomotive wasn't generally coupled up until a train was ready to head out. Government seals would mark the cars he was seeking, but one difficulty of picking up on them was the yard was engulfed in darkness and had no lamps like city streets. Under him the horse was moving along at a walk, the yard fanning out as it widened.

He rode along some boxcars, but found that some of them were standing with their doors ajar, and he pressed on. Another freight train announced its presence, passing this time to the south. Josh's horse didn't act as skittish, though Josh took a shorter grip on the reins, concentrating his attention on a locomotive with a coal-tender car hooked to it striking toward a distant siding.

"Could be the one I'm looking for," he muttered hopefully.

Closer to Union Station, it seemed there was more ground light, and his horse began to step easier over the rails. Some cars stood on the next set of tracks, with Josh riding alongside them, to pick up on the locomotive again. There he reined up and watched the locomotive roll backwards slowly to be coupled up to a string of around forty boxcars.

"Nope, don't believe this is the train . . . as it doesn't have any baggage or passenger cars mixed in with those boxcars." One thing he had to bear in mind too was the time and his promise to join Mike Garrison over at the Powder River Saloon. Spurring on, he let the horse lope along a stretch of yard barren of cars. What held him up then was that some men were clustered out back of the

Robert Kammen

main station, the glow of what they were smoking fireflies of light barely a hundred yards away. He could discern they wore the gear of railroad men, light blue coveralls and heavy shirts, and some others, maybe railroad detectives, were clad in rumpled suits.

Josh didn't hesitate but veered to the east, a route that would take him around the front side of Union Station, only to have the gelding's shod hoof strike a rail in a loud ringing noise. "Hey," someone yelled at the horseman, "what're you doing out there?"

Much to Josh's relief a passenger train that was gliding in cut between him and those who'd spotted him. Now if only he could make it without further difficulties around the main station and try his luck further north. Coming to the wide, tarred open space between the front of the station and the street, he veered away to go out into the street and head along rows of parked carriages and transom hacks. The worry in him then was that he'd been seen, and someone would alert Sergeant Hogue and others guarding that train.

"Got to keep going though . . . got to find Lanai . . ."

A light was on in Major George Devlin's second-floor apartment, a light that held Detective Garrison down below in his buggy. He kept glancing at his watch in the dim light beaming away from a street lamp, knowing that he had to leave in order to meet Josh Catlin at that saloon. There'd been little traffic out there on 34th Street, and now the sound of shod hoofs striking cobblestones brought his eyes to a carriage that had just pulled around the corner. The carriage pulled up across the street, and Garrison leaned back a little on his seat to keep from being seen, then he realized the driver was Doc Paul Catlin.

Whistling softly, Garrison waved the other man over, and Catlin came on foot but at a hurried gait. "Mike, thank God I've found you . . . and where's Josh?"

"Snooping around the railroad terminal."

"We have to get up by the amphitheater by eleven, Mike, or they'll kill Lanai Meling." He heaved up onto the seat. "A letter was waiting in my office when I got back. Seems they want to make some kind of deal."

Reining away from the curbing, Garrison said, "We'll have to worry about Josh later. What kind of deal? And was that letter signed?"

"No . . . and just that we'd better be there or . . ."

Garrison lashed out with his reins, and his horse picked up to a canter. "That amphitheater is a ghostly place at night—I don't like this, Paul."

"We're to meet them north of there, where that park is."

"Yup, I know the area. A big open space hemmed in by houses east and west and brush and trees north of that. A lousy place to make a last stand. They didn't demand any money in exchange for Lanai?"

Doc Catlin shook his head as Garrison lashed the horse into a gallop. "About a half-mile we'll come abreast of the amphitheater. What they want is to try and take us out. Rosewell Street runs right up past the amphitheater where it dead-ends at the park. Couple more blocks and we're there." At the next corner Garrison swung his buggy over and reined up hard.

"You're saying they're going to try and kill us . . ."

"What I'm saying, Paul. We don't even know for sure if Lanai Meling'll be there. But I do know this, Luther Radford can't afford to let you or me live, for that matter. He'll have some men with rifles holding in along those trees. I'm gonna cut over there, through that alley, work my way up along the park. What time you got?"

"Quarter 'til eleven."

"Cut it close, but we'll get there a couple of minutes before eleven. By then I should be up by those trees."

"What if they brought Lanai?"

"You're the college graduate, you figure that one out.

Radford, I doubt if he'll show. In any case it'll be somebody we probably don't know. Good luck, Doc."

Luther Radford figured he had to go out there to make
sure his enemies paid the price for all the trouble they'd
caused him. Plying the reins of his carriage was one hired
hand, and he'd sent the other one in close to the darker recess cast by the amphitheater. His carriage was holding in
behind one of the quadrangular ticket boxes. He consulted
his fat round pocket watch, and grunted out, "Less than a
quarter 'til eleven and where the hell is Sergeant Hogue?
But Hogue's a sly one, so I figure he's holding close by until the Catlins arrive. Driscoll, you ever kill a woman?"

"Nope, not yet, Mr. Radford."

"Neither have I, to tell you the truth." Puffing on his cigar, the sudden flare of light showed the smug set to the
rancher's face. And with reason, for tonight while attending the fights at the Denver Athletic Club he'd been
approached by no less than the chairman of the Colorado
Republican Party, asking him to run for governor. Naturally he had said yes, which made it even more imperative
that nothing go wrong tonight.

Setting that aside, he looked out at the wide expanse of
open ground across the narrow street. Beyond that lay the
treeline where his riflemen had sighted in their weapons.
Though the overweight Riddell was one of the riflemen,
and probably not all that happy at the moment at being
hunkered down in the brush, the man was a crack shot, as
was his ranch foreman. A warning word from Driscoll
brought him gazing to the east at a buggy just arriving
where the street dead-ended, where it hesitated, and when
it headed his way, Luther Radford leaned forward anxiously.

Doc Paul Catlin gazed ahead at the gravelly layout of a
baseball diamond in the southwest corner of the large
grassy park. Four poles formed a high wire-mesh backstop

and to either side were wooden dugouts sunken into the ground. Back of that at the street corner a street light was on, and beyond that lay houses sparking out more light. Here it is eleven, he thought nervously, and there's no sign of the kidnappers. His eyes fled north across the park to the trees and darker hump of brush punching along this side of a creek, a distance of at least two hundred yards. At that distance a rifle still had plenty of killing power, and he fought down his edginess as he reined up, for heading in from the west was an enclosed carriage.

"Mike," he said worriedly, "hope I've given you enough time."

Detective Mike Garrison's loping run through an alley had set off an alarm system of barking dogs, then he was leaping across a narrow drainage ditch hooking into the creek and vanishing under trees. He pushed through thorny underbrush, gripping his revolver and giving the park and the amphitheater beyond an occasional glance. He could also make out Doc Catlin waiting in his carriage, and Garrison knew time was running out.

Doubts began tugging at Detective Garrison, in that the sharpshooter could be holding by the amphitheater, or maybe one was there and another up here. Though the moon was out, it was of little help under the trees, but at least his eyes had adjusted to the quieter darkness. Crouching down under an elm tree, he gazed ahead, picking out shaggy clumps of brush any of which could actually be a man hunkered down with a rifle. He let his ears take over then, keening to hear any alien sound above the night sounds of the city. Pushing on for a few more yards, and about midway through the treeline, he froze, picking out amongst some brush a tiny pinprick of light.

From his vantage point Mike Garrison could also see out across the park. To his concern Catlin had moved his buggy on a little bit more toward a waiting carriage. "Closer to that street light. While this gent up ahead for damned sure has a scope hooked to his rifle. From this distance Doc'll have no chance."

The man driving the carriage had sat there for a few moments taking in the lone occupant of the buggy, and then Sergeant Guy Hogue tied up the reins and hopped down. He turned and swung open the carriage door and unsheathed his knife, which he used to cut the ropes binding Lanai Meling's hands and legs together. "Come on, bitch," he muttered derisively, as he reached in and pulled her out. Gripping her arm, he brought Lanai up to stand by his horse.

Doc Catlin had dismounted and he came forward uncertainly.

"You alone?"

"Yes, I am. Just what is it you want?"

"Where's your nephew and that detective? All of you were supposed to be here. But I'll tell you now, the way of it. I could kill her right here, Catlin. The deal is, you and your pals leave things alone. Pull away from this thing."

"And if we do you'll let her live . . ."

"I don't know, I don't like it Josh Catlin ain't here. And where the hell is Garrison?"

Over by the amphitheater, Luther Radford could barely suppress his anger, as the plan wasn't working out. What had the Cuban told him . . . that keeping her hostage could prove to be their ace in the hole. Yes, get her back on that train. Through his anger he muttered to his driver. "Dexter, kill that meddling doctor—now, dammit!"

The cowhand rose a little on the seat as he unleathered his six-gun, the shot he fired knocking Doc Catlin to the ground, and then Radford was yelling, "Hogue, get her back to the train! Come on, Dexter, drive us over there." Quickly their carriage swung out into the street, where the rancher gazed over at Catlin lying in front of his buggy.

"Dammit Hogue," said Radford, "by rights we should kill her right here. They must be hiding out close by."

"Maybe, but what the hell." Sergeant Hogue pulled out

his service revolver and snapped off a shot from his hip, the bullet striking Doc Catlin's horse in the head. The horse's front legs buckled and then it sprawled down, kicking a little until it died.

Close by where he lay, Doc Catlin could still hear, through the shock of being struck a grazing blow near the crown of his head, the mingled voices of the one called Hogue and the rancher. He lay motionless, knowing that if he did move the next bullet would slam into his body.

"Take care of her," Radford said as his carriage began rolling away.

Sergeant Hogue knew what the rancher meant, that someplace down the line he was to kill Lanai Meling. He jerked her around and back toward the carriage, as from the north guns began sounding.

When that first gun had sounded, Detective Mike Garrison knew it meant trouble for Doc Catlin. He had plunged on, as ahead of him a large, ponderous shape jackknifed up from the ground. Sensing the danger, the rifleman turned and fired, an errant shot that punched through the underbrush. Garrison triggered off two quick shots, scoring hits both times, and the rifleman toppled backwards and began rolling down the creek bank to splash into its brackish waters. Further along came the sound of a second ambusher plunging across the creek. Holding warily for a moment, Mike Garrison decided that the danger was past, and he broke away to begin running across the wide and dark expanse of grassy park.

He wasn't certain at first, but a concerned smile broke out when he saw movement coming from Doc Catlin. Winded, sweating, Garrison came onto the street and went to his knees to bring a supporting hand under Catlin's shoulders. "A fraction of an inch lower," Catlin said weakly, "and I'd be occupying a slab in my morgue. Seems they still have Lanai. And . . . and Mike, he was here, Luther Radford."

"The bastard wanted in on the kill. Now why did they have to take out your horse, Doc? Dammit."

"I'll be billing Radford for that amongst other things. Mike, they're taking Lanai back to that train. I expect it'll pull out tonight. And Josh is out there—"

"First we'll get you to a sawbones."

"I am a sawbones," he snapped. "Feel damned woozy, but now what?"

"That railroad yard covers a lot of territory. But at least we know where Judge Foley lives. He'll damn well issue a court order now, directing the police commissioner to take action. Lights are still on in that house beyond the park. Should have a horse and buggy and something to clean the blood from your head. Easy now, Doc."

"Don't fret about me. That horse, I paid a hundred bucks for it. Hope nothing else gets killed tonight, horse or man."

Seventeen

The word had spread throughout the railroad terminal to be on the lookout for a lone horseman. For Josh Catlin there'd been a few encounters with railroad workers busy with the task of moving about rolling stock. Once he'd ignored the warning words of a leather-lunged railroad detective, and as Josh had spurred away a warning bullet had sang by to bury itself in a boxcar.

His horse was tiring, but game to go on. He was way up north now, but glancing back he could still make out against the night sky the central switch and signal tower. Around him lay a complex system of interlacing tracks. He could well appreciate why the yard was busy around the clock, as freight trains kept on arriving, as did earlier a passenger train.

Josh simply couldn't tear himself away from searching for that train. Later on he could apologize to Mike Garrison for not showing up at the Powder River Saloon. He was willing to bet his horse that once he found the train the Cuban, Casandro, would be on board, and maybe Major George Devlin. Up ahead a little came the deep-throated chugging of a locomotive picking up speed. A flagman moved out from behind a line of cars and raised and lowered his lantern, signaling the locomotive to move ahead, with Josh cutting the opposite way toward more rails fanning into a siding.

For some reason he couldn't fathom, Josh check-reined his horse. Rows of cars occupied three sets of track, the cars holding closest to the edge of the yard drawing his interest. "A caboose hooked to less'n a dozen boxcars?" Squinting, he was almost certain a light was on in the caboose. From there he couldn't see what lay beyond the boxcars, then his horse shied sideways when someone yelled out it was the horseman. Looking that way, Josh spotted a pair of railroad detectives coming at a shambling run.

He spurred onward to come in between the two rows of cars. What lay ahead of those boxcars revealed to Josh a train ready to roll out. He knew without question it was the train loaded down with military equipment. Suddenly, his horse neighed a warning, which came too late for Josh Catlin. A dark shape hurtled down from the top of a boxcar and ripped Josh out of his saddle. He landed underneath his assailant, the wind knocked out of him, stunned at how quickly it had happened. The next instant the butt of a revolver came slamming into his head and everything went black.

The rules of the game had never changed for Sergeant Guy Hogue, for he'd just as soon kill Lanai Meling that night. But, to hold her hostage on the train, he'd come to realize, could pay them dividends down the line. At least the gunsmith's doctor brother was dead. Hogue had been forced to wait in his buggy for a work train to ghost by in the darkness of the railroad yard. He knew it was late, but he could sleep later when the train had pulled out.

With the passing of the train, he brought the buggy past the tracks and south toward the dim shape of a caboose hooked to boxcars. As he did so, his horse spooked away when a saddled horse suddenly bolted out of the darkness. "Easy," he snarled. Up ahead he could make out movement alongside the train holding the stolen military armament, and then a soldier pushed down a vestibule holding a lighted lantern.

"What have you got?" the soldier inquired.

"Don't rightly know," replied the man who'd used his gun on the horseman. "Awful young-lookin' gent."

From behind them Sergeant Hogue called out, "That's Josh Catlin. He dead?"

"Nope, but it won't take long to cut his throat from ear to ear."

"That rancher wants hostages. Might as well have another one. You, Benson, get this Chinese dame out of my buggy and back into that Pullman car. Then take the buggy and leave it up by the station." Guy Hogue hopped down from the buggy seat and came on to stare down at Josh Catlin. "Like that Mohican you hear tell of, he's the last of the Catlins." The toe of his boot lashed out and punched into Josh's neck and jawline. "Get 'em aboard, then hog-tie the son'bitch."

"We still leavin' come first light?"

Over his shoulder Hogue shot back, "Reason you ain't wearin' stripes, Muldoon, is 'cause you ask too many damn fool questions . . ."

The American woman Annie Wyatt had surprised Felix Casandro with her offer to take him out in her carriage to Union Station. They had left around four-thirty, after Casandro had spent the night at her house. To her he was still Rey Aguilar, man of sorrow and mystery. The most important thing of all to Casandro, however, was that Annie Wyatt was a woman of exceptional intuition and intelligence, someone he would very much like to see again.

"I just had this wistful thought."

She said, "You seem so sad, Rey. No . . . I know you will not be back."

"It isn't you," he said. "And I am not what I seem."

"Nor are you a Mexican." She smiled at him as he

brought the horse cantering around a dark street corner. "Cuban, I'm venturing. But whatever or whoever you are, Rey Aguilar, or wherever you go, I shall always remember the past few weeks."

He glanced at her snuggled in close to him on the seat. "*Sí*, Annie, I am Cuban. Who knows, afterwards, if I'm still alive, and my country is free again, there will be another *encuentro*. There is something . . ." At the next corner he took in the dark hulk of Union Station rising westerly.

Annie Wyatt refrained from speaking as his hand tightened on hers.

"There is a young man living here . . . whose father was killed . . . because of certain events. This is the way of this business, I suppose. But for you to deliver such a message could be dangerous. No, I . . ."

"No, do not leave it like this. Please, Rey, let me at least do this for you."

Nodding through his concern for her, he said, "His name is Josh Catlin. He lives with his uncle, the county coroner. We have much in common. Please, if you will, Annie, tell Josh Catlin that one of three men killed his father. One is a rancher—the others, I suspect, are military men. He will find out the rest of it. I . . . I wish I could do more for Josh Catlin. But the truth of the matter, Annie, is that at this moment my hands are tied."

He brought the carriage onto the street fronting Union Station. Slowing the horse to a walk, he brought the carriage up just north of the station and into the curbing. He gazed for a moment north along the dark recesses of steel rails and rolling stock; at that moment, the railroad yard seemed strangely silent. How could he tell her that now the full thrust of getting weaponry down into Cuba lay in his hands?

"Annie." Now his eyes centered on those of Annie Wyatt. "What can I promise you other than that I might see you again, or perhaps . . ." He brought her into his arms.

"At this hour," she murmured, "there are no passenger trains about. So I hope the one you're taking has adequate facilities." They shared quiet laughter, and a final embrace.

Quickly then Felix Casandro clambered down from the seat. He retrieved his luggage from the rear seat and came back to say, "Take care, my lovely Annie." Then he hurried across the sidewalk and soon disappeared into the darker labyrinth of the railroad terminal.

Judge Stanford Foley had never before suffered the indignity of being roused out of the bedroom of his palatial West side home practically in the middle of the night. He stormed downstairs gripping a Colt .45 and a coal-oil lamp and got even angrier when the doorpanes rattled again. Uttering a profanity unbefitting a judge, he unbolted and swung the front door open. "Now what in . . . ?" His words chopped away.

Said Detective Mike Garrison, "As you can see, Judge Foley, they tried to kill Doc Catlin—"

Beckoning them in, the judge brought them down the hallway and into the kitchen, where he put the lamp on the table. From a cupboard he removed a bottle of brandy. He turned and stared at the look of pain on Doc Catlin's face, the blood staining through the bandage wrapped around his forehead. "By they, you mean this Major Devlin?"

Garrison narrated what had happened up by the amphitheater. "I'll let Paul tell the rest."

"They assumed I was dead," said Doc Catlin. "Luther Radford was standing no more than five feet from me. Either Radford or one of his men fired the bullet, fortunately which just creased my head. Their intention was to kill all three of us."

"And," said Garrison, "they took Lanai Meling back to

that train, which by now has probably pulled out of Denver." He declined the offer of a drink.

Corking the bottle, Judge Foley said, "Doc, I expect you'll file charges against Radford and the others. But more importantly, right now we have to find that train. This is where the army and the Union Pacific enter into this thing."

"Sir, I'd be cautious about who I talked to over at Union Station."

"Not going through that pack of idiots." Judge Foley went ahead to the front hallway and into his study. "This new-fangled telephone was installed a month ago—now we'll see if it's worth the money." He picked up the receiver and turned the crank. "Howdy, operator, this is Judge—that's right, Judge Stanford Foley. Get me through to the president of the Union Pacific—that'll be Oakes Ames. I don't care what time it is! No, you won't get fired.

"Hello, Oakes, this is Judge Foley. Yup, it's about that matter we discussed this afternoon. Just you and I, Oakes, must know about this. That's right . . . we'll need a fast locomotive and coal-tender and maybe one passenger car. No, can't do that, Oakes. If we send word down the line to intercept this train they'll probably kill Lanai Meling." He hung the receiver back on the metal latch.

"Doc," said Mike Garrison, "you're not in any shape to tag alone. Besides, you've got your housekeeper and her husband to worry about. We'll need you here to make sure Mulcahan and Radford don't pull out on us."

"He's right," agreed Judge Foley. "We really don't know how many more are involved in this out at the arsenal, or just how many other ranchers. I've fired off some telegrams to the army. What is it, five o'clock?"

"A quarter after."

"That train could be heading east for all we know, for Topeka or Kansas City. Or down toward Santa Fe or Amarillo. And there are quite a few port cities along the

Gulf of Mexico. You say it'll be traveling under military orders?"

"It could start out that way. But remembering that Yardmaster Ralph Perrone has a hand in this." Questions danced in Garrison's eyes. "That train could get lost awful fast."

"Leave Perrone to me," the judge said. "Detective Garrison, you get out to Union Station and take charge of that locomotive. Meanwhile I'm going to use this phone and my federal powers to see that you get some help."

Eighteen

Union Pacific locomotive 441 left behind the awakening town of Castle Rock and pushed on into the light of a new day. The engineer was one of Yardmaster Perrone's trusted cronies working with a skeleton crew of three men. Orders so far were simply to keep pushing south as far as Pueblo.

Further back, Felix Casandro had the passenger car to himself. For some vague reason they hadn't wanted him in the Pullman car. He suspected that was an order issued by Sergeant Hogue, which hadn't been received by Major George Devlin all that well. There would be trouble, not only cropping up between the two men, but the make-up of boxcars and the passenger car, the Pullman and club car, would attract attention, since it rarely happened.

"It is a wonder this has not all come unglued before now."

Once they reached Pueblo and his men were aboard, it was time, Casandro had decided, to assert his authority over the military. And once he did, perhaps these *soldados* would leave. Then it would be better to uncouple the extra cars and turn it back into a nondescript freight train. The front vestibule door swinging open brought his eyes away from the passing landscape to the corporal who'd entered.

"The major wants to see you, sir."

He followed the corporal into the club car and eased across from Major George Devlin, who was sitting at one

of the tables. Further along the car other soldiers were
huddled at a table engaged in a poker game. No whiskey
bottles were in evidence, and that eased some of Felix
Casandro's concerns. He poured coffee into a cup as Devlin nodded at the meat platter. "You're hungry, help yourself."

"No, coffee will do. We have clearance down to Santa
Fe."

"Where we agreed to head, Senor Casandro. From
there you chart our course."

"I have given this much *consideracion*. But for now let us
not think beyond getting to Pueblo." The coffee was bitter
and not to his liking, but he drank it anyway, staring
through hooded eyes at Major Devlin over the rim of his
cup. "To be away from Denver is to get away from Luther
Radford's adventurisms . . ."

"I don't follow you, Casandro."

"This woman who was kidnapped. Radford told me
about her."

"If he did, then you know she's back on the train. I
wasn't involved with that."

"Perhaps," said Casandro. "It is the rancher's way to
leave no witnesses behind. Has he given orders that she be
killed?"

"Dammit, man, we can't let her live. She'll die the same
as that meddling Doc Catlin did last night. What the hell,
you'll be long gone down in Cuba. Radford's right as rain
about leaving no witnesses behind." Major Devlin, on the
verge of letting it slip that Josh Catlin was being held on
the train, let it pass.

"As you say," Casandro said softly. "We must leave all
thoughts of Denver and what happened there behind this
train. I have gone over the manifests. The armaments you
have sold to us will go a long way toward helping my
countrymen. Perhaps we will do business again."

"I've been thinking along the same lines. But this time
there'll be no rancher like Luther Radford muddying up

things. S'matter of fact, I've been in contact with your Cuban Junta people."

Was this all bluster coming from a man like George Devlin? A man whose authority aboard this train was being challenged by an enlisted man? Casandro would not press this, he would clutch to his breast the insecurities he felt about Devlin. After all, they were on the move, and as for Lanai Meling, a way must be found to at least get her off the train. To wage war on women, as the Spaniards did, marked a man as a coward or someone without conscience, such as Sergeant Guy Hogue. He would be the one to watch hereafter.

Up behind the vestibule door passing into the Pullman car lurked Hogue, the scowl on his face for the major and the Cuban conversing over an early breakfast. He'd overruled Devlin as far as Casandro sacking out in the Pullman car; not when they held captive two people destined for violent deaths. Swinging around, he went back up the narrow aisle lined with sleeping compartments and to the back section of the car. He had breakfast brought to him, and just a little water for the woman and Josh Catlin.

He was alone in the Pullman car, as Guy Hogue no longer saw any need to guard prisoners trussed up like hogs on their way to the butcher's block. With morning sunlight stabbing from the east, he reached over and pulled the shade down. He hadn't bothered shaving the last couple of days, a habit of his when out in the field, figuring that it gave him a mean edge. Right then there was a mean and ugly bent to his thoughts.

"So it's about time Josh Catlin learns what happened to his uncle." The only bad thing about the events of last night, in Hogue's opinion, was that someone else's bullet had killed Doc Catlin. "But the 'portant thing is the son'bitch is consigned to the pits of hell." The whiskey bottle he'd been nursing along was about empty, and he set it aside and shoved to his feet.

His stride was steady despite the slight roll of the car as

the track curled around a shaley bluff beyond which rose
Pikes Peak, still some distance to the south. He'd removed
his sergeant's tunic, under which he wore a thin woolen
shirt with black suspenders holding up his trousers. They'd
put the woman in the first compartment, which he entered
quietly, to find Lanai Meling gazing at him through fright-
ened eyes. Hogue knew that before her usefulness was over
and one of his bullets chased the spark of life out of those
eyes, he'd sure as hell plant his seed inside her. It wasn't
that she was anything special, but it was just that he'd use
her first and brag to Josh Catlin about how he had de-
spoiled her.

Roughly he untied the rope binding her ankles. He said,
"A damned shame you came all the way over here from
England to see Catlin. Well, you slant-eyed Chink, that's
all gonna change shortly. He's here, Catlin is"—he
brought Lanai to her feet—"in the next compartment
s'matter of fact."

He brought Lanai Meling out into the narrow corridor.
Pushing into the next compartment, displeasure deepened
the weather lines around Hogue's face when he saw that
Josh Catlin lay still as if sleeping. Then Hogue remembered with some annoyance that he'd hammered a knuck-
led fist into Catlin's head in response to a cutting remark.
Forcing her down into a kneeling position, he reached for
the can of water and doused its contents over Josh Catlin's
head.

Gasping, Josh tried springing up from the narrow bed
only to gasp in pain. *Where am I?* his mind screamed. For
some reason his eyes wouldn't focus in the suddenness of
what had just happened. One sensation that gripped him
was that he was drowning, and then the terror of it all
struck home. "You . . . bastard . . ."

"Look here, Catlin, look what I've brought you—"

Into sharp focus for Josh came the face of Lanai Meling.
She was alive, she was here, and these monsters held her
prisoner! The full thrust of what lay in her eyes swept

through Josh Catlin like the hot flames of a prairie fire, devouring everything in its path. He screamed out at her through the thick gagging cloth in his mouth. "I'll get you out of this . . . trust me . . . trust me . . ."

"Like hell," laughed Sergeant Guy Hogue. "She's here, Catlin, and alive. Which is more than I can say for your uncle."

With a strength born of desperation and fear, Lanai Meling lunged to her feet and threw herself down alongside Josh, feeling his closeness through the tears spilling unashamedly down her face. Fastening a hand in her long flowing hair, Hogue wrenched her away and back onto the floor. "Dammit, Catlin, that meddling uncle of yours went down with a bullet lodged in his head. An' once we get rid of you, and this woman, we got no more problems. Catlin, you lay there and think about this. Think about the pleasure I'm gonna have with your woman. Come on, damn you, come on."

With the slamming of the compartment door by Sergeant Hogue, to Josh Catlin came a helpless desperation and, though he tried to stem them, tears over the news his uncle was dead. They were few, thrust aside by the total helplessness of his own situation—and Lanai Meling's. The tepid water had served to revive him. By the light streaming around the edges of the window shade, it was daytime. This could only be the train loaded with armament for the Cubans. At least, through all that had happened, he still had the capacity to reason it out, which to Josh boiled down to the fact they were being kept alive for a particular reason.

"Dad," he murmured, "you were always fond of saying there is logic to every situation. The logic here is that troubled waters . . . exist back in Denver. That's it. And it is totally illogical to assume that Luther Radford is on this train. Which leaves us where? That once we are out of the way, these men will get away with this."

There were also the Cubans, Josh's mind raced on. No

doubt aboard this train headed for a southern port. At least . . . at least he and Lanai had a little time. He tried struggling against the ropes again with renewed vigor. He had to get free, and somehow get Lanai off the train. From there they could make their way to a town and send a telegram back up to Denver. "Damn," he cried out, though the sound of his voice was muffled by the twisted rag pressing into his mouth. He went limp, exhausted, and filled with a secret dread.

At least he'd left some of his possessions, including the bullet taken from his father's body, back at Mike Garrison's apartment. At the moment, there was still a lot of track between the here and now and southern Texas. "Lanai, somehow we'll get out of this—and how I love you."

No sooner had locomotive 441 pulled onto a siding just north of the main depot in Pueblo than Felix Casandro had smiles for five other Cubans hurrying into the passenger car. Down on the vestibule steps, Casandro gave the signal for the engineer to get the train under way. Then up he went into the car to explain to his countrymen what was expected of them from there on.

"You'll put on those uniforms, *compadres.*"

"Does this mean we have to pledge allegiance to the gringo flag, Felix?"

"Así, no, only that you will try to act like Yankee *soldados.* We will take turns standing guard duty with the men under command of Major Devlin."

"As you said before, Felix, only at night. The better to hide us Cubans." Displeasure ridged through the words of Dionicio.

"The idea was Major Devlin's," lied Casandro, for in fact that came from Sergeant Guy Hogue. In a way Casandro felt it would be to their benefit. Had all of them not operated at night before in raids against Spanish *soldados?* If things started going badly, the darkness would help them in case they had to take over the train. There was in him a growing sense of unease. The only reason for holding Lanai Meling hostage was because of what had happened in Denver, and even if they arrived at the Gulf of Mexico without incident he knew the woman would be killed.

"There is food and drinks awaiting you in the club car once you are properly attired. When you are done, do not linger but come back here, as these *soldados* have been drinking . . . and might cause trouble."

"How many days must we be on this train?"

"There could be *inevitable* delays. We know what is behind us." His studies of the routes trains took down through wide-reaching Texas and the other Gulf states was heartening to Casandro because of the interweaving main lines. Down in coastal cities lurked members of the Cuban Junta, there to help out when this train pulled in. But Felix Casandro had not revealed to anyone the specific route or port city. It was simply that he trusted no one with the information. So if they failed, he sighed, let his *compadres* with him on this train blame him wholly.

His eyes slid to the rear of the passenger car and beyond the vestibule to the closed door to the Pullman car, behind which was coupled the caboose. Further up was the club car, then the sealed boxcars. If trouble arose, it would be a simple matter to uncouple the club car and turn this back into a freight train. Earlier in the day while they were still approaching Pueblo, he had decided they would head for Amarillo instead of Santa Fe. And he said in Spanish, "I must see the major." Then he headed back toward the Pullman car.

With the sun coming low from the west Josh Catlin was grateful the day would soon end. Through the thin compartment walls he had picked up on sounds of Lanai stirring about on her bed, an occasional sob of pain coming to him. It had only spurred Josh on to greater effort in an attempt to loosen the rope snugged tight around his ankles. To do so, he'd been contorting his legs, to his hands bound behind his back. The racking pain caused by his efforts seemed to be centered in the healing wound at his side. Some time ago he could feel the knots giving, then more and more. He lay bathed in his sweat, his fingers cramped up and numb from the futility of trying to free himself.

There were times when someone passed in the aisle outside his door, and then go on. He hadn't eaten since yesterday, nor had anyone bothered to bring in some drinking water. A fleeing shadow passed across the window shade, distracting Josh from his efforts just for a second. Then, ignoring the pain and weariness he managed to open one of the knots, and another, and suddenly the rope loosened around his ankles. He used his feet to dislodge the rope. Then he lay back, exhausted and dragging deep draughts of air into his lungs, with an angry smile across his mouth.

"Now to see if my legs still work."

Swinging his legs to the floor, he sat up. Next he rose stiffly and just stood there, pondering over the plan he'd worked out that included freeing Lanai. He began bringing his knees up to rid them of stiffness and to get the blood circulating in his legs. The door—must find out if it's locked. To Josh's surprise, when he went over and turned to let his hands have a go at the door latch, it went down easily. "A break, at last."

Without warning, the floor of the car seemed to tilt at a sharp angle as locomotive 441 raced around a bending section of track. Loosing his balance, Josh lurched into the door, which sprang open. Still off-balance, he followed the open door out into the aisle.

"Senor Catlin?"

Josh swung startled eyes to the Cuban, Felix Casandro, coming down the aisle.

Major George Devlin's voice rang out from the opposite

direction, "Hogue, it's Catlin, he's escaped from his compartment!"

Drawing his revolver as he sprang to his feet, Sergeant Hogue bolted out into the aisle and said harshly, "Belly down, Senor Casandro, as I'm gonna kill the son'bitch! Which I should'a done last night!"

"No," barked out Felix Casandro. Instead of dropping down, he came on and moved around Josh Catlin to stare grimly at Sergeant Hogue.

Then the major appeared and said, "Dammit, Hogue, get a grip on yourself. Put Catlin back in the compartment and tie him up again. Do it, sergeant, now, damn you!"

Slowly Sergeant Hogue lowered his revolver. The cold glimmer still held in his eyes, but his anger had been redirected to the major. Somewhere down the line the showdown would come, with him in charge after he'd killed Major Devlin. He came on to force Josh back into the compartment. Quickly he closed the door, and just as quickly he used his revolver as a club, launching a blow that slammed viciously into the back of Josh Catlin's head, who pitched forward onto the bed.

"You son'bitch, this time I'll tie this rope so tight gangrene'll set in."

In the main part of the Pullman car sumptuously adorned in red velvet curtains and scrollwork around the windows and roof, the major stood confronting the Cuban. "So this is why," Casandro finally said, "I was told to stay out of here."

"We didn't want to trouble you with . . . security problems," Devlin said lamely.

"Your sergeant, either you control him or I will."

Major Devlin, gazing back into the Cuban's eyes, knew that was no idle threat. Pursing his lips, he gestured nervously toward the desk and the bottles of whiskey. "I want this to go as smoothly as you, Senor Casandro. But you see what I'm saddled with, Hogue and men like him." He sat down heavily behind the desk, the collar of his tunic askew and a day's stubble of beard on his face.

Casandro stood there for a moment as the compartment door was slammed shut, then the footsteps of Sergeant Hogue going to the front and out of the Pullman car could be heard. He sat down before the desk, on which also lay some maps. Pulling one over, he studied it covertly for a moment. "So large a country, your America. It seems we should slip through unnoticed. But there is your sergeant. I saw it, in his eyes. This isn't over between you two . . ."

"I know," Devlin muttered uneasily. "We've all got dirty hands, Hogue, myself, and especially Luther Radford. There he sits, back in Denver, protected by his money and self-esteem. While we're . . . but we're here, Casandro . . . and we have to make this go."

"I will tell you this," he said softly to the major. "The sergeant, he is a problem for both of us. And so are these hostages, the woman and Catlin. Catlin was only after the man who murdered his father. Then Radford in his arrogant stupidity saw fit to bring the woman into it."

"Worse than that, Casandro," said Devlin as he poured more whiskey into his glass. "Catlin's uncle, Denver County Coroner Paul Catlin, was killed last night. I had no part in that. Hogue, it was him and others. I'm afraid too much blood has been spilled . . ."

"We can do nothing about that now," said Casandro, though he knew that when the opportunity presented itself he would try to help the hostages escape. But only after they were down along the Gulf of Mexico. "Here, get word to the engineer to strike for Amarillo. Now I must get back to my men."

Nineteen

By the time a detail of soldiers from nearby Fort Carson had arrived at Union Station it was midday. Only when they had entrained and were underway did Detective Mike Garrison have a chance to discuss the situation with a puzzled light colonel of infantry named Karsten. Before the arrival of the military detail, Garrison had sought out and arrested Yardmaster Ralph Perrone, and in a spare office at Union Station the following sequence of events had taken place.

Garrison: "Where's Josh Catlin?"

Perrone: "Never heard of him."

Garrison: "You know damned well what I'm talking about." He hit the yardmaster squarely in the nose to have the man sag in his chair.

From Perrone came a mumbled: "Damn you."

Garrison: "Is he dead? Or is he on that train that pulled out of here around sun-up?"

Perrone: "You're the smartass detective. You tell me."

Garrison: "I don't have time to play games. You're part of this, same's Major Devlin and a rancher named Radford. Being part of a scheme to smuggle arms out of the country should see you serving ten to twenty." His fist shot out again.

Shocked and angry from the blow that about caved in

his right eye socket, Perrone: "You bastard ... I'll have your badge for this ..."

Garrison: "If it were only that. Two men were murdered, and last night a third, that being Doctor Paul Catlin. And you still say you know nothing about this?"

Perrone: "Nothing!"

Garrison: "Then you're free to go. But before you do, I'll be spreading the word you ratted on Radford and his rancher cronies. There'll be no train or railroad line that'll take you far enough to escape their wrath." He left the yardmaster in the room handcuffed to a water pipe. It had given Mike Garrison little satisfaction through his worries over what had happened to Josh Catlin. His patience had worn out by the time they were underway, but at least the action taken by Judge Foley had brought Lieutenant Colonel Karsten to his aid.

He went on, "... so Josh Catlin and the woman could be on that train ..."

"I know Major Devlin. Not all that well, sir. But to involve himself in something of this nature ..." Karsten was around five-eleven and greying at the temples. He was scheduled for retirement just before Thanksgiving, and he still hadn't gotten used to the idea that he or any of his men were in any danger, though what he'd just learned from Detective Garrison was shredding away any lingering doubts. "They have at least a six, seven hour head start on us. And, Mr. Garrison, to set things right from the beginning, I defer to your judgement in this."

"Colonel, this is a damned-if-you-do or damned-if-you-don't situation. Those Cubans badly need that military armament. So if we do catch up with the train, you have your priorities and I have mine. Which is prayin' and hopin' those hostages come out of this alive."

The roundup of those in the arms smuggling operation started out at Rocky Mountain Arsenal with the arrest of

Kevin Mulcahan by the Denver police. At first he resisted the accusing eyes of Doc Catlin, but he soon caved in when one of the detectives handling the questioning told Mulcahan he was charged with being an accessory to murder. From there the words gushing out of Mulcahan led them to the Powder River Saloon.

"I know this Deke Martin, Radford's *segundo,* as one bad *hombre,"* said Sergeant Doyle Hadley, a homicide detective. "Doc, maybe you'd better stay out here . . ."

"Not a chance," he replied, as some of the policemen and two detectives headed around to the back of the saloon. "Luther Radford could be here, as he owns the place. I just want to see the look on his face when he finds out I'm not dead."

"Well, you're the county coroner, so you know what a body looks like stretched out on a slab."

"Sergeant, if it's you going down"—Doc Catlin smiled impishly around the briar pipe clutched between his teeth—"I'll embalm you free of charge."

"Can't beat a deal like that. Okay, by now they're in place out back. Me and Doc'll go in first. And McPherson, put that billy club away until you need it. So now, boys, just tag along behind." The door stood open in the summery heat of late afternoon through which pushed the odor of tobacco smoke and the high-pitched laughter of one of the bar girls. Slowly Sergeant Hadley passed over the threshold, and with Doc Catlin a step behind he sauntered toward the long bar crowded with drinkers.

"Back at that poker table," said Doc Catlin, "it's Deke Martin sitting in with some other cowhands. How do we play it?"

"I'm kind of burly-shouldered so just hang in behind as we mosey back there. From what you told me, Doc, Deke Martin was up there too, laying in ambush with his rifle. Two others at the table are cowhands too, and they just might take exception to Martin getting arrested." He cut in between a piano and the roulette wheel, which was seeing some action to close, on the table.

It took a fraction of a second for it to register with Deke Martin that he wasn't seeing an apparition but that it really was Doc Paul Catlin. Seemingly by its own volition his right hand stabbed down to begin unlimbering his six-gun. Hadley, who had anticipated this, slipped a hideout gun out of his coat pocket, a .32 Smith & Wesson, their sixguns seeming to sound together, with the bullet from the *segundo's* handgun plucking at the sleeve of his coat. But Hadley had scored a hit into the lower portion of Martin's chest, and though the man sagged in the chair there was still fiery resistance etched on his face.

"Don't do it, Martin!" warned Detective Hadley. "And you men, back off."

Deke Martin could have fired again but chose not to as he let his gunhand drop limply to his side, the six-gun clattering into sawdust. "Dammit, thought we done you in, Catlin. Should have . . . made sure . . ." He coughed out blood around a go-to-hell smile, and then he slumped sideways and fell heavily onto the floor.

In the silence gripping the saloon, Hadley's voice rang out. "This is police business, so go about yours. You men, take care of the body." He swung away and followed after Doc Catlin making for the front door, through which they passed.

"If Luther Radford's still in town I know where he'll be."

"The Colorado Club."

"Yup, where he made his first mistake. I think the pair of us can handle this."

Easing into the front seat of his buggy, Hadley gazed at Catlin as he gripped the reins. "I don't see why not." He lashed the horse away from the curbing. "More than the look on his face when he sees you, Doc, it'll be pleasurable humbling Radford in front of those other cattle barons.

Your brother Jarvis now, a master gunsmith. He used to stop by just to talk about guns . . ."

"Somehow I get the feeling that Jarvis is waiting for us at the Colorado Club."

"You told me about this bullet you acquired . . ."

"This was all Josh's doing. What he calls his silent witness. Once we divest Radford of his sidearm, it won't take long to find out if he killed Jarvis Catlin."

"And maybe that Mexican diplomat."

To which Doc Catlin added, "Perhaps, but my worries now are for Josh and Lanai Meling. If they're on that train . . ."

Not since the beginnings of their dealings with the Cuban Junta had the three ranchers been together. Coming into Denver only that morning had been Reese Tillman, to get a room at the Colorado Club. Benton Wade had come in a couple of days before to have a doctor check out his heart, and he wished he hadn't, for Wade had learned he was suffering from high blood pressure.

Ironically they were gathered at the moment in the gun room at the club, the same room where Jarvis Catlin had spent his last conscious moment. With them was Luther Radford, and he was in a jovial mood for the train was headed out and in a little while they'd be immersed for the evening in a game of stud poker.

Reese Tillman cackled out, "This whiskey's smooth as a naked woman's thigh."

"What in tarnation, Reese," laughed Radford, "do you know about the lower workings of a woman? I know how you operated, hiking into one of them Mex shanty towns after dark to get fixed up." His grin widened as they clicked glasses together.

"Did you have to kill him?"

The question from Benton Wade, standing away a little, brought the response from Radford, "You mean Doc Catlin? Dammit, Benton, it was either him or us. And his nephew Josh, they latched onto him, too . . . and I reckon dead by now. I'd say our worries are over."

"Amen," echoed Reese Tillman.

"Benton," said Radford, "we've made a bundle out of this. Starting out this first go-around at shipping out these arms wasn't all that easy. Like beginning a ranching operation, you gotta work the wrinkles out. Just the other day I got another letter from the Cuban Junta asking if we can help them again. Here, Reese, pour some of that smooth-as-silk whiskey into this glass. And you bet'cha we'll oblige them Cubans."

"If you say so, Luther," murmured Benton Wade. Some of his old assurance came back, along with a quick smile. "I do believe I hear the riffling of cards."

"This is gonna," laughed Luther Radford, "be some night. With you, Benton, with your riffling of cards and Reese all hot and bothered about naked thighs. Come on, gents, I'm gonna divest you of those moldy old greenbacks you boys pack around."

Twenty minutes after he'd sat down to play Benton Wade was ten thousand dollars ahead. His worries, about his state of health and the other matter, dissolved in the smoky ambiance of the card game. The three of them were the only ranchers at the table. There were two businessmen, a banker, and a county judge, and the stakes were higher than usual, as Luther Radford had wanted it that way.

All of them were old poker adversaries, knowing pretty much how each man played, but even so, the no-limit game had given some of them a nervous edge. And despite Luther Radford's open show of joviality, inwardly he could feel vibrations of unease. That had, he told himself again, been a damn fool stunt, his going out to the amphitheater when he should have let Sergeant Hogue handle the whole affair. When the train reached Santa Fe, Major George Devlin was supposed to fire up a telegram as to how it had gone. He didn't anticipate any problems, since U.S. Army paperwork was honored up and down the line.

"You bet, Luther . . ."

"Oh, yeah . . . call that raise . . ."

"Four lovely ladies," grinned Reese Tillman as he laid down his hand to reveal the four queens.

Pushing away concerns he couldn't control at the moment, Radford said, "But these queens don't show any naked thighs, Reese." His smile froze around his cigar when one of the valets came in, trailed by a burly man clad in a rumpled brown suit.

"Sorry to interrupt your game, gentlemen," said Sergeant Doyle Hadley. "Evening Judge Bishop."

Irritably the judge replied, "Generally, Hadley, you're down arresting winos over on the South side. This better be good."

"This warrant I'm holding," said Sergeant Hadley, "is signed by Judge Stanford Foley. It empowers me to arrest those involved in the murder of Jarvis Catlin."

"How dare you come here and accuse . . ."

"Judge Bishop, shut the hell up before I arrest you for obstruction of justice. We can prove, Mr. Radford, that not only were you and your associates involved in Jarvis Catlin's murder, but that of his brother, Doctor Paul Catlin."

"This is ludicrous!" stormed Luther Radford.

"Further, that you and your associates have been involved in the illegal sale of U.S. Army ordnance to a foreign country."

"Luther," stammered Benton Wade, "what . . ."

"Shut up, dammit," Radford snarled back. "This is something we leave in the hands of our lawyers. I'm telling you now, Hadley, this is going to be your last day as a policeman. Jarvis Catlin committed suicide—everyone here knows what happened that night. His brother was here too, Doctor Catlin, he . . ."

"Did someone mention my name?"

Startled eyes flared to the open doorway at Paul Catlin.

"Luther," protested Benton Wade in a strangled voice, "you told me Doc Catlin was dead." His face had gone ashy; he gasped in pain and clutched at his chest, and then the rancher pitched forward to fold over the poker table.

Presented with the moment of truth Luther Radford clawed a hand under his coat for his six-gun. Then he went rigid when the barrel of Sergeant Hadley's service revolver nudged into his left ear, with Hadley rasping darkly, "Go ahead, make my evening complete. You, Tillman, lift your butt off that chair. Doc, get his gun and put them cuffs I gave you to use. Gents, I reckon this poker game is over. Unless, Judge Bishop, you've got something else to say . . ."

Twenty

In the dead of night locomotive 441 passed westward out of Amarillo. The headlight revealed to the engineer a few yards of glistening track and ghostly telegraph poles and switch targets. Adding to his worries were the overcast sky and lightning dancing some distance ahead. The scraping noise made by the coal-tender shutting the furnace door brought his eyes back inside the cab. "Mort, what do you make of all this military security?"

"I'm not paid to make anything of it, just to shovel coal into this hog of a furnace."

The engineer shifted slightly and gazed past the tender car to the dark silhouette of a soldier sitting atop the boxcar. A bad place to be if they ran into that storm, lamented the engineer. All he'd been told was to keep the train heading westerly. All the military goods packed in those boxcars could only mean the army was about to get in another brush-fire war with either Mexico or some Central American country.

When he looked back again, the soldier was gone, and the engineer shrugged and said, "Nobody within twenty miles of us, and here these bluebellies are sulking about this train armed to the teeth. The army—nothin' about it makes any sense."

The thoughts of the engineer were echoing in the mind of Felix Casandro, who was walking carefully on the top of the boxcar. "It makes no *sentido*, Major Devlin trying to drink himself into a stupor." It could be the man had simply given up command of his men to Sergeant Hogue, along with the chore of getting rid of those hostages. For if it came to a showdown, the sergeant would disembowel the major like a plumb chicken. Or it could be, mused Casandro, part of the blame was his, that he should have let Major Devlin help him plan the route down to the Gulf of Mexico. Tonight, though, he must worry about Sergeant Hogue, that there along the isolated stretch of prairie land death could claim both the woman and Josh Catlin. He couldn't shake loose from that, which was the reason Casandro had issued his men special instructions.

They involved the Cubans slipping quietly out of the passenger car and making their way up outside ladders and onto the roofs of the cars. Their intention was to seal off the club car, where all of the soldiers except for the sergeant and Major Devlin were gathered. He came to the back end of a boxcar, hopped to the roof of the next one and went on at a crabbing walk to crouch down by two of his men. He said over the strong breeze clutching at his face, "If you hear shots, you know what to do."

"*Si*, Felix. These *gringo soldados*, all of them are drunk. Despite my hatred for the Spanish, they would never let their *soldados* act in this manner. If we free these hostages, what then?"

"I don't know," Casandro said truthfully. "Keep watch. Though nothing might happen, but . . ." He slipped further back along the roofs of the cars and to the caboose, where he went down the back of it and slipped inside.

Unfortunately for Felix Casandro, he couldn't see what was happening in the Pullman car. There was a temptation to go in and have it out with Sergeant Guy Hogue. He resisted that, as he pondered over the awful responsibility thrust upon him of making sure the train kept rolling southerly. So many lives depended on him and his *compadres*. To have to share the responsibility with men indiffer-

ent to the cause of *Cuba Libre* ate at his belly. The truth was
he needed the major when they got into more populated
areas of the Southwest, as the major knew all of the proper
words to say to military and civilian authorities, and the
necessary papers were still in the incapable hands of Major
Devlin.

"This is no good, this waiting." To him came over the
clacking of rails a muffled thunderclap. No, wait, for patience can be a weapon, he thought. And though he held
in the caboose, Felix Casandro knew that tonight he would
take control of the train. If it came down to it, he held no
scruples over doing away with the murderous Sergeant
Guy Hogue.

He couldn't shake it away, the face that kept coming
back out of the dark edges of his memory. All she'd been
was one of many Cheyenne squaws amongst others being
butchered by elements of the Ninth Cavalry. She hadn't
even whimpered as his knife had sliced a path from her
pubic hairs up her distended belly. It was her eyes, blazing
out a defiant hatred, that had told Sergeant Guy Hogue he
was killing only the body of a Cheyenne woman and not
her true being, her soul.

"Well, she's dead," he muttered as he stared around the
club car from where he sat by himself. All of them except
for the major and the Cubans were gathered in there, either playing cards or drinking whiskey. They would all be
nursing headaches come sun-up, and owly-eyed. He didn't
particularly care. Some would desert once they rolled into
southern Texas, an idea that even appealed to him. But tonight he had a chore to perform.

He rose and left without being noticed. Back in the connecting vestibule he paused for a moment to peer out at
the dark countryside, as he set the way he would do it in
his mind. The major, drunk as he was, wouldn't even
know what had happened until afterwards. First he would

take Catlin back into the caboose, to plant a bullet at the base of the man's skull, then come back into the Pullman car and have his way with the Chinese woman before he killed her.

Pushing into the Pullman car, Hogue passed quietly along the narrow corridor. Unlocking a compartment door, he left it ajar as he entered and took out his knife to cut the ropes away from Josh Catlin's legs. There was enough light in the compartment for him to see the glitter of Catlin's eyes, and he murmured in a soft-ugly voice, "You couldn't leave things alone, boy. Just had to stir things up." Roughly he lifted Josh up from the narrow bed, only to have Josh sag down on legs numbed from being tied too tightly.

"Come on," Sergeant Hogue muttered, pulling his victim erect. He managed to walk Josh out into the corridor, and from there prodded him back into the main part of the Pullman car.

Frantically Josh's eyes stabbed over at Major Devlin, slumped forward where he sat at the desk and snoring away. He grunted in pain at the sharp jab of Hogue's gun in his back, knowing he was about to be killed. A hard shove from the sergeant sent Josh Catlin stumbling toward the back door, and Hogue was there to open it and force Josh on through the vestibule into the caboose.

"In a couple of minutes, Catlin, you're gonna be what's known as trail-kill. The vultures are gonna be pluckin' out your eyes while I'm back there in bed with that woman of yours." Just as he wrapped his hand in Josh's hair and began forcing him toward the back door of the caboose, a voice sang out damn near Sergeant Hogue's ear.

"Drop the gun, Hogue!"

Sergeant Hogue's reaction was instantaneous, that of spinning and firing at the vague form of Felix Casandro; only his bullet went awry. Not the quick response from the Cuban's six-gun, two shots that tore into the sergeant's midriff. Hogue stood there though dying, not realizing it, his thumb trying to pull the hammer back on his .45 service revolver, a Colt. For some strange reason it lacked the strength to do so.

"Damn . . ."

"Pow!" The bullet penetrated Guy Hogue's left ear, and the night became a lot darker as he plunged dead at Josh Catlin's feet.

"Easy," Casandro said tautly. "I mean no harm to you, Senor Catlin." He moved in closer and stared back at Josh, with his teeth flashing whitely in a quick smile. "Right now my men are taking over the train." He used his knife to cut the dirty piece of cloth away from Josh's face, and the rope away from his wrists. "There, sit, over here. The major, as you may have noticed, is no threat." Stooping, he retrieved Sergeant Hogue's revolver, which he handed to Josh. "Do not be alarmed when the train stops. It will be merely to get rid of some unwanted passengers. As for Hogue's body, it will also be cast off our train." Giving Josh his knife, he spun away and pushed into the vestibule.

Josh Catlin found that his hands were shaking so badly that he had trouble holding onto the heavy revolver. The knife, why had the Cuban given it to him? Of course, to cut those ropes away from Lanai! Thoughts of her brought Josh lurching to his feet. He made his way into the Pullman car and past Major Devlin, who was still spread out over the top of the desk, and then a trembling hand unlocked the compartment door. He darted inside but held back a little to let her probing eyes adjust to the variance in light.

Finally, and what seemed an eternity to Josh, a smile beamed out of her disbelieving eyes. He dropped to his knees and gathered Lanai Meling into his arms and held her close, whispering, "You know I love you."

She mouthed the words through the gagging cloth.

"Now, just nod your head in response to my question."

He laughed softly, joyously, enjoying the moment. "Will you marry me?"

The strangled words came out louder as her head bobbed up and down. Amusedly he cut the gag and the ropes away as the train began slowing down quickly. He said to dispel her alarm, "It's the Cubans, they've commandeered the train."

"I see. You, Josh Catlin, have a mean streak a mile wide. Marry you—are you sure?"

"More sure of this than anything else in the world." He helped her stand, and they moved slowly out of the compartment, with Josh Catlin unaware that he was gripping the gun that had been used to kill his father. As they stood there looking at the major beginning to stir about, the train jarred into motion. As it picked up speed, he caught a glimpse of men spread out straggily alongside the right-of-way.

In a moment Felix Casandro came alone back into the Pullman car. He'd holstered his gun, and glimpsing Lanai he removed his hat. "Senorita, I am glad the worst is over for you."

"But . . . why are you doing this?"

"Josh, it is because I cannot tolerate any longer what these men have done. Now that I have given you back your lives, I must ask a favor—" He walked back with them, where Lanai slumped onto an overstuffed chair. He gestured toward the major. "From here on he will be of little use to us."

"Then why didn't you throw Devlin off the train with the others?"

"For two reasons, Josh. I need use of his papers and his uniform. And he must be brought back to Denver to testify against the others. You are about the major's size . . ."

"Me, pose as an army officer?"

"I have told no one else"—with an easy casualness Casandro lifted the revolver out of his holster and stepped up to the desk to strike Major Devlin alongside the temple—"about my intended route down to the Gulf of Mexico." Grasping the major by the shoulder, he brought the man's upper body from the desk and let it slump back into the chair. "This map here, Josh, we have the junction of five railroad lines midway between El Paso and Fort Worth. At this junction and easterly, railroad traffic picks up. Once we are past this and into Louisiana I am hoping to rendezvous along the Mississippi River with some *compadres*. From there, Josh, the boxcars will be loaded aboard barges."

"Which you plan to float down the river and into the Gulf and hopefully to Cuba."

"Without your help, Josh, we will fail."

"We will do it."

Both of them looked over at Lanai Meling.

"I guess we will," Josh agreed.

Twenty-one

About forty miles west of Abilene the main line of the Texas and Pacific Railway formed a junction with three other lines in the Callahan Divide. At that junction of steel rails the decision was made by Detective Mike Garrison and Colonel Karsten that the train they were chasing wouldn't head east toward Abilene, but would take the most direct route cutting down through the Lampasas Cut Plains.

Away back at Coldwater, a town up near the Texas-Oklahoma border, they'd been flagged down and handed a message which told of some cars being detached from the train they were after. Further along at another town, another telegram told of a work crew on a repair train discovering the body of a soldier.

As locomotive 441 came pushing into San Angelo, it was to seek a siding to be replenished with coal and water. Daylight was pushing away the last flickering stars when Mike Garrison hopped down from the vestibule and held to wait for Colonel Karsten. He took in a canvas-topped wagon pulling away from the depot, coming toward the train. "At least," he said to the colonel, "we'll have food on board."

"I'll second that, Mike. That dead soldier—they must be having trouble aboard their train."

"If so, we might have a chance. I'm glad it's someone wearing a uniform and not one of those hostages."

"Seems there's another message for us," said Colonel Karsten as a man wearing a visored hat appeared on the platform and began waving a yellow piece of paper.

Handing the telegram to the colonel, the stationmaster said, "Seems you boys took the wrong route."

"Yup, Mike, that train passed through Abilene sometime last night. This means we're out of it. Damn the luck. But why? It doesn't make sense pushing on through Fort Worth."

"It doesn't," said Garrison. "Unless they figure they'll run into too many troops down along those Texas coastline towns. Seems they've won, for now."

"Maybe not. These tracks will take us due east for about a hundred-and-fifty miles where this line hooks up with the Missouri Pacific mainline coming down from Fort Worth. In fact, Mike, it's shorter this way down to the Gulf. If my recollections are right, San Marcos is located at this junction. We can fire off a telegram which'll bring troops in from Austin to set up a barricade."

"After that, Colonel Karsten, we'd better get up a head of steam."

About an hour after locomotive 441 had pulled out of San Angelo, the ammunition train commanded by Felix Casandro was approaching a railroad bridge spanning the Red River in northern Louisiana. Casandro felt easier now that Texas lay behind them. The only car offering them comfort besides the caboose was the club car through whose open windows came more humid air. While some of his Cubans were back in the caboose standing guard over Major Devlin, Dionicio was up with the engineer, the remaining Cuban having been pressed into duty as cook in the club car. Lanai Meling and Josh Catlin were studying a map with Casandro.

"You look good in that uniform."

"Be sent to Leavenworth if they catch me," Josh grinned. "You said, Felix, this is the biggest railroad terminal in northern Louisiana."

"As you can see, several major railroads come through here. There are many lines heading southward toward New Orleans and the Gulf of Mexico. Which one to take—"

The lighter clacking sound made by the train wheels told them they were passing over the bridge and slowing down quickly, and the reason for it was soon evident when one of the Cubans shouldered in through the front door to say excitedly, "There are *soldados* up by the signal tower."

"As we expected," Casandro said tautly. The order he'd issued to the Cuban holding in the locomotive cab was for the engineer to take to one of the many side tracks and hold among other rolling stock. He moved over and thrust his head out of an open window, as did Josh. They could make out uniformed men spread along a passenger train holding this side of the large terminal building into which trains passed to disgorge passengers. Slowly their train eased away from the main line to pass behind a long line of freight cars, where it came to a halt.

"This is not over yet, Josh." He pulled away from the window. "It is not by accident we came here to Shreveport, because we need a diversionary tactic which we can only find here at Mantua Junction, as railroad men call this terminal. A switch engine, to be precise. You know what to do, Dionicio?"

The Cuban turned to the map table and gestured with his finger at one of the red lines marking railroad tracks. "It seems, *amigos*"—a confident smile danced in his eyes—"the Louisiana & Arkansas Railway will have another loco engineer to worry about. *Si*, Felix, it shall be no problem stealing a switch engine and coupling it up to some boxcars. Then we tear like mad *hombres* past those *soldados* guarding the main depot and head south. A few bullets fired over their heads will make them angry enough to chase us."

Grasping Dionicio's hand, Casandro said, "It will be dark soon. You should wait until then . . ."

"No, I want them to see us. Don't worry, down the line someplace we will abandon the train and head into bayou country. Even these *soldados* fear the swamps. See you in Havana."

"Ver usted en Havana," Casandro echoed as Dionicio hurried out of the club car.

"If this works, Felix, we can use one of these other mainlines heading to the southeast."

"No, we are venturing due east to Vicksburg, that is if all goes well. One other thing, which is of some minor importance." Felix Casandro smiled at Josh and at Lanai Meling, who'd come over. "All of my men will be on that other train. Leaving we three saddled with the *responsibilidad* of completing our overland journey to Vicksburg and the Mississippi. What I am saying, Josh, is that you can leave now, you and Lanai. I will understand . . ."

"No," Lanai said quickly. "You saved our lives. Even by going the rest of the way we can never fully repay you for that, Felix. And we must not forget our prisoner, Major Devlin."

"Yes, Devlin," said Josh. "The wisest course would be to turn him over to military authorities at Vicksburg. And in full uniform. Which reminds me, I'm wearing his."

"Lanai, take my revolver and go and check on the major. Though he is trussed up like a chicken, one never knows. Josh and I will go now to keep our engineer and coal-tender company."

Easing out of the club car into the darkness of the still and humid night, Josh and Casandro hurried up to join the rest of the Cubans clustered by the locomotive. One of them said, "Up a quarter of a mile on that siding, a switch engine has been moving boxcars. Taking it should present no problem. Dionicio and Blancas have gone on ahead to scout it out, and now we join them. *Hasta la vista.*"

Quickly, as the rest of the Cubans vanished into the inky darkness, Josh clambered up behind Casandro into the locomotive cab. Tersely Felix Casandro detailed to the engineer their plan of action. He downplayed the presence of the soldiers in the railroad yard as he added, "Now you know our route."

"Due east along the Illinois Central line. How far, though?"

"Until you run out of track."

Soon they lapsed into silence, though the locomotive vibrated around them, while the sounds of the yard told them of the dangers to come. Softly the Cuban said to Josh, "You'd better go back and check the train over. Hold it, what's that?"

What they'd heard was the crackling of rifle-fire over the blaring of a steam locomotive whistle, and as Casandro told the engineer to get ready to move the train, Josh scrambled down and ran back to find the caboose and Lanai Meling. As he took in Major George Devlin tied up where he lay stretched out on a narrow bunk, the train lurched forward, slowly, inching past their protective covering of empty freight cars, and soon the main station came into view. He said, "Those soldiers are piling back onto their train. I expect they'll be taking off after those Cubans." He watched until the troop train had pushed away, then he walked Lanai up into the club car.

"Now it's just us and Casandro to see that this train completes its journey. Denver, even London, seems ages away. After all that's happened . . ."

"I wouldn't change anything, Josh. Only that I wish your father were still alive."

Josh Catlin laid his eyes upon the depot falling back to his left as their train pulled onto a set of tracks curving easterly. From there they picked up speed, and as Lanai folded into the curve of his arm she said, "Felix said we'll be there before sun-up."

"We'll make it."

And they did arrive along the fog-enshrouded levees guarding the lower Mississippi River a little before sunrise. Before long there began the business of moving boxcars onto barges, but Josh and Lanai knew their journey had ended. Perhaps it was only beginning for Felix Casandro and the Cubans who'd been there when the train had pulled in out of the night.

A carriage had been put at Josh Catlin's disposal. He'd changed back into his own clothing, and the only thing that remained was to go on into Vicksburg. They'd spoken their farewells to Casandro, and with Josh helping Lanai onto the front carriage seat he murmured, "We could be arrested."

"But at least not for a couple of days. By that time the Cubans will have those barges way out at sea. What about the major?"

Josh turned on the seat and gazed back at Major Devlin, in uniform now and wearing handcuffs and leg irons instead of binding ropes. He felt no pity for the man, even though the words Devlin had spilled out had been consigned to a paper resting in Josh's coat pocket. The one thing eluding Josh had been that Major Devlin kept denying he knew anything about the death of Josh's father.

Shifting on the leather-padded seat, he gazed at the locomotive which had brought them there from Denver. Still coupled to it was the coal-tender car, and an idea flared in Josh's mind as he watched the engine back up to retrieve the club car still hooked to the caboose. "You know, Lanai, that engineer is determined to get his train back to Denver. Well?"

"You mean . . . why, yes, luv, as we came, so shall we return. Does that include Major Devlin—"

"All three of us," he grinned back. "Us to get married,

my dear Lanai Meling . . . and Devlin to face a long prison
sentence or a hanging."

"Damn you, Catlin, I'd rather take my chances down
here . . ."

"Perhaps, Major, but our train awaits."

"It was Sergeant Hogue—he killed your father. Now
you know. He was ordered to do so by Luther Radford.
Now I've told you everything. Let me go and you'll never
see me again."

"You know, Devlin," Josh said sadly, "a man like you is
no good to anybody. Let you go—why not?"

"Josh," Lanai said with some alarm, "you can't mean
that?"

Hopping down, Josh Catlin opened the back carriage
door, where he stood staring at the major. Then he fished
out a key and unlocked the handcuffs, after which he tossed
the key at Devlin. "I'd get rid of that uniform, as you're no
soldier. I'm still tempted to simply blow a hole in your head.
But somehow the greater punishment is to let you find a
rock to crawl under. Those barges, I'd forget about them
too, Devlin, that you or these Cubans were ever here tonight."

When Josh stepped around the carriage, Lanai was waiting for him. He grabbed her hand and they broke into a
run toward the locomotive, spilling out noise as it was
about to get under way. They ran past the coal-tender who
was heading back to get into the cab of the locomotive,
and he shook his head around a wide smile as Josh and
Lanai eased up to enter the club car.

Josh said, "Seems as if Felix Casandro is still here.
Would be nice to have him as my best man. But I reckon
we can talk the coal-tender or the engineer into standing
up for us."

"At the first town we reach, Mr. Catlin."

THE BLOOD BOND SERIES

by William W. Johnstone

The continuing adventures of blood brothers, Matt Bodine and Sam Two Wolves — two of the fastest guns in the west.

BLOOD BOND   (2724, $3.95)

BLOOD BOND #2:
BROTHERHOOD OF THE GUN   (3044, $3.95)

BLOOD BOND #3:
GUNSIGHT CROSSING   (3473, $3.95)

BLOOD BOND #4:
GUNSMOKE AND GOLD   (3664, $3.50)

BLOOD BOND #5:
DEVIL CREEK CROSSFIRE   (3799, $3.50)

BLOOD BOND #6:
SHOOTOUT AT GOLD CREEK   (4222, $3.50)

BLOOD BOND #7:
SAN ANGELO SHOOTOUT   (4466, $3.99)

Available wherever paperbacks are sold, or order direct from the Publisher. Send cover price plus 50¢ per copy for mailing and handling to Penguin USA, P.O. Box 999, c/o Dept. 17109, Bergenfield, NJ 07621. Residents of New York and Tennessee must include sales tax. DO NOT SEND CASH.